DISHONOR AMONG THIEVES

CALLIE CHASE

CALLIE CHASE

The characters in this book are entirely fictional. Any resemblance to actual persons living or dead is entirely coincidental.

Copyediting by Jenny Rarden
Cover illustration by Matt Hubel
Cover design and typography by Michael Lee
Interior formatting and design by Michael Lee

ISBNs:
Print trade paperback: 978-1-959415-00-8
Ebook: 978-1-959415-01-5

This book is dedicated to Davaggio. I needed aid! And there you were. None of this would be possible without you.

And to my family:

Dad, you believing in me the way you do is a bigger gift that I can ever repay. I love you, Dad. Thank you for helping make a grown daughter's dreams come true.

Mom and T, I pray the view from Forráheim is beautiful and that you're celebrating. I love you.

And to the best sister I could ever have hoped for in this lifetime, you're next.

CONTENT NOTES

Dishonor Among Thieves contains depictions of some violence, sexual situations, reference to parental death, and references to mistreatment of an animal (off the page) which some readers may find uncomfortable or disturbing.

Although this is a work of fantasy, care has been taken by the author to ensure that violence is not gratuitous in any way. If you are a reader who is concerned about the content in this book, please refer to:
www.calliechase.com/content-notes

I have taken great care and hired professional editors and multiple beta readers over multiple drafts to ensure this book is free of errors. Should you find anything that you think is an error or typo, please contact me at author@calliechase.com and I will review it and respond personally to your inquiry.

Thank you for taking the extra time to reach out to me!

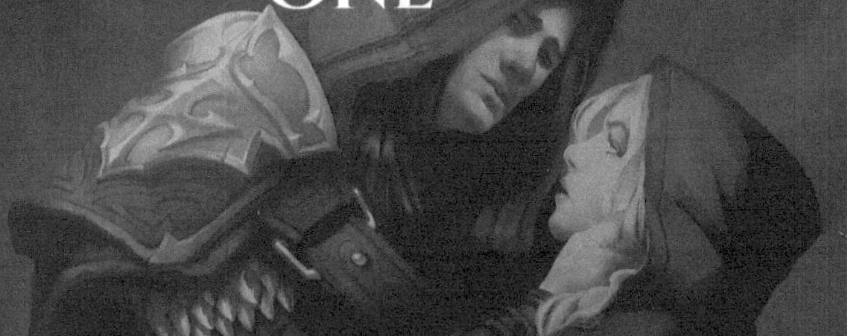

If there was anything that turned my stomach faster than the smell of rotting fish, it was the sound of a man's desperation. I'd hoped an inn with more animal heads on the walls than customers in the chairs might sell something a little less pungent than fish head soup this late in the season. Too bad the men here sounded luckless, and the food...meatless.

I tucked my chin to my chest and held my breath as bowls of something fishy, steaming, and questionably less than fresh passed by high over the head of an overworked woman.

"Heads up, toes in!" she bellowed.

Bits of brownish muck splashed from the bowls onto her tray as she stepped past salt-warped chairs and boots.

"The one that trips me, tips me!" Her rhyme earned brash laughter from a few who must have heard the warning before and were already moving their feet.

The crowd of customers was small but boisterous. Men with yellowing teeth clinked their mugs of ale. Bits of partially chewed bread flicked onto their beards like embers popping from a dying fire. I scanned the crowd, taking in everything. And everyone.

In a dark corner, a man touched his nose to the neck of a girl whose flush and giggle suggested she was not yet his wife. Two older women sat together on a bench, slurping as though competing to see who could finish her ale first. A half-asleep man, tufts of gray hair sprouting from his ears and nose, nearly fell off a backless chair at the bar.

"Oy! What you havin' tonight, gentlemen?" The buxom barkeep looked over two men sitting across from each other at a small table.

The taller one had his back to me. The hood of his dark cloak was tugged back, revealing hair that looked black in the firelight. His long hair didn't necessarily mark him as wealthy, but I knew no laboring men whose hair looked expensive and well-kept. The second man at the table wasn't nearly as refined looking, but his booming voice and strange accent drew me in. I hung back in the shadows watching, taking it all in. After both men had placed their orders, the barkeep grabbed her tray and headed back to the bar.

I followed after her, wedging myself between mister hairy ears and a younger man who seemed intent on counting every bubble of foam in his mug of ale.

"Excuse me, miss!" I worried one of my last precious quarter-pennies between two fingers, the firelight reflecting on the dull edges of the coin.

The girl pointed at me, then jerked a thumb toward the back. "Whatcha need, sweetie? I got a line of hungry men ahead of ya. Ya gotta speak up if you wanna get noticed."

Getting noticed was the opposite of what I wanted. But I nodded and gave her a gracious smile. "You're too kind, thank you. My lord back there. The gentleman with the long hair." I flicked a glance over my shoulder. "Did he order the fish head soup?"

"Aye, he did. One for him and one for his friend." She waggled her brows. "He's pretty, that one is." I assumed she meant the one whose face I hadn't yet seen. His companion wasn't a man that even a barrel full of ale could make "pretty."

I nodded. "The pretty one, yes. He's so very sorry for the trouble, but he's asked that I change his order. Do you have any meat?"

"Do we have any meat? Of course we do! What's he fancy? Sausage? We got a real pretty sausage plate…"

The fact that she'd called both the man and the sausage pretty gave me pause, but I figured a plate of anything would be more substantial than late-season soup.

"That'll be perfect. Just perfect," I said, smiling and looking down at my hands. I tapped the bit of coin against the bar. "Should he give this to you now? Or do you prefer it after the meal?" I held my breath, knowing what I'd do if I were her. Take the money now. The promise of future money was never as good as a coin in the hand. But I was fairly certain this woman was nothing like me.

She crowed with laughter and waved me away. "Go on, now. I'll fix your lord right up." She winked at me. "Maybe then he'll toss more than a quarter-penny my way."

I nodded at her predictable logic and the flirtatious suggestion in her voice, then stuffed the coin back into my traveling pouch. "May I wait here?" I asked, leaning against the bar. "The gentlemen are…" I rolled my eyes and mimicked the movements of their jaws as they talked.

She shouted at the drowsy man who was about to tip over and pounded against the bar with her fist. "Vigi, go find a chair with a back. I'm not going to lift your arse off the floor if you fall. Let the girl here..." She lifted her brows at me. "What's yer name, girlie?"

I debated giving her a fake name but then provided just my nickname. As small as the shire of Fish Head End was, it would be impossible to track me down anywhere in the Realm of Tutovl with just that. "Brex."

"Vigi!" she crowed. "Give Brex here yer seat. Go on, now!"

The man blinked his swollen eyes and dug a finger deep into his fuzzy ear canal, then shrugged a shoulder before stumbling to his feet. I nodded my thanks and sat, trying not to cringe at the damp heat of the stool that seeped through my thin dress and cloak. The girl behind the bar nodded at me.

"Whatcha drinking, Brex?" she asked. "Ya fancy an ale?"

My shoulders sagged in genuine relief. "Ale would be fantastic." She sloppily filled a mug and dropped it on the bar, then took off to deliver more bowls of soup.

I sipped my ale, trying not to smirk. The gentleman with the blue-black hair had no idea he would be paying for my drinks, but if his fine cloak and manners were any indication, he had more than enough means. *Only from those who can spare it*, I reminded myself. And it wasn't really stealing. Or even lying— not really. I was benefitting from a bit of misinformation. Nothing more than that.

Now, what I planned to do with the plate of sausages once they arrived... That *was*, in fact, stealing.

"Look a'that," the barkeep preened when she returned. She set a steaming meal before me. "Told ya they was pretty!"

I looked over the dish and took a quick count of the sausages, then frowned lightly. "Oh no," I said, trying to sound dismayed. "Have you any shaved onion? I know he'd fancy a bit on the side. No insult to the cook," I added. "These look delicious. In fact, could you bring a few more sausages? My lord has quite the appetite."

"You got it." The woman behind the bar took off into the kitchen while I helped myself to two of the pale links. I chewed them and swallowed as quickly as I could without choking. Then I wrapped a third in a bit of clean rag from my traveling pouch and tucked it away beneath my cloak.

"'Ere ya go." The woman loaded the plate with four more sausages and a pile of thinly sliced raw onion.

The smell made my tummy lurch, but I put on a huge smile. "Absolutely divine. I'll take this over myself. Thank you so much!"

"Yer a godsend." The barkeep whirled off to break up a fight near the door. "Oy!" she bellowed. "Oy, you! Put that chair down before I put *you* down!"

I finished my ale and grabbed the plate of sausages, then headed to the table where the gentlemen were still deep in conversation. I nodded my apology without looking at either of them. "The soup will be up shortly."

The gentlemen held their conversation while I set the sausages in front of the pretty man. "What's this?" he asked. "I thought we ordered two soups."

I avoided his eyes, knowing full well the best way to blend in was to be seen but not *seen*. "Apologies, sir. I can take it away if..."

"That looks damn good, Neo." The rough man with the strange accent reached a hand across the table and stabbed a link with the tip of his eating blade. I was hardly dressed the part of a barkeep or pub servant, but I'd been counting on a man like him lacking in attention to detail. "Girl," he said, without bothering to look at me, "bring another round of ale."

While the gentleman was engrossed in his meat, I tapped his near-empty mug with one hand to distract him from the quick movement of my other hand into the pouch that hung over the back of his chair. It took mere seconds to feel about the contents and tuck a couple of coins from his pouch into my sleeve. He had plenty in there and would not likely miss those I'd taken. At least not before I managed my escape.

"Of course, sir," I said, acknowledging his order of ale. I could have whispered I was a keeper of magic, a vampire maiden—any of the illegal, forbidden, or forgotten truths of our Realm—and he would not have noticed. The men already had their heads low and had resumed their friendly, but heated, conversation.

The pretty one, Neo—if that was his name—was indeed pretty. His long dark hair glittered black in the dancing firelight, his eyes an unusual shade of gold ringed with brown. I urged myself to look away from his face, somehow both rugged and alluringly refined. The longer I looked, the more likely he would be to look back. And I was none too excited to be remembered.

Neo leaned forward on the table, his eating blade lying untouched on the table beside him. I made a note that he didn't seem too hungry, which must have meant he'd eaten plenty already. I was certain he was the easier mark of the two. I would have congratulated myself on my instincts, but there was no time for that just yet.

"Trond, I need to hire someone," he said, persuasion heavy in his deep voice. "I can't very well be in two places at once..."

I dragged myself away from listening to their conversation and bustled back to the bar. The barkeep's thin brows were raised as she looked at me expectantly.

"Exquisite," I gushed. "He's quite happy with the sausages. And the onions." I winked at the woman with a satisfied nod. "He's asked for another round of drinks to wash them down."

"Happy to oblige." The woman dropped two full mugs on the bar, no longer interested in making the long walk past boots and skirts if she had a willing assistant to do so in her place. "Another for you?" she asked.

I helpfully grabbed a rag that was lying on the bar and wiped the sloshed contents as I nodded, accepting her offer. I busied myself tidying, making myself useful and trying not to grin. Some people made taking advantage of them too easy. But I reminded myself I wasn't doing anything to hurt the woman. Now that I had a few extra coins, courtesy of the gentleman's pouch, I'd leave her a little something as a show of thanks. After all, I was technically helping her do her job.

"Look at that!" she said, nodding approvingly at my work. "I'll put ya to work back here if you ain't careful!"

I was always careful. It was how I'd survived this long. But I tipped my mug of ale to the woman with a demure smile and drained the entire drink in a few thirsty gulps. I savored the warm wash of bubbles in my belly which mixed nicely with the sausages. Then I grabbed the full mugs and headed back to the gentlemen's table.

I set the mugs down just as Neo, the pretty one, leaned forward, stabbing a long, strong finger against the surface of the table. "Be reasonable, man! I'll pay handsomely. Consider it a break from the rigors of the road. The responsibility. The danger... All you need to do is watch the estate. I will take care of your every need. Meals, chores... I need someone to stay there who's not afraid of every sound that goes bump in the night. It's an easy job, Trond. Give that knee of yours a chance to really heal."

The second man, the un-pretty one called Trond, didn't seem at all interested. He belched loudly then grabbed the mug I'd set on the table and got to work filling the space that fragrant burp had freed up. "I'm no caretaker, Neo. Sounds to me like you need a wife. Not an old—" The man flicked a glance at me and paused as if unwilling to admit what he was really was in front of a stranger. "An old friend," he said, settling on an innocent word.

Neo chuckled and shook his head, the long ends of his hair dusting his forearms as he leaned forward. "It's because we're friends that I'm offering this job to you. My brother's new wife has a sister, a gifted healer. I'll send her over and get you fixed up once and for all. No more bloodletting and—" he waved a hand toward his companion's knee "—booze."

"I love my booze!" Trond didn't bother looking at me as he fisted the mug and took another long sip. "And the bloodletting isn't half bad." He rasped a long, wet laugh that ended in a cough. While he was clearly a man of means, his demeanor was rough. I took him for a merchant of some kind. Merchant...or maybe a raider, which made both men that much more interesting. "Caretakin' ain't for me, Neo. You know that. I've got a crew to support..."

That sealed it, then. Merchants didn't have crews. Most thieves did. My ears perked up to catch the details of whatever job the gentleman had that paid handsomely.

As I walked away, I brushed the unattended eating blade from the table and caught it, completely unnoticed, in my palm. I looked it over in my hand, quickly assessing its condition and value. The carving on the handle was simple, the shade and complexity of the dark rings in the light wood revealing that it was locally made from birch trees native to Tutovl. That meant the gentleman was likely not from a remote shire or even another Realm. The blade was well-sharpened and cared for, and its joint was well-oiled. No jewels that I could pluck out and sell, but this would easily bring in a coin or two in any square in the Realm. I snapped the blade into the handle, slipped it into the pouch beneath my cloak, and headed back to the bar.

With a few bites of sausage and two full mugs of ale in my belly, I was growing tired. I'd made sufficient profit for the night to hit the road. I reached for the charm that hung between my breasts and stroked the smooth round stone on its length of leather for protection. For luck. Then I dropped a quarter-penny on the bar while the barkeep was back in the kitchen shouting her orders to the cook.

I tugged my hood over my head and was just about to head for the door when I felt a hand at my elbow.

"Miss?" The pretty one's face loomed above me.

His eyes were golden fire—the intense blaze searing me to my core. My stomach sank and my feet itched, knowing that I'd stolen from him. But looking at the angles of his face, the dusting of evening scruff that covered his strong chin, it was difficult to resist getting lost in a face that was equal parts complicated and perfect. I'd known many unusual people in my life, but this man was exceptional. His voice was low and gritty, but his refined words filled my ears like a song.

I shook my head. I'd been in the company of children too long. New people and places were almost intoxicating. I tried to deny the response of my body to the man. The last thing I wanted was to be distracted by a pretty thing—except the pretty thing I'd stolen. I took a breath and planted a puzzled look on my face, dragging my eyes away from that molten stare.

"Excuse me, sir. I was just about to leave." I ducked past him, my hand on the trinket around my neck for good luck. As I passed by, I swore I caught a whiff of him. Heat and spice, smoke and something harsh and primal—like new blood and rich, fresh earth. I turned my cheek, curious about the fragrance that was so familiar, for a moment I wondered if I knew him.

That was impossible, though. I didn't know anyone, not in these parts. That's why I was here. Still, something deep inside me felt a connection to him. A bond that reminded me of home, of family—neither of which I had. I shoved aside all thought. I couldn't trust anything that wasn't real, and feelings like this for a strange man were among the least trustworthy things in the Realm. And worse, I certainly wasn't about to let my crime be discovered because I was transfixed by a mark with beautiful eyes.

I darted between chairs and stepped over boots as I made my way toward the front door. I ducked my chin as I hurried past the companion of the pretty gentleman who was shoveling sausage and onion into his already full mouth. Pushing the door of the pub open, I slipped into the crowded village square. Disappearing into the sea of bodies should have been easy.

But the gentleman was not only handsome, he was quick.

"Miss," he called, waving a hand in the air. His cloak parted as he waved, revealing a midnight blue doublet that stretched across a muscular chest. His arms were strong, and even his fingers looked like they might crush mine if he caught hold of me. And yet his voice, luxurious and low, flowed over me, the noise of the square disappearing until I felt that we were the only two people standing under the quickly darkening evening sky. "Miss? I think you may have something of mine."

By the gods... I hadn't taken this one to be so attentive. Careless, handsome, rich—that's how I'd pegged him, but the only part that was not lining up was the careless bit. He trotted after me, his tall form towering above the slow-moving villagers in the square.

The night air was chilly with a bite of salt that pleasantly teased my nose as I stood in place and considered my options. Denial was easy, but if this one got handsy, I'd quickly be discovered. As he closed the gap between us, I tried another tactic.

"The job you spoke of, sir," I said. "I'd like to be considered. I'm hard-working, honorable, and—"

He coughed into his hand, quietly repeating, "Honorable?" under his breath.

I backed two tiny steps away. He truly did suspect me, after all. I'd not been as quick or as discreet as I'd hoped. We were in public, and I was certain I could easily outrun his fine, slippery shoes. Especially after giving him a good shove to his middle, but I'd not been accused just yet. There was still plenty of time to work this out.

"I'm afraid I don't understand," I said, trying to make my sweet voice sound genuinely confused.

"I believe," he said, nodding at me, "you may have accidentally taken my blade. It was on the table when you delivered our food. I thought it might have slipped onto the floor, but perhaps I am mistaken." He paused, his unusual eyes surveying me from top to toe, as if trying to figure out whether he'd assessed me incorrectly. I heated under his gaze, and tried to convince myself I felt the spark of warmth only because his eyes were so unusual.

"About that job you spoke of inside," I pressed, trying to distract him from his purpose in chasing me down. "What does the work entail?"

He shook his head, a frown marring his full lips. "It's not a job for a—"

"For a woman?" I barked. "Sir, I'll have you know—"

I was about to berate him for making assumptions, when a torchbearer wandered past, dragging a small cart behind him.

"Beg yer pardon," he said, the small man struggling toward the row of lamps that lit the village. "If yer strangers to these parts, you may not know about the curfew. There's a turn-in order. Goes into effect about a quarter hour from now."

"A curfew?" I echoed, trying to edge the panic from my voice. "Why is it not posted anywhere?" I'd checked the shire-reeve's notices when I arrived in town this morning. There had been nothing of the sort mentioned anywhere.

The old man, his shoulders stooped with age, shrugged. "Curfew's been in place so long, hardly a soul in Fish Head End don't know of it." He struggled to climb down from the box he'd climbed on to reach the flames of the lamp. I reached out a hand to help him.

"Lot of good that does travelers. People just passing through," I muttered, but then quickly adjusted my face into a calm smile. "Thank you for the warning, sir. I'll make haste to take shelter for the night."

The older man squeezed my hand and dragged his cart off to stoke the rest of the lamps in the square. "Be safe, little lady," he called. "The sea trolls get hungry after dark."

"Sea trolls," I sighed. With two sausages in my belly and one in my purse, I'd make a fine meal for a sea troll. As bony as I was, I might fight one off by tossing the sausage I'd stolen and making a run for it, should I find myself in the jaws of the nocturnal beast.

At the mention of trolls, the gentleman's face grew dark, and I noticed small scars marring his features. His full lips looked as though they'd been smashed and roughly put back together. A tiny scar on his lower lip peeked past the day's growth of thick, black facial hair. One of his eyebrows looked broken too, as if a fist had separated one brow into two and the parts had stitched themselves together without the aid of so much as an ointment.

"Miss, you'd best go back to your duties," the gentleman said, looking sincerely concerned and even a little confused. "You must know the night belongs to the sea trolls."

I barked a laugh, despite how rough it made me feel beside the well-dressed and well-spoken gentleman. The night no more belonged to those rocky beasts than it did to me or to the pretty man standing before me. We were all vulnerable to the whims of the gods—even the trolls. "I'd like the job you're offering," I repeated.

The gentleman shook his head. "The position...has been filled. My friend has accepted it. I'm afraid it's no longer—"

I shook my head. "Your friend—" I lowered my voice, trying not to sound like I was threatening him "—is a raider. Raiders rarely turn honest. The thieving life...it's far too difficult to leave. The risk, the excitement. I don't see a man like him managing a household for you. Isn't that what the job is?"

Leaving the criminal life behind wouldn't be at all difficult in my case, but that was not information he needed. I watched his face as he considered my words.

"You seem to have picked up an awful lot of information while serving us dinner," he grumbled. "But I'm sorry. The position is not available." He looked me over again, the evening breeze teasing wisps of his raven-black hair over his face. He searched my face and my form, as if expecting to see his missing blade fly from my hand. He'd find no evidence, no matter how long he looked. "You'd best get back inside," he reminded me curtly. "The hour of curfew draws near."

Before I knew it, he'd leave. Go back into that pub, or to an inn, and I'd be jobless still, with no better prospects in sight. I would need shelter soon as well, but first, I wanted something else. Something bigger. I wanted that job. With no background, no skills, and no references, this might be my only chance. A desperate stranger and even more desperate girl. Could this be the will of the gods? The gentle assistance of my sister nudging the fates to guide me?

I didn't think I'd ever know. But I did know that I couldn't let him walk away without trying one more time to secure something that would get me off the streets and in possession of a steady income. "Why did you follow me out here, sir?" I asked, taking an instinctive step closer to him. I'd never been a woman who used seduction to get what she wanted, and I didn't think I could seduce this man if I had all the forbidden magic—which meant *any* magic—in the Realm on my side. But still, I boldly took hold of his arm. "Was there something you wanted?"

He took an uncomfortable step back, shaking his sleeve free of my touch and lifting his hands so I could see they were empty. "I thought... I'm missing my..." He shook his head. "It's not important now. Forgive me. I see I was mistaken."

"I believe you need something. *Someone.* Someone who is clever and brave," I pressed, angling my chin to get a better look at the marks on his face. "Someone who is one step ahead of whatever problems you're having. Because you do have problems, don't you?"

He shook his head. "No, I... No. I'm not having any problems. And you, you already have a job, miss. You'd best return to it."

"I'd like the job you spoke of inside," I said. "I'm a most agreeable worker. I can cook, clean, manage horses." I pulled his knife from my traveling pouch and flipped it open, pointing the blade harmlessly toward the ground before securing it closed again. "I can find lost things," I said. "And you, sir, look lost."

Those honey-gold eyes traveled over his knife before hardening like spun sugar as he glared at me. "I didn't lose that. You took it. Why? Why would you endanger your position at the pub by stealing from a customer?"

"That?" I asked. The door of the pub slammed open as the flood of customers left, heading for inns and cottages and stables—wherever it was they'd spend the hours of curfew. Safely inside places no sea troll would venture, even with all this human meat about. "I don't work there," I said with a shrug. "Just passing through."

The pretty man's mouth fell open. "How could you... You stole from me? And then you demand a job?"

"I'm applying for it," I clarified, extending the handle of his knife toward him. "I'm a problem solver," I explained. "I need a job. You have one. And here, see? I'm returning an item of value that somehow, perhaps through inattention, you misplaced."

"Misplaced inside your cloak?" he gritted, but he sighed and accepted the knife from me. He tucked it away and turned his back on me. "Seek shelter," he advised as he turned away. "You may think yourself clever, but you'll be no match for a hungry sea troll." He looked at me over his shoulders, his uncanny eyes meeting mine. I thought I heard him add, "Or one like me."

"If you change your mind," I shouted, before losing his glossy hair and broad shoulders in the crowd of villagers, "I'll be in Fish Head End until morning!"

He stopped before heading back inside the pub. "I won't." His luxurious voice turned stony.

I watched him disappear inside, then turned and tucked my head, flowing through the square with the crowd of common folk. He might have believed he was done with me, but I had no more time for stolen sausages and pilfered coins. What I did have was a few more tricks up my sleeve. And I'd use every one of them to get what I wanted.

TWO

It turned out the pretty gentleman was a liar. Those honey-gold eyes were not sweet, but hid the bite of something much more dangerous.

Given the curfew in place, I secured a room at the local inn, a place that offered rooms by the hour or at a steep discount for those who stayed an entire night. The woman at the front desk eyed me with concern, as if I didn't know what sort of shire I'd wandered into. I gave her a grateful smile and let her know I was a girl just passing through who'd had no idea there was a curfew in place. I just needed a safe roof over my head before departing Fish Head End in the morning.

"Lucky you'll be leaving these parts," she grunted, passing a key across the counter. "Not much honest work left for a young one like you."

I accepted the key without bothering to correct her about my age. I looked younger than my twenty-four years, but if she gave me a little extra courtesy, I wouldn't argue the point.

"Settle up in the mornin' when you return the key," the woman reminded me. "Water's included in the rate, but any food or drinks'll be extra. Got a horse?"

I shook my head. If I had a horse, I would've considered riding it through the night to someplace without a curfew. To someplace that wouldn't cost me half the coins in my purse for a place to rest my head. She tapped a long finger on the counter as I headed up the stairs to my room.

"Lock yer door, missy," she reminded me. "Nights're rough around these parts."

I nodded, appreciating the warning. I'd slept in scarier places most of my life. A strange room at an inn by the sea filled with displaced lovers and drunks would probably provide one of the more restful nights I'd had. I unpacked my meager belongings and nibbled the last cold sausage I'd taken from the pretty man's dinner.

"Should have taken a bit of bread too," I mused, before stoking the small fire in the room. I examined every inch of the place for anything of value, but the room seemed outfitted for neither luxury nor comfort.

A washing bowl filled with what looked like clean water and a handful of clean-ish looking rags rested on a plain plank table. Just enough twigs and lengths of wood to keep the fire burning through the night were bundled near the very small fireplace. I'd learned long ago to inspect abandoned fires. Ashes and embers could be unusual sources of treasures, as things rarely burned the way people thought they would. I pressed my fingers against the charm around my neck, sending a silent prayer to my sister.

I'm trying, I told her, knowing that my words would never reach her. But still, if I believed that the necklace connected us on some level, it couldn't hurt to make an effort to nurture the bond on this long, lonely night.

I poked the embers at the base of the fire with one of the longer twigs, digging for anything that might be of value. All I got for the trouble was a nose full of ash, so I tossed the twig on the fire and stripped off my thin shoes.

There was no furniture in the room save the modest bed, but at least that was more than a coarse, hay-stuffed sack tossed on the uneven floor. There was a real wooden frame under the mattress, narrow but solid enough to hold my weight when I sat. The pillow was soft beneath my head, softer than I expected. Exhaustion and the promise of uninterrupted sleep had my eyelids feeling heavy. I got up, hung my cloak on a hook by the door, and secured the lock. Once I blew out the candle, I returned to the bed with something like relief filling my chest.

As I closed my eyes, I emptied my mind, casting out as many worries as I could. Sleeping in a bed like this, protected from the elements, with a real pillow under my head, was a rare indulgence. I hated to waste a night of comfort giving in to the terrors that had driven me from home. Those would chase me down soon enough. Of that I was certain. For tonight, I was hidden away. Safe.

Home. Such a fool's notion. As if someone like me, an orphan, an outcast, could ever hope to call any place home. I'd been living a life as a burden to those around me for so long, just sleeping someplace away from the shouts and the whispers, the overwhelming feeling that I simply shouldn't be there made the night's rest more peaceful than I could have hoped for. Yet the sensation of peace wasn't to last. I had an escape to make, and I'd need to be clever about it.

The next morning, I opened my eyes before the sun rose, my bare toes poking out from the ends of the coarse blanket. I stretched and groaned, briefly contemplating how long I could stay here. How many nights of peace the money in my bag could purchase honestly. Maybe I could settle in a shire like this. Take up a rag and a spot behind the bar and serve ale day after day. I could imagine worse fates. Had seen many people whose lives had been ruined by indulgent dreams and pointless hopes. Maybe someday I'd stop wanting a better life and I'd accept the life that I'd been given by the gods. The life that, whether I liked it or not, I was destined to live.

As if stealing and saving and keeping secrets could be called living. I could hardly call what I'd been doing survival.

I didn't want much. Just a place to rest my head and a steady enough stream of income so that I didn't have to ration every bite, every sip, every quarter-penny. Constantly worrying about the next moment and whether want would weaken me, tire me, or destroy me completely.

Just one of the coins I'd picked from the purse of the man at the pub would be enough to cover last night's stay. Should I settle in, spend it all and stay another? Maybe the barkeep would hire me, or the kind lady at the desk would take pity on a motherless, homeless wretch and help me find a job.

Thinking about work reminded me of the handsome gentleman from the pub. His blue-black hair and strange eyes had been haunting, but there was something else about the man that made his job so attractive. He seemed like the type of man who'd never known want, whose home would be filled with food and luxuries like feather pillows and furniture covered in costly fabrics. Any man who wore vibrant colors had to be a man of means, and if he was hiring a caretaker—if he'd come to Fish Head End to seek out a trusted friend for the job, he had to have wealth that required a person of some trust to secure it.

That was a job I wanted. That was the work I needed.

Money meant opportunity, and I was more than ready to create the change in fortune that I sought, even if I had to do so through less-than-honest means.

I sighed, tossing and turning in the unfamiliar bed. The ease of a safe night's rest was vanishing like a fog with the appearance of the morning sun. No matter how I tried to cling to the lazy luxury of sleep, my heart beat faster with every moment that passed. This was not my destination. Just a stop on the road. I'd best get on before fate or fortune intervened in a way I did not want. Preserving the few choices I had was the only aspect of my life that brought me comfort.

I kicked off the blankets, washed my face, and ran my fingers through my hair, wondering what manner of breakfast I might find before slipping into the crowd and disappearing along the dusty road. While I pondered the issue of my next meal, I stamped out the fire from last night and doused the last of the embers with the used chamber water. Then I packed my bag, slipped into my shoes, and remade the bed exactly as I'd found it.

I didn't dare hope that the innkeepers wouldn't remember I'd stayed here, but with the plan I had, it was possible, *possible*, that I could slip out without paying. I peered out the north-facing window and took in the dark square. The lamp lighter was already on duty, dragging his cart behind him as he extinguished the lamps now that the risk of trolls and other beasts that attacked in the night was diminishing with every ray of the rising sun.

I stood at the closed door of my room and quietly turned the lock. I heard nothing in the hallway—no early risers, no staff—so I crept from the room and secured the door behind me. I tiptoed down the stairs and breathed a sigh of relief. There was no one working. No voices prepping teas and bread or hauling fresh water in from the well. The place seemed blessedly deserted. I walked quickly toward the abandoned front desk and slipped the key to my room onto the counter. I closed my eyes and rubbed the charm around my neck, thanking my sister for keeping an eye out for me.

Except I thanked her a bit too soon.

"Oy! You there! Girlie!" Gone was the matronly woman who'd been so concerned last night when she'd rented me the room. Now, a grizzly older man with a robust belly that strained the fabric of his filthy tunic popped up from behind the desk.

"Oh!" I exclaimed, a hand to my chest. "You startled me!"

"You startled me," he said, glaring, "into thinking I was about to get taken for the price of a night's stay! You checkin' outta your room?" He picked up the key I'd left on the counter and inspected it before using it to pick at something stuck in his front teeth.

My stomach rolled over, and I brushed away the sudden urge to clean my hands on the folds of my cloak. I thought fast. "I paid for the room last night," I explained. "I was only intending to sleep a few hours, and the nice lady I spoke to…"

"Ain't no nice ladies workin' here," the desk clerk rasped. "Certainly nobody nice enough to give a room away for free."

"It wasn't free," I insisted. "I paid for the room last night. If you'd only give me a chance to explain—"

The man didn't seem convinced, and I suddenly realized that the kindness of the old woman might not have been kindness at all. I may just have fallen victim to a scam of an entirely different sort. I cursed myself for being so naive, so foolish as to think there was any real compassion to be had from strangers. I'd not make the same mistake again.

"Explain it to the shire-reeve," the man groused, ringing a bell he kept behind the counter. "Billy boy! Oh, Billy, run and grab the shire-reeve, and tell him to bring his cuffs. Looks like we got a thief needs taking in."

"I'm not a thief!" I exclaimed, panic seizing in my chest. I could not be taken into custody. I'd never have the means to pay the fines for my confinement, and I had no faith whatsoever in the justice to be found in this remote shire. I had to get out of here, no matter the cost. "How much do you think I owe you?

Surely we can work this out." I reached beneath my cloak to stroke the stone around my neck, seeking out the comfort of my sister's touchstone. "Please," I insisted. "This is just a misunderstanding."

"Full night in a room with a bed and a fire..." He counted something out loud on his fingers before proclaiming the amount that I owed him. "Four silver," he said. "And that's before I inspect the room for anything missing."

"Four silver! Anything missing?" I echoed, my voice indignant, despite my fear. "There was nothing in that room but a handful of twigs for the fire and the bed! Do you think I've somehow managed to slip the bed out the window and will be scurrying off with your flea-infested hay? This is preposterous! I could rent every room in this place for the night for less than four silver!"

The amount he demanded was at least four times the amount I would have paid for the room if I'd actually planned to pay for it. I was certain now that I had fallen into a trap, a web that I only hoped I was clever enough to escape.

"Billy!" the clerk shouted again, swearing under his breath. "Don't you make a move, missy! Once my boy is up, you'll answer to the shire-reeve, you will!"

"Four silver?" A deep voice behind me caused my shoulders to sag in defeat.

Not him. Not the pretty gentleman. If he'd heard that I was being accused of slipping out of the room without paying, I had no doubt he'd be happy to add my theft of his blade to the list of complaints that would be lodged against me.

I was just about to turn and argue with him too, when he slipped beside me, leaned forward, and planted a strong hand on the front desk. "That sounds like an unfair rate to charge a woman for a single night's stay," he mused, cocking his chin at the clerk. "If I'm not mistaken, the woman who was working here just last night offered me a room for a single silver." He flicked a glance at me, his face impassive. "And she sent up tea and biscuits before bed."

"Tea and biscuits!" I exclaimed, but the gentleman waved away my words.

"Where is that Billy of yours?" he asked, his thick brows furrowing in concern. "I suspect the shire-reeve would like to know just how many innocent strangers passing through Fish Head End have been cheated by...what's your name, sir? I'd like to know the name of the man who's attempting to scam innocent women traveling alone. And perhaps even myself. One coin silver for a night's stay in a place like this..." He looked up at the ceiling and then back down at the floors, his lips pressed thin. "Nothing short of outright thievery."

"Never you mind, sir. Never you mind." The clerk waved a hand at me, his eyes wide as he took in the man's fine clothing and sleek hair. "I must be mistaken about this one."

"*This one?* Are you referring to the lady?" His voice was imperious, and the clerk quickly warmed.

"The lady, yes, of course. This...*refined*...young lady right here." The clerk was scrambling now, pulling out some kind of ledger from behind the counter. "I'll just check the records... I'm sure I can sort this out and we can all be on our ways then, eh?"

The gentleman peered at the ledger before yanking it from the innkeeper's hand. "This?" he challenged. "This is your ledger?" He flipped through the pages. Not a single word or figure was recorded. "I think the shire-reeve would be very interested to see whether your *records* and your taxes are in alignment." He touched a fingertip to his lips. "Fraud, theft, manipulation... I don't know the law in this shire, but I suspect there will be sufficient cause for an official investigation. Where is that Billy after all?"

"All right." The clerk yanked his blank book back from the

gentleman and slammed it closed on the counter. "Ya made yer point, sir. The young girl's room is on the house. Now I'd ask ya both to take yer leave."

The man with the sleek black hair dropped two silver coins on the counter. "I trust this will more than satisfy my bill. And any expense you've incurred from the lady's stay." He set a key almost identical to the one I'd been given on the counter, then turned to me. "Shall we?" he asked, offering me his elbow.

I frowned. I'd gotten away without paying for the room, not thanks to my wits or skill, but thanks to this man. If the shire-reeve had been called and I'd become embroiled in some type of scam... My heart sank as I realized even the shire-reeve might have been in on the ruse. What if he'd come and placed me under arrest? A sour taste filled my mouth as shame flushed my cheeks.

I slipped my hand in the crook of the gentleman's elbow and turned to look over my shoulder at the clerk. I wrinkled my nose and stuck my tongue out at the nasty little man, giving in to my more immature impulses. Then I lifted my chin and followed my companion into the square. As soon as we out in the sunlight, I yanked my hand from his elbow.

"You're welcome," he said, nodding at me.

"I was not going to thank you," I seethed, angry at myself, at the situation, and unable to control my fear from exploding from between my lips. "I had the money to pay for my room! I did nothing wrong!" I stopped my rant and glared at him. "Why are you here? I thought you said last night you'd be 'gone from Fish Head's End by morning!'" That last bit I said in a low voice intended to sound like his.

He didn't appear amused by my mockery.

"That's true, I did say—"

"You lied!" I snapped. "Why are you here, then? Where's the friend you dined with at the pub last night? Or aren't you a close enough friend to be invited to his home to wait out the curfew?"

The man's eyes darkened at my words. He pointed behind him. "My *friend*," he said, making it sound like his dinner companion was not a friend at all, "had too much ale to make it back to wherever it is he's staying. I suspect if you and I hadn't just been kicked out of that inn, we'd see him rolling out of a room with one of the ladies from the pub sometime around noon."

"We weren't kicked out," I insisted. "I was sorting out a misunderstanding."

"A misunderstanding which might have found you in shackles and answering to the shire-reeve had it gone on much longer." He sighed as though I were exhausting him. He tugged his hood over his hair and stared at me, his bright yellow-gold eyes boring into my face. "Again, you're welcome."

He turned and strode toward the village square. I watched him walk away, realizing if he was still here, there was still a chance to persuade him to give me that job.

"You owe me," I called out. "We're nowhere near the point of me thanking you!"

He stopped fast, the hem of his cloak skimming the dusty path. "Debt? You believe I owe something to you?"

I took off at a run, catching up to him and peering up at his face. The rays of the early morning sun reflected off his unusual eyes, making them seem even more golden than they'd seemed in the pub. "You do realize," I said, "that you bullied that man. Manipulated him with your wealth, your means. I don't condone what he was doing. The greedy little goblin is a common thief." I shuddered, trying not to let the irony of my accusation slow my argument. "But what you did? That was an unequal transaction."

"Unequal transaction," he echoed, his voice sputtering in

disbelief. He narrowed his eyes and leaned close to me. "And yet it appeared to me when I stepped in and spoke up—on your behalf, I might add—that you were on the losing end of that unequal transaction."

He was not wrong there.

I sighed. "Please. I feel as though we're talking in circles, but truly, we have no dispute with each other." I met his eyes, thoughtlessly reaching for the charm around my neck. My fingers itched, and I was badly in need of comfort. "I need a job. If you're still looking for a caretaker..."

He shook his head. "No," he barked, far too quickly. "This is not work I would entrust to one like you. It's far too dangerous. Get yourself home or someplace safe. The world will eat alive innocents like you." He began walking toward the stables, his steps long and his stride quick.

I struggled to keep up with him. "You have no idea how far from innocent I am," I blurted out, immediately regretting my choice of words.

He turned and looked at me, a sly smirk on his full lips. "Is that so?"

I quickly shook my head, trying to clear my thoughts. "You said the job was dangerous. I've seen quite a bit in my life. I am trustworthy. I can manage any task..."

"Except perhaps paying for a room without being accosted by the innkeeper?" His voice was irritatingly smug.

"That's not fair." I followed him through the square as he walked at far too great a speed. "I cannot be blamed for someone else's lack of honor. Can I? How is what happened my fault?"

He reached the village stable and turned back to face me. "I'm not blaming you for that, what happened back there. But I'm unconvinced that you have any right to demand the job that you should not even be aware I have. You were listening to my conversation. I know I was charged for more sausages than my companion and I ate. And then, there's the matter of my eating blade…" He handed a quarter-coin to the stableboy. "I'm here for the blood bay," he reminded the teen.

"Lord Oderisi, yes, sir. Give me just a minute, sir." He quickly ran to retrieve the man's horse while I took note of his name.

"We may not have met under the most flattering of circumstances, but I am capable." I looked around the stable to make sure we could not be overheard. "Please," I whispered, letting the word slip softly between my lips. "I would not ask so passionately if I was not in extreme need of honest work."

He ignored me completely, as if I were not even there.

"You and your friends," I pressed. "What kind of work do you do? Piracy? Coastal raiding? I fear neither troll nor man. Nor monster." I'd begun to assume the work he needed was someone trustworthy to watch his manor, maybe pose as his wife or sister to keep his butler and crofter honest while he was away on raiding adventures. There could be no one better suited to that work than me.

Lord Oderisi clenched his hands into fists, only releasing them when the boy led back a beautiful bay. He took the animal's reins before leading her past the stable and into the quiet square. The vendor stalls were coming to life, bakers and fishmongers, tailors and other tradespeople opening carts and shops to begin the work of the day. I sniffed the air and my tummy growled, reminding me that I'd need rations before leaving this place.

He stroked his horse's neck and looked over her hooves and mane before climbing astride her. "You're persistent," he said, adjusting a scabbard at his waist. "Which means you're foolish. Dangerous. You know not what you ask, and yet you insist on something that remains impossible."

"Where I come from, persistence is a virtue," I implored.

"And thieving?" he asked, giving me a look. "Is that a quality of the virtuous where you're from?"

I glared at him, wondering exactly why I felt so compelled to push for this job. He hadn't attempted to prosecute me for the stolen eating blade. He'd come to my defense at the inn, even though he no doubt suspected I had no intention of paying for that room. He'd reacted visibly, looking uncomfortable, perhaps even insulted when I accused him of taking the upper hand in an unequal transaction.

Living as I had the last few years, I needed to be incredibly astute at understanding people. Predicting when and how their patience grew thin. Anticipating the limits of their generosity. Knowing what mattered most to them, so I might exploit those things they cared about. My entire life had been a struggle to prove my worth to those who might betray me, use me, or otherwise neglect me.

This man had a job, and I was no more than a day or two away from desperation, starvation, and many other conditions that were graver than most I'd faced in my twenty-four years in this Realm. If I admitted to myself that I'd planned to gain the trust of a wealthy man, loot his manor, and take off with whatever I could sell as quickly as I could do it, I could never have pursued the job so passionately. I was not a criminal, not deep down. I'd been driven to take what others might spare only so that I might survive. I could make a fresh start. But I never would if no one ever gave me the chance to make an honest wage.

"I am sorry, sir," I said, lowering my chin but not my eyes. I looked into his face and nodded. "If you'll take a chance on me, I vow to you, on the safety of my own sister, I'll not steal from you again."

When I mentioned my sister, he flinched, his body giving

away something about his heart. He had a sibling. A family. People he loved whose needs mattered so much that he might be swayed by the smallest display of honesty from me. I was certain of it.

"Where is home?" he asked. "Where are your people from?"

I shrugged. "I was raised in a foundling home in Byrlad," I admitted. "I don't know who my people are or where we're from."

He closed his eyes, and his shoulders seemed to lower. "You mentioned a sister... Are you the eldest?" he asked, as if he already knew.

"I am," I admitted.

He sighed and led his mare close to me. He peered down at me but then climbed down from his horse. "What is your name?" he asked.

He held a hand out to me, and I almost laughed. Any weapons I might be hiding wouldn't be shaken loose by his gentle handshake. But if it made him feel more secure to shake my hand, I'd oblige.

"Brexia," I said. "Brexia Eloise." I took his hand and held it firmly, allowing him to give mine a slight shake. When his fingers closed around mine, I couldn't help closing my eyes just momentarily. Warmth flooded my body, as if his very touch moved something within me. Handsome, powerful, and dangerous. Working for a man like this might not be the uncomplicated opportunity I hoped it would be.

"I am Neoruzzi Oderisi," he said, holding fast to my hand.

"*Lord* Oderisi," I corrected, watching his golden eyes trace my face, my hair, my lips.

He breathed deeply through his nose and released my hand quickly. "I prefer Neo," he said. "First names equalize the transaction."

I smiled in spite of myself. Neo Oderisi was a clever man. I appreciated that. He wasn't just a pretty face with a purse full of silver.

"Are you familiar with Omrora?" he asked.

I squinted up at him, the sun beginning to shine on my face. "Never been, but it's west of here, correct? A small shire, close to the capital?"

He nodded. "If you still need a job in a week's time, and if you can find Omrora, then maybe I'll consider you. Bring your sister," he suggested. "I'll have space for two to stay."

Then he climbed on his horse, urged her into a trot, and rode away.

I had one week's time to make it to Omrora and convince this lord to give me that job. There was only one small problem.

My sister was most likely already dead.

THREE

"Come, girl." I turned around and nodded at the Coldblood Trotter following a short distance behind me.

It had been just over twenty-four hours since Lord Neoruzzi Oderisi told me to find him in a week if I still wanted a job. I'd spent the day wisely, which was how I ended up leading a small white mare, her mane and tail dark as the cones of an ironbark pine, into the small village in the shire of Omrora just a few hours after sunrise. I didn't expect to see signs pointing me to the estate of Lord Oderisi; neither did I expect the name to be so provocative when I did inquire. I stopped first at a place I suspected a man such as him would be well-known: the farrier.

"Good day, miss." The woman in the farrier's shop peered at the condition of my mare with an obvious look of distaste. "This horse looks like she's had a spot of trouble. How can I help?"

The front of the shop was little more than a workbench with a chair, but behind the entrance was a pristinely kept stable bustling with activity. Apprentices worked furiously in stalls, while a supervising farrier wandered between the humans and animals giving corrections and praise, critique and insults.

"Watch it...watch it!" A man with his hair tied back in a thin, straggly ponytail tapped the blunt end of a whip against the straw-covered ground as he leaned over the work of a sweating young boy.

I could hardly stem my curiosity at the activity behind that wall but had a goal in being here that would not be quickly accomplished by distraction.

"Trouble," I repeated, bringing my attention back to the farrier. "Yes, you see, I've only just rescued her," I explained. "She was in the employ of a man who didn't have the patience the breed requires."

The woman came around, her expression softening. "By the gods." She stood a respectful distance away from the horse, but her eyes trailed over the many old, well-healed scars on the horse's body, as well as a few newer injuries on her face. "Trotters are the gentlest of creatures—when handled right. Who in the Realm would lose patience with an angel like this?"

I nodded and took a step closer to the woman. She looked visibly relieved when the mare stepped with me, keeping a close distance between our bodies. "I was able to take her off his hands," I said, shaking my head, "but I've just arrived in this shire. I'm on my way to a new job and wonder if you might look her over and put the charges on my employer's account?"

The woman pinched her lips between two fingers and looked at me sideways. "Your employer?" she questioned. "And who might that be?"

I gave her the pretty man's name but did not get the reaction I'd expected.

"Oh no." She shook her head. "We don't maintain an account for Lord Oderisi. I wouldn't be able to do that for you."

She looked me over, as if trying to decide whether I was trouble or if I was unaware of the trouble I was in. "What kind of work were you hired to do?"

I shrugged. "To be honest, I'm not entirely clear. Household staff of some sort. I believe he has a butler and a crofter, but needs a household supervisor."

Even as I said it, the story sounded off. The woman stepped a bit closer and lowered her voice.

"You have family, girl? Someone to look out for you?"

I didn't hesitate to reassure the woman, even though my words were completely untrue. "I do," I lied. "I met Lord Oderisi while he was traveling. My people know exactly where I am."

She nodded but didn't move her fingers from her lips. "You rescued this mare, you say?"

"Just yesterday," I confirmed. At least that much of my story was true. I'd decided to start the journey to Omrora on foot but encountered a drunk merchant beating the trotter with a wooden club. The man was a savage. Had two other horses tied to a cart that looked completely broken and beaten down, but this girl was separate, unattached to the cart and the only immediate victim of the man's temper. "Ran across a merchant whose daughter had died. This was her horse," I said, stroking her mane with gentle fingers. "I'd like to believe he took his grief out on the horse, not that that's any excuse."

The farrier nodded and looked distraught. "Have you anything?" she asked. "Anything you can spend?"

I shook my head. "I spent my last coins getting her away from the merchant."

That also wasn't true, but this lie didn't sadden me. I had in fact spent the last of my coins paying the merchant for a place to stay overnight. In his stable. With the abused horse. The fact that we fled together before sunrise didn't mean that I had not truly spent the last of my money on the horse. Just not in the way the farrier might believe.

"But I have a job, ma'am," I assured her. "If you're able to care for the horse, I'd be happy to take a note to Lord Oderisi. I'll ask him to pay you out of my earnings. I understand I'll be given lodging and food, so any extra will come here to pay off my debt."

The woman looked worried, and not only about the cost of cleaning up my horse. "Do you know anything about the Oderisi family?" she asked. She looked deep into my eyes, the maternal affection there making my heart catch in my chest. No one had looked at me that way in so, so long. I wasn't sure I could remember a time when I'd seen such unrestrained concern directed at me. I remembered the treacherous innkeepers and wondered if this might too in some way be a scam, an attempt to part me from my money.

"I don't mean to frighten you," the farrier rushed on.

I shook my head in answer to her question. "I do not know anything about them," I admitted. "I'm a young girl far from home in need of work. The gentleman was nothing but kind when he offered."

The woman considered me a for a moment and then sighed. "Well, I cannot very well let this horse walk around in that state. And you, dear…" She shook her head. "You put your own safety at risk riding her. Come. We'll find a way."

A swell of gratitude bloomed in my heart. "You'll help me? And her?"

The woman nodded, all business now. "Consider it done. We offer credit to many in this shop." She sighed and shook her head. "We spend half the time giving credit to local men who drink up the money they should be putting toward their debts. I couldn't live with myself if I didn't offer you aid." Her smile was warm, and she reached out and clasped my arm with a hand. "You rescued her. I'll pay that kindness back to you, girl."

I stared at the woman in a state of near speechlessness. She would extend me credit simply because I had said I'd been kind to the horse? What a far cry from the innkeepers and the care and treatment I'd know thus far.

"Thank you," I said, a flush heating my cheeks. "I...I am truly in your debt." I gripped the charm around my neck and vowed that if this woman helped me, that I would, in fact, repay her. No matter what effort was required, I would not disappoint the faith she'd placed in me.

"What's your name?" the woman asked.

"Brexia," I said. "Brexia Eloise. Brex for short."

The farrier introduced herself as Laura and took the reins of the trotter from me. "Come on back," she said. "You're far from home, and I think there are a few things you might want to know about the Oderisi brothers before you accept that job."

Brothers.

I knew it. I'd thought Neo had said something about having a brother with a wife whose sister was a healer, but I'd been too focused on the sausages and the eating blade to catch the details. Now I could be certain—Neo had a brother. And I guessed the softness I'd detected in him could be attributed to affection for his sibling.

I followed Laura through a door that led to perfectly orderly stalls where a dozen horses were being cared for. She situated my mare and opened a ledger to record the services and the prices for the work the trotter would need. She called over an apprentice, who sucked his teeth when he got a look at the mare's hooves.

"She's a rescue," Laura said, swatting the boy's shoulder. "This kind young woman has given the horse a reason to hope.

Let's not penalize her for whatever marks or signs of neglect you find." She turned to me. "Has she a name?"

I nodded. "I've been calling her Sara. I think she prefers it to whatever she was called before."

Laura took gentle hold of Sara and nodded. "She's as lovely as a Sara should be," she said. "Todmund! Get Sara here fixed right up. Give her a thorough look, and be quick about it. Miss Eloise doesn't have all day."

The apprentice took charge of Sara while Laura took me under her wing. "Now," she said. "Come with me. Let's have a friendly chat."

By the time Sara was ready to ride, my ears were full of stories about the Oderisi clan. The mother, wrecked by love, who'd lost not one, but two spouses over the years. Her first husband, Neoruzzi and Rainieri's father, had died when the boys were very young. Her second partner's illness had nearly bankrupted the family, but Laura assured me that the Oderisi gentlemen still had some means.

"That's what worries me," she said quietly, as though one of the family might be nearby to overhear. "The younger one, Rainieri... He married a local girl, a common scrivener, just a few months ago. She was also from a very, very troubled family."

If trouble followed the Oderisi family, then I would fit right in. I thanked Laura for her concern and information.

"A young girl all alone so far from home," she said, looking me over kindly. "I trust that those boys have the means to pay you. But with a wife and the wife's sister all living under one roof, I can't imagine why they need more household staff."

I shrugged. "Maybe that's why? The mistress of the manor and her sister moving in doubled the number of people living under one roof. I know I'd want to hire a girl if I were newly wed and had only my sister on hand to help."

Laura reached a hand for me and did something that nearly broke my heart. She tipped my chin with her fingertips and looked me squarely in the face. "Be careful there, my dear," she said. "Things in the Realm aren't always as they appear. Put your safety first. Protect your mind, your honor, and your spirit at all costs. There's no replacing you, you know."

I knew that just as well as anyone but nodded my thanks. Then, in a moment of genuine appreciation, I grabbed the fingers that had touched my chin and squeezed them warmly. "Thank you, Laura," I said, emotion clogging the words in my throat. "For being so kind to a stranger. I'll not forget all you've done. And I'll be back to pay what I owe if Lord Oderisi doesn't handle it first."

She nodded and squeezed my hands back. The charm at my neck seemed to warm, and I released her fingers and stroked the pendant. I took Sara back from Todmund, who looked right pleased with himself and his work.

"She's so beautiful! She's nearly a new animal," I breathed. "Thank you for your good work, sir."

The boy flushed at the praise but got right back to business. "I put a bit of ointment on that gouge on her face," he said. "She took it like a champion, but if you can find some more, you'll want to keep the wounds clean so they don't get infected. She's got a good appetite and a very pleasant temperament. I'd trust anyone I loved on this horse," he assured me.

"We'll use this," Laura said, pressing a series of symbols into a smooth length of green wood. "Not all of the guildmembers can read, so we still use tally sticks in these parts. You can go ahead and put your name right here."

I looked over the markings on the wood then pulled my own dull eating blade from my traveling pouch to carve my name into the stick, binding me to repay the amounts I owed for Sara's care. Once my name was on the wood, Todmund split the young piece of greenwood in half, and handed one part to me. The other half he hung with an iron nail on the back wall of the shop. Mine was not the only tally stick on the wall, which made me feel quite a bit better. I tucked my half of the stick into my cloak and made a vow to myself.

This was one bill I would not run out on. This place, this farrier, had shown me kindness that might just be a sign of a fresh start. A new way.

But before I let myself be carried away dreaming of independence, wages, and a right proper purse full of hard-earned coins, there was one last thing standing in my way. I still needed to convince Neo Oderisi to give me a job.

FINDING the Orderisi manor was much easier than I expected, although Laura couldn't give me very specific directions. She was very well-acquainted with the younger Oderisi brother, Rainieri, as he had a fondness for horses and kept a full stable. Laura generally sent me off the village roads on a path that led north.

She assured me I wouldn't have to travel far but suggested I make haste to reach the manor before dark. "This is vengersax territory," she'd reminded me. "If you don't have them where you came from, you'll do well to carry a torch in the dark or get yourself inside long before nightfall."

I'd heard plenty of stories growing up about the beasts that roamed the Realm, "winged daggers" like the vengersax who preyed on men's eyes and tongues after sundown. The things that went bump in the night where I'd been could compete with any beast I'd find here in Omrora. I was certain of that but would nonetheless remember her warning.

With her clean, new shoes and a belly full of fresh grass

from the grounds outside the stable, Sara seemed far more comfortable, and I was able to ride her through the village and along the dusty path. Just as twilight descended over the hills, I spotted lights burning in a manor that was almost indistinguishable from the horizon of dark clouds.

As I nudged the mare toward the exterior gates, I noticed something glowing off in the distance. Curious, and a bit concerned that I'd happened upon a fire, I dismounted the horse and led her gently toward the gate. I peeked over the chest-high stones, the top of the gate grown thick with winding vines of smilax. The long thorns looked mature, as though they'd been growing for decades. The plant's purpose was neither flower nor food, but covering the top of the gate to prevent the admittance of any who weren't welcome.

I climbed astride Sara and urged her closer to the gate, peering past the brambles to the unusual glow ahead. I lost my breath as I stared at the haunting aura around the property. While the stone wall itself was grown high with the distinctive heart-shaped leaves and jagged thorns of the smilax vine, behind the wall, the ground was grown over with a thick, dark reddish plant—a sedum, I believed.

But it looked like no sedum I'd seen before. Even more strange was the way the densely flowering plants *glowed*. If it had been rainy or humid, I might have believed there was a dense fog that hovered over the hills of the Oderisi estate. But from here, the ground, thick and overgrown with plants, glowed with a mist as red as blood.

Sara whimpered slightly, as if to warn me away, but the plants had the opposite effect. I was transfixed. What kind of magical place was this, where the ground seeped blood and the walls were reinforced with natural weapons? I might not be able to get inside quickly or easily, but I was certain this had to be the right place. This would be my place of employment. My home. I just had to find a way inside.

The sun was setting, which meant I'd need a torch or would need to take shelter. Both Sara and I would be exposed if this really were the hunting ground of the vengersax, and I had no interest in losing my horse's or my own eyes to the winged monsters. Large as geese, toxic saliva, and beaks so sharp they could slice through a man's hand, the vengersax were like every other monster in the Realm—better avoided than confronted.

I calculated the distance between the gate and the front door of the manor and realized quickly that the gate might just be unlocked. I rattled the lever, and to my relief, the latch gave way and the gate freely opened.

Just as I was mounting Sara and preparing to ride past, a cart pulled by two horses emerged from the back side of the property. The horses were at a canter, a young man at the front urging the horses ahead. Torches hung from hooks mounted on top of the cart. As they passed quickly over the grounds toward the road, a woman with hair pale as moonlight stood and waved to the driver to stop.

"Hello, there!" she called, standing to greet me as the cart slowed. "Are you here for the healer? I've been called away to attend a fever in the village, but I expect to be back in a few hours." Her face was lovely, but she looked over my scarred horse and my humble dress with concern. "My dear," she said, "you have no torch. You mustn't be out after dark."

She motioned to the driver to wait as she leapt from the cart with one of the lamps in her hand and walked over to greet me.

"I'm Odile," she said, looking over my face as though surprised that someone she did not know was calling for her services. "Take this lamp and go right up to the house. The vengersax won't attack if there's light, but still. I'd take no chances if I were a girl alone." She held the lamp up to me, but I shook my head in refusal.

"I'm looking for Neoruzzi Oderisi," I said. "And I'm quite well, thank you. I don't need the services of a healer."

"She might," Odile said, nodding at Sara. "Go on inside. Neo will get you the help you need." She gave me another strange look but then quickly softened to a smile. "Neo didn't mention he was expecting anyone," she said. "But you're welcome here. I hope you'll excuse my haste."

She climbed back into the cart, looking very concerned at my lack of light.

"Are you sure I can't offer you a lamp? You'll go right to the house?" she asked, her pretty face pinched with worry.

"I'll run her up that way," the driver offered. He was a young man, likely no more than a teenager, with a flop of reddish-brown hair and an easy smile. "I'm Flynn," he said, waving a hand at me. "I'll grab a lamp and run ahead if you'd like me to show the way, miss."

"No, please. You have a sick person waiting. Thank you for the hospitality. I'll hurry inside." I waved at them and urged Sara inside the stone wall. I peeked over my shoulder to see Flynn jump down from the cart, close the gate behind him, and then he and Odile took off, their lamps glowing orange as they bounced along the path toward the village.

Once the steps that led to the manor were in sight, I leapt from Sara's back, ducked my head into my hood, and moved swiftly through the dark toward the door. Sara snuffled the air, stamping lightly on the ground as I knocked, keeping my ears tuned for wing beats overhead.

"Hello?" I called, knocking hard against the door again. My voice might have been a little shakier than I would have liked, but all this talk of vengersax was unnerving. I was growing cold and tired, the rumbling in my belly reminding me that I'd not eaten anything but a few wild carrots I'd shared with Sara. Just as I was about to pound a third time, I heard the click of the latch and the door slowly opened.

A small woman with a shock of white hair answered. "Hello, there. Can I help you? Are you here for the healer?"

I suddenly understood why the manor gate was unlocked. If Odile expected callers any time of the day or night, it would make sense to keep the gate unlocked but the manor itself locked and secure.

"Good evening, ma'am," I said. "I'm sorry to intrude at this hour. I'm here to see Lord Oderisi. Neoruzzi Oderisi."

The woman's mouth fell open in surprise, but she quickly opened the door in welcome. "Of course, miss. Come in, come in. You must come out of the night."

She didn't even ask my name before she shouted into the darkness behind her. "Dale! Dale, come quick. Lord Oderisi has a visitor!"

I stayed outside with Sara until an elderly man came round to the front door, smoothing the long graying strands that fell over his forehead.

"A visitor at this hour! For Neo?" The man squinted at me but quickly broke into a smile. "That mare needs a nice quiet place to rest up while you visit. May I, dear?"

"Slow down, slow down, Dale. Don't go running off into the night. Your eyes may not be what they once were, but those nasty vengersax will still take a bite of you if you give them half a chance." The woman rolled her eyes and held out a lamp for the old man. "My husband," she said with a cheeky grin. "I married him for his looks, not his wits."

Dale shrugged and said, "And you were right lucky to land me! I'll have you know, my hand was highly sought after back in the day..."

She sighed and nudged him through the door. "He may

have a bit of a faulty memory, but he can be trusted with your mare. What's her name, dear?"

"The horse is Sara," I said, trying to keep up with the easy chatter and loving manner of these two. "And I'm Brex. Brexia Eloise."

"I'll take good care of her, miss," Dale said, holding out a well-veined hand.

After grabbing a lamp, Dale took Sara's lead.

"Sir!" I called out before he could hobble too far.

He stopped and looked back over his shoulder.

"I've only just taken Sara in," I explained. "She's brand-new to me, and as you can tell from her face, I believe she's known rough treatment." I reached for his arm and squeezed gently. "I mean no insult to you, sir, but I don't know her temperament well yet. I'd urge you to be careful and to know that she might react poorly if she feels unsafe."

Dale's face sagged as though his heart were breaking open in front of my eyes. "Oh, my dear, sweet girl. Both of you, that is. I know just what she needs. I'll take good care of her. In the morning, Rain will pay her a visit. He's got a special way with horses. We'll have her feeling right with the world before you know it."

He clucked his tongue and scurried off toward the stable.

"Miss?" The woman waited at the door, motioning me inside. "Come in, come in. Please."

I clutched the touchstone around my neck, a sudden rush of emotion freezing me in place. I'd been so certain that what I needed was a job. A place to stay, a source of income. Truth be told, I'd expected to scout the house for valuables. Stay long enough to learn the secrets of the manor, collect a paycheck, and fill my purse with as much as I could sell on the road before going back to the foundling home. To the place where I hoped I might buy my sister's freedom. Assuming that she was still alive. Assuming I was able to find her. I had every reason to believe she was dead, but still I clung to a weak hope that I would see her again. This job was a means to a very personal end.

I hadn't considered that the manor would be filled with people who might treat me kindly. Whose warmth might shift something inside my heart and soul in such a way that my plan, while necessary, would seem cold. Calculating. But now was not the time for second-guessing.

As I stepped inside Oderisi Manor, I held my breath and my ground. I was here for one reason, one purpose. No amount of kindness to me or to my horse could shift me from my goal. My life and that of my sister, if she was still living, depended on one thing and one thing only. I'd need to toughen myself—push myself harder and farther than I'd been pushed yet. The sweet old couple, the pretty gentleman, this warm home with the magical glowing flowers and beautiful land were not mine, would never be mine. This was a job, and a temporary one at that.

I gripped my sister's stone in a shaking hand as I reminded myself why I was here: to take what was here for the taking.

"I'm Antonia," the woman explained as she locked the door behind us. "I'm the Oderisi family butler. I've managed the household since Neoruzzi and Rainieri were little boys." She gave me a wink. "Sometimes I still call them Neo and Rain, even though they're titled gentleman now. Well, Neo holds the title now," she explained. "Rain did for a time too, while his brother was...unavailable." She trailed off, leaving me to wonder what the story was there.

Why would a younger brother assume the property title for any amount of time? And then return it? I was certain there was a mystery there that would unravel if I let Antonia speak freely. There would be plenty of time for that once I got settled in.

"Why don't you have a seat?" Antonia gestured toward an ornately carved wooden door that was slightly ajar. "I'll call for Lord Oderisi. Have you eaten, dear? Shall I bring tea or some supper?"

I was about to ask for as much food as she could spare when a voice behind me froze the blood in my veins.

"Brexia? What, by the gods, are you doing here?"

A pair of golden eyes met mine. The man was glaring and storming past Antonia to meet me. He was closely followed by another man, one with long, sand-colored curls and stormy gray eyes, his angular chin covered by a scruff of facial hair.

"Neo!" Antonia clasped a hand over her mouth. "Mind your manners. This girl is our guest!"

"This *girl* is a thief," Neo barked. "And the fact that she's here now when I *told* her..."

I held up my hand and shook my head. "I beg your pardon. If this is about the matter of your eating blade—"

"So this is her?" The blond man cocked his chin and looked me over with a smile. "This is the woman?"

"Hold your tongue, brother," Neo seethed.

The shorter of the men walked up to me, his hand extended. "I'm Rainieri Oderisi. Neo's younger brother. My apologies for his lack of manners. He's only recently been dismissed from prison and doesn't fully remember how to behave in polite company."

"Rain!" Neo's eyes flashed, and he crossed his arms over his chest.

"Prison?" I reached out and tentatively shook the younger man's hand. "I don't suppose he was apprehended for stealing? He seems to have a great preoccupation with thieving."

Neo sighed and pushed past the ornately carved door. Inside, a beautifully appointed sitting room was warm, a fireplace bricked with unusual black stones ablaze with a roaring fire. Luxurious blood-red fabric covered long settees adorned with so many plush pillows, I wasn't certain how anyone would dare sit on them. Neo paced the length of the room, sighing dramatically while Antonia glared at him like he was an ill-mannered child.

"I was just about to offer our guest some supper," she said. "She looks as though she could use a good meal and a long rest."

Neo dismissed her with a wave. "Fine. Bring her all the food in the house. She's particularly fond of sausage and ale."

Rain smirked at his brother and motioned for me to join them in the large sitting room.

"So, Miss Eloise—" Rain began.

"Brex is fine," I corrected, watching Neo as he gathered speed and paced more frantically across the black tile floor.

"My brother here, despite his lack of manners, has spoken of very little but you since leaving Fish Head End yesterday."

I flushed and looked between the brothers. "If his current mood is any indication, he's not had the most pleasant first impression of me."

Rain laughed, his face warm and inviting. "His current mood is his forever mood these days." He walked to the window and clapped his brother on the shoulder. "I'll leave you two to talk," he said, but before he left, he leaned close to his brother and spoke softly under his breath. I don't think whatever it was he said left a favorable impression on Neo, because he snorted and pulled away from his brother's hold.

Rain strode through the room, pausing beside me before leaving.

"Brex," he said. "I know my brother and I have a difference of opinion on many topics, but we'll both agree that a young woman cannot be turned out into the night without home or host. I'll have Antonia prepare a room for you and will bring my wife by to meet you before the household retires. You'll be welcome here for the night, no matter what that one says."

He hooked a thumb toward his brother then left the room, closing the heavy door behind him. Once we were alone, neither Neo nor I spoke. And then, of course, we both began speaking at once.

"You shouldn't be here," he said. "I told you not to come."

"That's not true! I thought I would be welcome," I said, unable to keep the hint of embarrassment from my voice.

I grasped the touchstone around my neck and remembered my pride. My purpose. I had nothing to be ashamed of. Other than a few stolen sausages and a couple mugs of ale, there was no debt between this man and me. Other than the natural imbalance that the circumstances of our lives had created. And for that, I should be angry—not ashamed. If he had any sort of a moral compass, he'd feel the same.

Neo uncrossed his arms and sighed but clamped his lips closed, so I went on.

"I need a job, and I thought you'd give the one you have to someone else if I waited until next week. It's rare that passion and initiative is discouraged by an employer, but I'll make a note you prefer your staff...to be what, exactly? Lazy? Indifferent? Unmotivated?" I probably should have moderated the tone of my voice, not to provoke him into further anger. But when I challenged him, he didn't react, just looked me over with obvious uncertainty.

Those honey-gold eyes seemed intent on learning all my secrets. He stared at my face, my lips, my eyes, as though I was a puzzle that could be fitted together if he just looked long enough.

"Who are you, really?" He crossed the floor, his fine shoes echoing on the polished tile. He stopped a few inches from me and explored my face with his molten gaze. "You *overheard* that I had a job—which, by the way, was intended for my friend. A man with whom I have long-established history and trust. What if the work was unsavory? Involved a criminal aspect to it? Who are you, and why are you so blasted persistent about working for me?"

I had no chance to explain when he whirled on me anew, pointing a finger in my face. "Your sister," he demanded. "Where is this sister you spoke of so poignantly? Does she know you delivered yourself to the doorstep of a strange man, demanding employment, the details of which you know nothing about?"

At the mention of my sister, I felt suddenly weak and overly hot. I loosened the laces that fastened my cloak and set a hand on the back of one of the lush settees. "May I sit?" I asked quietly. "I will be honest with you, but I've not eaten since last night and the day has been taxing. May I please take a seat and perhaps trouble you for some water?"

Neo's eyes flashed something hard, as if he were fighting any feelings of compassion I might have evoked. He still didn't trust me. One stolen eating blade and couple of bites of his dinner, and I was no more than a common thief to him. Even if his reaction wasn't unreasonable, I had my dignity. I'd not stay where I was not wanted. The feeling was altogether too familiar and made the emptiness of my stomach fill with queasy discomfort.

He grunted under his breath before disappearing into a shadowy corner of the room. I heard the sound of water pouring into a mug.

"Here," he said, his voice tight. "Take a seat. Have a drink."

He extended the mug to me, and I accepted it with relief, my fingers brushing his as he passed me the beverage. His hand was strong, and the tops of his knuckles scarred in a way I hadn't noticed the other day. I considered taking hold and looking at them, inspecting his hands for the stories they kept hidden, but I stifled the impulse. If the man were to eventually be my employer, displays of intimacy might send the opposite impression I intended. No matter how irrationally drawn to such displays I might be.

"Were you truly in prison?" I asked, gently perching on the edge of the furniture and sipping the water he'd poured. It was surprisingly cool and delicious, almost sweet, unlike the well water where I came from.

"In a manner of speaking, yes," he said. "Through no fault of my own, of course."

I bit back a smile. "Of course," I agreed.

Just then a loud knock at the door announced Antonia's arrival with a butler's cart. "Oh good!" she exclaimed. "Happy to see you've been offered water and a place to get comfortable." She glared at Neo and then nodded at me in approval. "I'll have Dale clean your cloak for you, miss, and your shoes if you'd like."

I shook my head, my mouth already watering at the promise of the food spread out on that cart. There were crisp apples, their pinkish-green skins promising sweetness. A selection of cheeses and breads, a bit of salted meat, and even a bottle of wine. I counted two mugs and wondered if my reluctant host would join me or watch me while I ate and drink my fill at his table.

"This is wonderful," I breathed, leaping from the settee. I wanted to hug the woman, and tears stung my eyes. "I've not seen a meal like this in…" I choked back the words I wanted to say and simply admitted, "A very, very long time. Thank you. Thank you for your kindness. This is most generous of you."

She seemed moved by my sincerity and sent another glare Neo's way before she reached for my cloak.

"No, no," I said, refusing to let it go. "I don't believe I'll be staying. I don't wish to put you to any further trouble on my behalf."

Neo's head whipped toward me when I said I wasn't staying, his glossy black hair reaching nearly to his elbows.

"Not staying?" Antonia echoed. "Not staying? That's foolish, girl! You cannot leave before morning. You'd be ensured an attack by air or worse." She turned on Neo and pointed at him. "Neo, please. Whatever issue you may have with this young girl, make her feel welcome. I'll not have a sleepless night because we sent an innocent out into the dark."

"Innocent," he muttered. But he waved a hand, and with a disgruntled chortle, Antonia left us alone.

Although the food was sitting right there in reach, my hands felt grimy from the horse and the road, and I just couldn't stomach eating while Neo was pacing the room in a frenzy, no doubt trying to figure out the easiest way to cast me from his manor for good.

"I'll not be a burden," I said, lifting my chin. "Why don't you leave me here? I'll eat, sleep the night right here where I sit, and be gone in the morning before I can trouble your household further."

Neo turned and looked me over, the intensity of his golden eyes sending chills down my back and arousing an uncomfortable heat in my belly. "I thought you were here for the job," he said. "Now all of a sudden, you're anxious to leave?"

I closed my eyes and swallowed a sip of water then set the mug on the cart and stood. I paced the beautiful room, moving away from Neo. The corners of the large room were dark, as no lamps were lit. Only the roaring fire in its enormous black hearth sent light and heat through the room. The floors were a smooth, glossy tile with thick woolen rugs set away from the fire to soften the sounds of footsteps. When I moved out of the warmth of the flames, the space felt empty. Dark. I wrapped my hands around my arms and stared into the fire. My expectant host cleared his throat impatiently.

"I am an orphan," I explained. "A foundling. I was rescued by a woman who was not my birth mother when I was only three." I sniffled and rubbed away any traces of grief as I spoke. "My mother, the woman who took me in, didn't survive long. She was alone in the world as well. I have never been able to understand why one such as her would claim me for her own. Would put herself through the burden of raising a little one, as she herself was an outcast."

I swallowed hard and looked at Neo. I had no reason to trust him, so I withheld the details about my adoptive mother that I knew would put him off. What she really was. An unholy, forbidden creature the name of which even now I feared speaking.

If Neo knew anything about my life before, anything about the secrets I was bound to keep, he might cast me out, dark of night or not. So I told as much of the story as I dared.

"She passed when I was very young. Just a girl of eleven. She knew she had little time left and installed me in a foundling home in a small shire called Byrlad. Have you been?"

He nodded his head. "Passed through at least. Of that, I'm certain. Go on."

I stared into the fire, stroking the charm around my neck. "I was well treated there."

That was the truth, in a manner of speaking. I'd been fed and not abused in the ways some might presume. But my life there was far from safe. Not at all peaceful.

My voice was quiet, but I could not keep the emotion from my words. "I should not have been allowed to stay. I didn't belong there. By the time the woman who ran the home knew as much, it was too late. I knew her secrets, and she mine." I met the man's bright eyes and glared at him. "Secrets bind people in devastating ways," I said.

"Secrets," he echoed, a surprising concern in his voice. He strode behind me at the fire and reached a hand to touch my shoulder.

I lifted my chin, just peeking over my shoulder where his hand rested against the rough material of my dress. He withdrew, yanking his fingers away too quickly, before I could take a moment's comfort from the touch. But I knew deep down there was no comfort to be had here. Even if he was moved to a moment's kindness, it was already gone.

"You were never harmed?" he asked, his voice composed.

I nodded. "No serious harm of the physical sort was ever directed at me, nor at any of the foundlings. I made myself useful but, sadly, was unable to learn any trade that might have been gainful outside of the home. I was unable to leave, to seek a marriage, a guild for training or education. I remained there, in a place that was never meant for the likes of me, until just a few days ago when... Well, I've obviously left the place."

Neo stepped beside me, lifting his chin as if fighting the words on his lips, his hands clasped together in front of his chest. "And what of your sister? Was that a lie, then?"

"A lie?" I turned on him. "My sister," I seethed, "was my sister by bond, not blood." I gripped the charm around my neck and closed my eyes. "She was special. Not meant for this world," I whispered. "And as far as I know, she's no longer in it."

"I don't understand." Neo reached a hand toward my necklace but stopped short of touching it. Of touching me. "Is your sister dead or alive?"

"It depends on who you ask," I spat bitterly. "She disappeared just over a week ago. Left of her own will or taken, I'll never know. All that remained of her was this necklace. I found it hidden under my pillow as I tried to fall asleep the night she disappeared. The caretaker of the foundling home refused to speak of her. Every child eventually leaves, but most depart with a special meal, gifts, and well-wishes. Ginevra, my sweet little Gini, disappeared without so much as a goodbye. She would never, ever have left me that way. I'm certain of it. But I don't know that I'll ever know for sure what's happened to her. I was cast out of the foundling home when I was caught looking through the books for any sign of where she'd gone."

"I...I'm sorry." Neo looked at me curiously, as if trying to puzzle through what I'd told him. Doubt and distrust set his mouth into a hard line, despite the hint of concern that lit up his eyes. "So you looked at the records to see if there were notes or clues as to what happened to the girl?"

I nodded. "I was discovered, of course. And when the caretaker found this around my neck—" I stroked the charm on its slim length of leather— "I was accused of stealing it. They tried to take the one thing I had that let me know Gini loved me. The only clue I had." I sighed, my shoulders sinking. "After an entire lifetime in their care, I was branded a thief and tossed aside."

Neo paced away from me, dropping down into a velvet-covered armchair. "So you're on the hunt for your sister. And you need a job, a place to live. Money."

I nodded. "Whether or not I'm ever able to find my sister, I have no home to return to. No savings, no skills."

"And yet you mean to offer yourself for employment here?" His voice lacked judgment, but rather sounded curious.

"Managing a household is something I can easily do," I assured him. "At any given time, I was responsible for the care and maintenance of up to a dozen foundlings. Each with very unusual needs."

I clamped my lips together, hoping I already hadn't revealed too much.

"I assure you, I only stole from you in Fish Head End because I had nothing. I am not heartless, nor am I selfish. Your fine clothes, your hair... You are by all appearances someone who would not be greatly harmed by the loss of a few sausages and mugs of ale. Your meal filled my empty belly. Had I kept your knife, I would have sold it to purchase only what I needed to survive. I am not proud of what I've done, but I hope you see the necessity that drove me to it and do not judge me harshly."

"By the gods." Neo dropped his face into his hands and raked his fingers from the stubble on his chin to the top of his glossy hair. "I can't... I don't..."

"Please." I walked to his chair and sat on the settee so our faces were nearly level. I licked my dry lower lip, pulling it into my mouth absently as I weighed my words. "I cannot go to a pub or a guild and provide a reference or demonstrate even the slightest bit of skill or training. I have nothing. No people to vouch for me. I'm a ghost out there in the Realm. It's as though I didn't exist all those years I was hidden away. I do have skills, though. I can run a household. And you need a caretaker. Don't you see?"

I leaned forward, knotting my fingers together while I wished I could clasp his hands in mine and make him see. Make him understand my sincere plight.

"It was the will of the gods that I ran into you the way I did, just when you were looking for help."

Neo's eyes darkened and he rested his fists on his knees. "You know not what the gods will for me. It would be better if you had nothing to do with my dark destiny." He stood to move past me, but I stopped him, unable to resist reaching out and gripping his arm with my hand.

"Lord Oderisi, what's happened to you? Why were you in prison?" I hoped I would not push him too far with the question. If he would answer, if he did so honestly, gaining entry to his secrets might bring about the same kind of dark pact I'd had with my caretaker. But it soon became clear that Neo had no desire to bind himself to me in any way.

"My past is no business of yours," he said, his voice deadly serious. The hairs on the back of my neck and arms stood, reacting not so much in fear, but in warning. "I do have a job. You're correct in that. But the job is not here, Brexia. My household manages itself fine. I have neither the desire nor the means to put you to work under my roof."

"What, then?" I demanded. "What am I to do?"

Mine were not his problems to sort, I understood that. I'd come all this way, stolen a horse, and traveled far beyond familiar lands in the hope of some opportunity... I'd been such a fool. Fear ignited in my chest. If he turned me away, I might not just be hopeless, but truly defeated. The plan I'd concocted began to burn up in my mind.

"Please understand," I said, swallowing back my shame. "I came here for the job. And I cannot leave. I will work hard, dutifully serving—"

"Stop! I know not what will become of you." He stared into the fire, his face revealing not even the slightest trace of emotion. "But I cannot help. The work I have was intended for someone I trust. Someone I've known a long time. It's far too dangerous for a young woman. I cannot be responsible for what might happen."

"Are you willing, then, to take responsibility for what happens if you turn me out?" My fingers tightened on his arm, and he looked down at the contact. I hastily withdrew. "I am stronger than I look. Braver than probably anyone you've known."

He barked a laugh, but I held fast to my plea.

"There are things I have seen, things I know, that cause me to fear nothing in this Realm. Nothing the gods could send can hurt me more than the loss of the only person I've loved. The loss of the only family I've known. Not just once, but twice."

He flinched, and I remembered what the farrier had told me about his mother losing not one but two loves. Maybe he and I were more alike that he cared to see. Not that I would point that out. I felt certain nothing I could say at this point would recommend me to him. Nothing would change his mind and heart now. If he were unmoved by my story, my vow, and my pleas... Nonetheless, I would not be able to sleep if I did not ask one last time.

"I can do the job. Please. Reconsider. Let me try. If I'm unsuccessful, I'll understand if you dismiss me. But until you give me a—"

"No!" he roared, turning away from me and striding toward the door. He yanked it open, his molten eyes hard, his lips pressed thin with fury. "Eat the meal my butler has prepared. Rest the night in safety. No one will disturb you here. But in the morning, take your leave. There is no work for you here. Nothing you say or do will change my mind on the matter."

He left the room, closing the door loudly behind him. I sat in stunned silence, the crackling of the fire doing little to ease the chill in my heart. For so long, I'd carried the secrets of others. The weight of duty, of responsibility, was truly now gone. Had vanished along with my sister. Perhaps I was a fool to think I could land a position that would bring me quick coin, access to goods, and a way to go back to Byrlad with enough power to demand answers. To demand the foundling home reveal what had truly happened to my sister.

With every passing day, she might be in danger, sick, alone. I had been powerless to stop her disappearance. And despite my best efforts, I might remain powerless to fix it.

My rumbling stomach reminded me that while I had a weary heart, my body wouldn't stop functioning. A lack of food might weaken my mind, drive me to make mistakes or choices that I would regret when the soundness of my circumstances improved. I reached for an apple and instinctively slipped into it my purse. I filled my traveling sack with all the food it would hold, and then I opened the wine and filled a mug.

I walked to the corner and found the water Neo had poured me to drink. Not wishing to waste good water, I poured a bit of it onto one of the clean rags on the butler's cart and wiped my hands clean of the grime of the horse and the road.

Tomorrow would come before long, and if I were cast aside again, at least I'd leave with a full belly and full purse for my trouble. Then I ate, the food at first sour in my mouth. But quickly I set aside my emotions and focused on the fact that this was the most healthy, delicious meal I'd had in as long as I could remember. I devoured everything I hadn't stuffed into my pouch—the meat, the cheese, the bread. All of it.

Only when I'd finished two mugs of wine did I give in to grief. I rested my head on the plush pillows, images from my memory preventing sleep. My sister's face, my old room. Tears fought hopeful dreams, but I must eventually have dozed off. I had cried myself out of tears when the door opened and the butler Antonia crept into the room. I heard her soft steps, but I did not dare move to thank her or even to speak. She'd insisted that Neo *not* send me away, but I was fearful. Uncertain.

People's minds and hearts changed so suddenly, with so

little provocation. I would not do anything to provoke a change in the woman who had so far treated me so kindly. I squeezed my eyes shut and stayed motionless on the settee. Just the thought of what these people must think of me brought another wave of tears upon me. But I held them back as best I could.

The simple reality was that I'd failed. I had come to Omrora for work and to quickly amass what I needed to go home and find Gini. But now, I had no job. There was nothing in this room but furniture and fire. Nothing to take. Nothing to sell. Nothing but an empty butler's cart and a few morsels of food.

The soft pillow beneath my cheek would be pulled away come morning. That grim reality was very, very difficult to face. Silent tears rolled down my cheeks as I felt a hand on my brow.

"You'll find some fresh water for you if you wake in the night, dear one," Antonia said. Whether she knew that I was awake or not, I felt she did not mean to disturb me. She stroked my hair back from my forehead and covered me with an incredibly soft blanket. Her hand lingered on my head, and she whispered something I couldn't understand. A blessing, I hoped. A curse, I feared, until she said slightly louder, "Sleep well, dear girl. You are safe here. You can rest without fear."

She hobbled away from me, checked the fire, and added a few small twigs to the blaze. Then she placed a heavy iron grate in front of the flames to prevent sparks or embers from escaping and setting fire to the rugs or furniture in the night. Finally, she hobbled from the room, closing the door behind her.

I heard voices in the hall but kept my eyes closed, not wishing to engage in further conversation, no matter who was outside the door.

"She's asleep, Rain. Let her rest. She looks exhausted. We'll make introductions and set her up in a room tomorrow." Antonia's voice carried through the quiet room.

"My brother is intent on sending her away in the morning." The voice, much softer and gentler than Neo's, echoed through the closed door.

Antonia said something, but I couldn't make it out over the sounds of their retreating footsteps. I was nearly certain before the voices faded completely away that I heard something turn, a lock perhaps, containing me within this beautiful cell for the night.

There were windows and I had everything I needed in reach. I'd escape if it came to that. No doubt Neo wanted to contain the rooms I might raid to just this one. He didn't want me to stay, so my containment was by no means imprisonment. It was little more than an act of damage control. A way of showing exactly how little trust he put in me—an unarmed, homeless, useless girl.

I turned onto my side and burrowed my face into the soft pillow. I'd probably take it with me in the morning. Out of spite. After all, I was a criminal. Not to be trusted in this house. With Neo's job. With anything. I might as well live up to the expectations of me, low as they were. I drifted off into a fitful sleep, my fingers wrapped around my sister's touchstone.

Help me, Gini, I prayed. *Help me so I can help you.*

It was probably better that I moved on from this place. I hadn't told Neo the whole truth about the foundling home. Yes, I'd been bound to stay there, working under lock and key, maintaining the secrets of the children who passed through those rooms year after year after year. But when I finally left, I'd fled. Escaped. I'd not been cast out. Not been accused of thievery. I'd stolen nothing, taking nothing from that place. Except the secrets that would forever bind me to it.

I couldn't tell Neo why I'd been unable to leave. Why I only left once my sister disappeared. Whether I'd been forced out or left of my own will didn't matter any longer. What he needed to know—where I was from, how little I had, why I was so insistent in my pursuit of his job—none of that would matter come morning.

As I drifted off to sleep, I dreamed of golden eyes, a barren manor, and visions of hills drenched in blood.

"Hmmm, which one...You...or you?" I fought waking the next morning, running my fingers along the perfect seams of the pillows beneath my head as the tiniest hint of sunrise pressed against the window glass. Despite how emotional I'd been, I did fall asleep, and oh, by the gods, I'd slept soundly. Haunted by unusual dreams, yes, but still... It would have been impossible to deny that soft pillows, a warm blanket, and the comfort of a full belly led to an incredible night's sleep. Too bad it wasn't going to last.

I traced the stitches on the pillows with my fingernails, wondering over the talented craftsperson whose hands had once so perfectly guided the needle to make such a luxurious item. Perfect flowers were embroidered in wreaths along one of the pillow's edges. Another was trimmed in a short, soft fringe.

Maybe I'd find someone willing to teach me tailoring. Embroidery, even. I'd mended plenty of clothes over the years and was not terrible with a needle and thread. I was no artisan, but who was until they'd been gifted time to practice and reliable guidance? If I needed to create a new life for myself, I'd need to find work that was meaningful, fulfilling. Honest. But until then...

"It's decided, then," I said.

I grabbed the flowered pillow and rolled it tight between my hands, crushing the downy feathers inside. I had a momentary twinge of conscience as I slipped the pillow beneath my cloak, tying it tightly into a small bundle with the leather strap from my pouch. I'd never promised Neo that I wouldn't steal from him again. Well, maybe I had made such a promise back in Fish Head End, back when I thought the wealthy lord would be my future employer. But now? He was nothing to me. Nothing except a man who had more pillows than heart.

The pillow was mine now. His rotten heart would remain his problem.

I gathered my things quietly and checked the handle on the door. It was not, as I'd expected, locked, so I was able to slip into the hallway with my full purse. I heard the soft echoes of sounds carrying through the hallway. The voices of Antonia and Dale, no doubt readying the household for morning. Cooking, cleaning, laughing. I shouldn't have been surprised they were awake at this hour, but I hastened to the front door, unwilling to engage the members of the Oderisi household. Especially not the heartbreakingly kind old couple. I had a pillow to smuggle out and a horse waiting for me. The day ahead promised hardship and heartbreak. The sooner I set out on the road, the sooner I might find some kinder path.

I tread softly across the expansive property, peering down at the sedum that covered the land like a lush blanket. I wondered about the red glow I'd seen on the plants last night and knelt to inspect the perfectly coiled blooms. In the early morning light, I could see there was something growing on the petals of the sedum, something that might have been algae or perhaps a type of moss. It was dark red now, the color of dried blood, not the vibrant, nearly glowing red I'd seen last night. The plant life, like the man who owned this manor, would remain a mystery, though. I was not meant to stay here, and I tread cautiously through the sedum until I reached an expansive field of grass.

When I reached the stable, I shoved the door open and wandered through the stalls looking for Sara. I realized as I peeked at the bays and other breeds the family kept that I would not be able to repay the farrier who had treated Sara with such kindness. The reality of that brought a pang of sickness to my heart.

Maybe I would stay in Omrora. Maybe I'd find other work here, or, I thought sadly, other petty thefts that would allow me to make good on my debt to the farrier before making my way onto the next village. I sighed but brightened when I noticed the distinctive dark mane of my sweet mare Sara peeking up from behind a low wooden stall. Her white muzzle looked far brighter than it had yesterday, the gouges on her face almost impossible to perceive.

"My girl," I whispered as I approached, mindful that a stablehand might be about. "What's happened to your lovely face? That must have been some ointment—"

As I approached the stall, I realized Sara wasn't alone. There was someone with her. I approached quietly, my breath stalling in my chest as I recognized the sand-colored curls of the younger Oderisi brother.

I reached for my necklace for comfort, immediately regretting the stolen pillow. What was he doing here with my horse? Hoping to stop me before I left with my contraband? How could he have known? How could he have discovered I'd taken it already? My mind raced to find an excuse.

"Lord Oderisi," I said. "Good morning. I...I—"

At the sound of my voice, the man's back stiffened and he

froze, his hands splayed on Sara's neck. For a moment, neither of us moved, and I couldn't quite make sense of why. I had the pillow I'd stolen tucked deep within my belongings. Why didn't he turn to me? Accuse me or dismiss me?

"Sir? Is everything all right?" I echoed his name and stepped closer, but one of his hands flew into the air.

"Don't!" he shouted, his words oddly slurred. "Stay back!"

"What are you... Are you quite all right?" I reached out to touch his shoulder just as he whirled away from Sara. He covered his face in his hands, seeming at odds with himself. But finally, he dropped them, revealing a sight I would not soon forget.

Rain's gray eyes glowed blood red, an unnatural, unholy color. The whites of his eyes were streaked with dark veins that cast a sickly, horrific glow to even the parts that were not red. Instead of his perfect, handsome smile, a pair of elongated teeth —like the fangs of a snake—peeked between his lips. A trickle of vibrant crimson stained his lips.

The fluid was blood. My horse's blood. My eyes flew to her neck, where two puncture marks, the same distance apart as Rain's fangs, were scarcely visible through her white coat.

I swallowed hard, speechless but not shocked. Rain seemed stuck in the same reaction, his eyes slowly resuming their normal appearance as he stared at me.

"Rainieri? Rain? How is Sara this morning? Did you give her a bit of that venom of yours?" Dale wandered into the stable, looking from Rain to me to Sara and then back again before his mouth fell open. "Oh, by the gods. Oh no. No, no, my dear, I... I thought you'd sleep well into the morning. Oh, by the gods." Dale dropped his face into his hands and staggered against the wall for support. "Oh no. No, no, no. My lord, I'm..."

I held up a hand and shook my head. "It's all right," I assured him. So much made sense now. So much about Neo, his job, his attitude. Everything. "You've helped her," I said, nodding at Rainieri. "I can see the wounds on her muzzle have already begun healing. Even the older scars look less prominent. Thank you."

Rain wiped his mouth with the back of a hand, his eyes fully returned to their stormy gray color and his fangs retracting back into the perfect but otherwise very average-looking teeth I'd seen when I met him yesterday. "How?" he sputtered. "How do you not react with fear? With horror? How do you know about the healing effects of the venom?"

I truly wished in that moment that I hadn't stolen the pillow. That I had nothing to hide. Because my time at the Oderisi manor was far from over.

"Let's go back inside," I suggested, sighing deeply. "I'd like to talk to your brother again. I suppose we all have some explaining to do."

"BY THE GODS, brother! How could you be so careless!" Neo picked up a roughly split log from beside the hearth and hurled it furiously against the wall. It struck the stone, leaving little more than a faint mark and a tiny, pathetic bang as it clattered to the floor.

I was seated back on the settee where I'd slept, my cloak tight around me to hide the food and the pillow I'd stashed away. Rain was sitting on the armchair near me, his head in his hands, his elbows propped on his knees. He was the picture of guilt-laden misery.

"It's all my fault, sir," Dale said, his voice sincerely apologetic. "I thought the lady was sound asleep. I'm the one who suggested the mare might benefit from a bit of venom. She's been through so much but seemed so very trusting. The injuries on her face, the old scars. I... I never thought, never dreamed..."

"This has nothing to do with you, Dale. Don't trouble yourself." Neo stormed through the sitting room, the hard heels of his fancy shoes echoing against the floor tile. He seemed to intentionally avoid the woolen rugs so he could noisily work out his rage through his feet.

Antonia wheeled in the butler's cart, her face flushed and pinched. "Now before you get yourself all worked up, Neo, the girl's got to eat." She stooped beside me where I sat on the settee and put a hand on my shoulder. "Have any of you brutes bothered to ask the girl if she's all right? She just walked in on the lord of the manor drinking the blood of her pretty mare. Is she in shock?" She rested the back of her hand gently against my cheek. "Lovely, can you say something? Are you all right?"

Since I walked in on Rain feeding from my horse in the barn, I'd been contemplating how to play out my reaction with the family. If I overacted, played the terrified girl—no. That would never work. It wasn't me. Even if I didn't have the history with vampires that I did have, I was no performer. I couldn't pretend to feel anything other than what I was. But this did provide a delicious amount of leverage. I only needed to understand how to use it.

I reached for Antonia's hand and squeezed it. "I'm fine," I said, sincerely. "Truly. Thank you for your kindness. You're the only one who seems not to blame me for this."

"I do not blame you," Rain said immediately. "I'm the one who should have been more careful. Asked for your approval to treat the horse and then sent you away where you wouldn't see exactly how I planned to help."

Neo alone looked at me with fury and distrust in his eyes. "Speaking of that... Tell us, Brexia. Why do you show no fear?"

he asked. "No surprise? Why do you look as though you've bested us all in a game of cards?"

"Really?" I spat, but I refused to stand from the settee lest I accidentally drop the pillow and food supply. I stomped my foot, but my soft leather shoe provided little more than a disappointing slap beside Neo's angry footfalls. "You think not to ask if I'm scared witless? You suspect me even now of some nefarious doing because I'm *not* a blubbering mess?"

"Rain?" A stunningly pretty girl with long brown hair and thoughtful eyes appeared in the doorway of the sitting room. She wore a linen shirt tucked into a pair of loose-fitting breeches. Her clothing struck me as unusual but wonderful. I immediately appreciated her willingness to dress for ease and functionality and wondered if someday I might be able to do the same. To be so confident, so safe in my home that I could make choices based on my own free will and desire, not the demands or conventions of those around me.

"My love," the woman asked, "what happened?"

Rain strode to the door and clasped the woman in an embrace, resting his forehead against hers before kissing her lips. "Oh, Gia, I've made a terrible mess, I'm afraid. One that cannot easily be tidied."

The blonde woman I'd seen in the cart last night—Odile the healer—pushed her way past Rain and came to me. "What happened?" She scowled at Neo. "This is the girl who came looking for you. I thought you'd given her shelter for the night. What happened?"

Odile immediately began touching my face, checking the flush of my cheeks, and asked me to open my mouth and show her my tongue.

"Have you taken ill?"

I grabbed her hands and kindly squeezed, turning my face away from her nervous examinations.

"I'm fine!" I said loudly, trying to quiet the chatter in the room. "I'm well, please. Well enough, that is."

Neo crossed his arms over his chest, the fine burgundy doublet he wore today embroidered with gold-colored thread making his eyes seem more yellow than brown and his black hair even more glossy and beautiful. He truly was a sight to behold, his chest broad and his legs thick and tall even as he stormed about the room. Like a raging, angry prince. Too bad his heart was filled with bile, and his face, as handsome as it was, bore a scowl sour enough to curdle milk.

"Can someone please explain what happened?" Odile sat beside me, placing a protective arm over my shoulder.

Neo rolled his eyes at her gesture of concern, and I shook my head.

"How do you stand him?" I asked her, curious if Odile and Neo were somehow connected. A couple, perhaps?

"He is my sister's brother-in-law, and that makes him family," she said, her tone making it clear that she was not in any way entangled with Neo romantically. I flushed at the fact that I was even momentarily curious about that. "He's a good man once you know him," she continued, her voice softer. "He's been through a lot. More than any man should. But there are times when he lets the darker aspects of his vitality get the better of him."

I couldn't help making a face at that, twisting my lips to one side in disapproval. I was hardly moved to compassion for a man who'd heard about my own painful circumstances and had nonetheless tossed me into the street. Turned me out. Yes, with my pockets full of food and a pillow he'd not yet discovered I'd taken, but still. It was difficult to feel compassion for him when he'd shown me nothing but contempt since I'd arrived.

"Please, Neo, Rain, one of you. Start at the beginning." Rain's wife walked up to me, her hand extended. "I'm Gia

Lestalinn, wife of Rainieri Oderisi," she said. "I'm so very sorry to meet you under these circumstances. If I only knew what the circumstances were!"

I shook the lovely girl's hand. "Thank you for your hospitality," I said, silently praying that my pillow crime wouldn't soon be discovered.

"Enough," Neo sighed, a bit less bark in his tone. "Brexia, you now know the household. Antonia and Dale, my butler and her husband. Rainieri is my younger brother." He closed his eyes, as if withholding some complaint or insult, and then continued. "Gia is Rain's wife, and Odile her sister."

"Ah-hem." A throat was cleared from the doorway, and the redheaded boy from last night waved at me. "I'm Flynn," he said. "Part-time cart driver, all around apprentice to the needs of this fine enterprise."

"Enterprise?" I echoed.

"Flynnie..." Gia said, her voice heavy with warning.

A warning to be quiet about their business? The longer I stayed among these people, the more I realized their secrets were many.

"Flynn Serlo, out!" Neo pointed at the door. "You have work you should be attending, do you not?"

Flynn scrambled away, closing the door behind him. "Nice to see you again, miss!" he called through the closed door.

"That boy has a weak spot for pretty faces," Gia said, shaking her head.

"Enough," Neo boomed, pointing a finger at his brother. But I was certain his eyes trailed over my face when Gia called me pretty before he angrily looked away. "To summarize, my brother decided this morning to drink from Miss Eloise's horse, who I understand suffered injuries before she was rescued from some rather unfortunate circumstances."

"I believe the mare was abused," I clarified, a sincere frown on my face.

Gia's hand flew to her mouth, and she nibbled nervously on a nail.

"And then this morning, our guest decided to escape from the sitting room like a thief in the night. She happened upon my dear brother just as he was drinking the horse's blood."

Gia gasped, her face drained of its color. "She saw that? She witnessed it?"

"I'm terribly sorry," Rain said miserably. "I had no idea she would be awake."

"I am furious at your carelessness, brother, but that is a matter for another conversation. The situation we find ourselves in is not solely your fault." Neo glared at me, his long hair falling in menacing panels over his face. "She is a guest here! She should never have been sneaking about the property. Who knows what dangers she might have encountered! Even worse, after a night of hospitality, who slips away without so much as a goodbye?"

"Neo, that's ridiculous." Odile shook her head, her lack of patience with the man matching mine. "She is a guest here, not a prisoner. It was simply an unfortunate accident. She might have stumbled into any of the rooms and seen something else that..." She looked from Rain back to his brother. "Something else better kept private."

Neo pointed at his brother, his golden eyes flashing dark. "Nonsense. She's a thief and she's trouble. And now, thanks to you, she *knows*."

Gia joined me and her sister on the settee. "Brexia," she said gently. "You seem altogether too calm for someone who's just seen what you have. Are you all right, truly? Are you in shock?"

Before I could answer, Odile scooted closer to me. Surrounded by the sisters, one on each side of me, I could see the resemblance. While Gia's coloring was dark and Odile so very fair, there was no denying they were sisters. The likeness and their obvious bond made my chest ache with longing.

"You knew, didn't you?" Odile asked. "This isn't the first encounter you've had with vampires?"

I nodded and looked down at my lap, my hands nervously reaching for my necklace.

"I have known such creatures exist. I've known for many years." My voice was steady, but I avoided looking at Neo as I spoke. "I of course had no idea there were any here." I looked at Rain and then back at his wife and her sister. "Are you...? All of you?"

Antonia barked a laugh. "Oh, girl, would that I were a vampire." She patted her forehead. "What I'd give to get rid of these lines!"

Dale walked over to his wife and kissed her cheek. "The lines are the best part. Each one is a reminder of the many years we've been blessed to share."

"Only my brother and I are," Rain offered. "My wife and her sister... They're not, but they've had trouble over the years from our kind. And now that we're family"—he nodded at Odile— "we are bound together by blood as well as love. We're fortunate to have absolute trust in Antonia and Dale. They are as close to us as family. No, they *are* family. Such loyalty and discretion as we've enjoyed with them since we were young boys are among the rarest of qualities. I trust you know too well how the common folk view our kind. What dangers there are for those like us, if our truth were to be discovered."

"And what about me!" A muted voice filtered through the door. "You have my trust as well!"

Rain shook his head, a grin on his lips. "And Flynn, of course. He's part of this household now, but he's all human."

"A bumbling one at that," Neo grumbled. Then he turned

his attention back to me. "Now that we've played the who's a vampire game, I'd like to know a little more about you, Miss Eloise. How are you so unafraid? How do you know of our kind? Are you one of us?"

That was one thing I could not lie about. Wouldn't. I'd never sipped blood, nor would I ever. Couldn't, not even to pretend I was something I was not. I'd tried once. And learned the hard way that there were limits to the games I could play. Even when my survival was on the line.

"I am not," I said, not mentioning the many times over the years that I'd wished, hoped, prayed even, that I could be more than what the gods had made me. "I'm fully human. Through and through."

Odile nodded, and Gia took my hand and gave it a reassuring squeeze.

"I'd like to be alone with Miss Eloise," Neo said, his voice unreadably cold. His face unflinching in its appraisal of me as he addressed his family.

Family. It struck me then that even an angry, brooding vampire like him had a family. People to argue with, to cast from a room. To blame for mistakes and to share secrets with. People like Gia and Odile, who expanded their family through marriage and love. The ache in my chest swelled to despair, but I lifted my chin and nodded. "I believe you're right. We should speak privately."

Antonia and Dale left the room, nudging the boy Flynn, who was still listening in the hall.

Odile gave me a quick hug as she stood from the settee. She assured me if I needed anything that she'd be in her workshop creating a salve just for Sara. "I'll be just upstairs. Although I believe she'll be a lot better now that she's had the venom," she said kindly, "it can't hurt to have something more, just in case."

Gia gave me a reassuring squeeze to my shoulder before taking her husband's hand.

"I am truly sorry, Brex," Rain said, his voice low and his eyes meeting mine for just a moment. He humbled me by kneeling on the tile floor before me and extending his hand. "Truly. I thought I was doing something kind, something to help..."

"I'm sure that was your intention." I squeezed his hand firmly. "And I am grateful for it."

I gave him a flat smile and held my breath until the entire household had left, closing the door behind them. Then, I was alone with Neo. Now the truth would have to come out.

Once we were alone, Neo fell silent. No stomping of feet, no pointing, no accusations. The crackling of the fire was the only disruption to the absolute peace of the room. Not peace, I supposed. There was nothing calm or comforting in the agitated clamp of his lips, the furious set of his brows as he just stood there and stared at me.

"Have you decided?" I finally asked, stretching my legs before me and leaning back slightly against the pillows on the settee.

Neo walked close, his hair cascading over his shoulders. He stood before me, transformed into a furious, angry beast. His once-golden eyes glowed a sickening, bright red, and his scarred lips parted to reveal a pair of long fangs. "Decided what I should do? I believe I should kill you," he seethed, glaring at me. "End this nonsense once and for all."

I stifled a yawn. "Ah," I said, drawing out my words, boredom coating my tone. "I see. You'd like to try and scare me into cooperation? Into being coerced or controlled. Is that what you've settled on?"

He growled, a vicious, terrifying sound that rattled from deep within him. Yet, I would not be startled into submission like a deer surprised by a hunt. He had no idea how much worse

I'd seen. How much more terrifying the other beasts were that roamed this Realm, and how I'd faced them. And lived.

I leapt to my feet and grabbed the front of his doublet in both fists, yanking his face close to mine. "Is that what you mean to do?" I seethed, his breath sweet against my skin. "Intimidate me? Terrify me?" I released his garment and turned away in disgust. "You'll have to do more than growl like a rabid dog if that's your aim."

As soon as I released him, the flames of my anger swelled, and I turned on him again. "No," I exclaimed. "You, a petulant, selfish little man, you do not scare me. If you want to kill me, if that's how you manage your—" I swept a hand around the empty sitting room—"your household, then fine. Take my life and be done with it. But unless you plan to do that, put those fangs away and speak to me as what I am. Someone who has far more power in this moment than you do."

Neo's mouth fell open as his fangs retracted into his mouth. His eyes resumed their normal honey-gold color, and he cocked his chin at me. "You are an infuriating, dangerous, reckless woman," he seethed. "Why would you provoke me? If you know what I am, you know what I'm capable of!"

"I know what all people are capable of," I said simply. "And I've already told you. There is no more powerful bond than the bond of secrecy. And now, I know yours." I stepped close to him and reached out to touch his face. "These scars," I said. "You're a vampire. Naturally quick to heal, as long as you drink blood at least every third day. For these scars to mark your face permanently, that means you were likely tortured. Deprived of blood. Beaten. Mistreated, I would assume while you were imprisoned. The marks on your face no doubt match the scarring in your heart from what I can only imagine was a horrific circumstance. Whether deserved or not, you, Neo, have known unspeakable suffering."

Neo lowered his chin, moving his face closer to mine.

"I do not fear your kind, nor do I fear you," I said, watching his eyes flutter closed as I ran my fingertips along the fullness of his lips, the poorly stitched flesh of his broken eyebrow. His beauty, the warmth of his flesh under my hands, dissipated my anger to something like frustration. Impatience, diluted with compassion. He had to have been cruelly mistreated to bear the scars he did. I knew how painful the wounds that left visible scars were, and while my own injuries might not have marred my face, my heart was no doubt as broken and battered as his.

His lips parted as I traced his scars, scratching lightly against the stubble on his chin. An unexpected erotic heat flooded my body, and my fingers froze. His eyes flew open, and he took hold of my wrist and gently moved my hand from his face as if he too felt the power of something unspoken flow between us.

"You enrage me," he whispered. "What are you? If you're to possess my secrets, it's only fair I possess something of you."

I walked away from him, heading back toward the settee. "You'll never possess any part of me, Neoruzzi Oderisi. I don't give myself freely, and you're not a clever enough thief to steal what little I do have."

"Is that so?" He crossed his arms, watching my every move. "You might be interested to know my family business—the enterprise Flynn spoke of—is, in fact, thieving."

I took a seat, leaning back against the cushions and meeting the angry vampire's eyes. Then I burst into a fit of laughter. "The gods indeed intended us to meet when we did!" I said. "You're a family of vampires and of thieves." I unfastened my cloak and let the garment drop to the settee. "It looks more and more certain that the job you spoke of was meant to be mine. And now, in fact, you might just owe it to me."

Neo watched me, his gaze heating and his lips parted as I

removed my traveling purse from the strap around my waist. I untied the leather that had compressed the embroidered pillow.

"But before we speak about the specifics, I should return this pillow to where it belongs."

"Tell me everything." Neo sat beside me on the settee, his back straight and his eyes boring into mine. "Start at the beginning. When you learned of my kind, how you first encountered us. *Everything.*"

I reached for the embroidered pillow and gripped it between my clammy hands. It didn't bring the comfort my sister's touchstone provided, but I picked at the threads and savored the smooth, luxurious fabric, wishing I had a way to ease the confusion and indecision of this moment. I'd not prepared what to say. I didn't know quite what to do.

"By the gods, Brexia." Neo raked a hand through his hair and released a sigh. "Please." His voice was more gentle than it had been yet in the very short time I'd know him. "Let's start over, shall we? Equalize things between us. You know my secrets—some of them, at least. I want you to trust me with yours. Please."

I had no way to evade the truth. I didn't have the heart to lie about things so tender, so true. If he were patient enough, I would speak, and this wealthy, titled man, this vampire would see me laid bare. And that terrified me from the tip of my head to my toes. What might he do once he knew everything? I was not in such a rush to balance things between us, unless in so doing, I had some kind of guarantee I would not be cast out. Shamed or rejected beyond what I already had been. I nervously twisted the pillow between my hands.

"Brex." His voice was surprising. Gentle. "Why don't we start by setting down that abused pillow. If you need to tear something to shreds while you talk, I offer this." He set the pillow aside, and he set one of his hands atop mine. He grinned, an unexpectedly kind gesture that lightened the burden of indecision in my chest. "You know I'll heal just fine, no matter the damage you might do to my fingers."

I lightly squeezed his hand and returned the smile but then pulled my hand away and laced my fingers together, forming a tight fist in my lap. "I admit, I am afraid." His body shifted beside mine, but I didn't look at him. Didn't want to face the reactions he would make to my honesty. "I've had few friends in life. And I don't yet know whether you might become a friend... or a haughty adversary."

"I have been called worse," he said with a chuckle. "By my own family, no less. I'll do my best to keep my bad attitude in check if it will help you speak freely."

I stood from the settee and paced toward the window. Beyond the confines of the manor walls, the sun was shining. Outside, the shire of Omrora was blessed with a beautiful fall day. I was certain Sara would be grazing the free-growing sweet grass beyond the stable. Common folk would be readying for work. Of course, in my mind I imagined the ideal, the kind of routine that I'd always imagined other people lived. Children running off to chores with full bellies and hearts. Loving spouses sharing kisses and the quiet intimacy of shared lives. I put a hand against the cool glass and thought back to my earliest memories—which were nothing like my fantasies.

"My mother was a vampire," I said simply. "Not my birth mother. I know nothing of my people before my mother saved me. I only know that she would not speak of the conditions she found me in. Where or how I was born...to whom. I was just a babe of three, and as far as my memory reaches, I remember only one mum."

I pictured my mother as vividly as if she were standing behind me. Smelled the scents of the smoke she used to anoint our one-room cottage with sacred burning wood. The cloudberry tea she steeped with a touch of wild honey as a special treat when I was sick or cross. "She was a wonderful woman," I said, a surge of longing and affection making it difficult to speak. "How she thought a vampire alone could raise a child..." I shrugged. "She was so beautiful, so kind." Her hair a rich vibrant brown, coiled in perfect curls. Her eyes were as dark as the midnight sky, alive with loving sparkles that rivaled the stars. I smelled the perfume of her skin as strong as if she were standing behind me, the physical memory bringing tears to my eyes.

Neo didn't move, didn't speak to interrupt, but I felt his gaze upon me, watching me.

"I grew up understanding that my mother needed blood to survive." I turned to face him. "She told me the origin of the vampires. Was always very honest about what she was, and I believed with all my soul that the vampire was a holy creature. Descended from the gods."

"What did she tell you?" he asked.

I claimed the velvet armchair before leaning back and settling in, holding on to my charm for comfort. I recounted the history that my mother had shared. The parts that most people knew, but which time and the rules of jealous monarchs had forced the common people to suppress. As if suppression and forgetting could ever completely erase truth.

Back in the earliest days of creation, a goddess gave birth to a son. The babe's father was a jealous god, believing the child was not his. He accused her of infidelity and threatened to destroy the child before its mother's eyes as a test of his paternity. The goddess had not been unfaithful, but fearing the wrath of her mercurial lover, she hid the babe, banishing her son to a cave nestled deep in a fertile valley to be raised by loving nymphs. She would take no chances with her beloved child.

The nymphs, creatures of wood and water, forest and mountain, were attentive guardians of the infant god, but they struggled to feed him. All the milk the nymphs could spare was not enough for their own children and the voracious child-god. Even the milk the animals of the land could provide was not plentiful enough for the insatiable infant. His surrogate mothers feared that the child would die of hunger and bring the wrath of the goddess upon them. Before they lost him to starvation, in desperation, the nymphs fed the baby the one resource they had in abundant supply: their blood.

While at first they feared the consequences of such a meal, the child didn't just grow—he thrived.

I flushed as this part of the story Neo knew no doubt knew, despite its more intimate themes.

"He grew up to be a powerful lover," he supplied, a wry grin on his face.

I nodded, thankful that he'd spared me the embarrassment of saying it.

"You know the rest of the story, then. When he was fully grown, the young god fathered the first of his children with nymphs who had grown up alongside him. Not with the sisters and mothers who'd raised him, of course, but the daughters of those powerful beings."

When the god grew up, he left his sanctuary with the

nymphs forever. By then, he'd spent years perfecting the art of making love. It was said that his offspring numbered in the hundreds. But the selfish god abandoned his children to the care of their mothers. The nymphs quickly learned that what had been created could not be undone. The offspring descended from the blood-drinking god were destined for long lives, exceptional strength and healing, and an unquenchable need for the blood of the living to survive.

"My mother told me that the children born of those unions eventually left the sanctuaries of the nymphs. At first, some sought to find their father. But over generations, they scattered among the various Realms of Efimia and assimilated into the human world. Unfortunately in many places, like here in Tutovl, they found they were not loved by their common brethren."

"Many of us would say we are hated, despised," he said quietly. "We are both of Efimia, of this physical world, and yet not entirely part of it. Destined to hide what we are, to do what we must to survive in secret, even though we have no more choice in the matter than we do over the beating of our hearts."

"My mother spoke of other powers, as well. Powers that are different for each vampire." I licked my dry lips, my mother's whispers echoing through the vast distance of memory.

"Descending from nymphs means that most vampires have other unusual gifts. For some, a siren-like talent for song. Others connect to the natural world—the air, water—in ways I cannot imagine," he explained.

I lowered my eyes, defying the danger of speaking of this long-buried truth. "The vampires of Tutovl have been hidden and suppressed for so long, my mother never knew if she had other abilities, other gifts. She always longed to learn. To live someplace where she could discover her talents and freely develop them."

"This is the not the Realm for any like us to be free." Neo's voice was raw with rage and something heartbreaking. Regret? "Our own bodies, the very makeup of our souls is the stuff of gods, and yet, we are cruelly judged. Shackled by fear which is emboldened by law."

My heart raced as he described feeling exactly the way I had my entire life. We were not so very different, and that awareness made me feel oddly connected to this man. This vampire.

"I agree with that, but my mother taught me the most powerful truth in the universe is balance. No amount of suppression over the generations could kill one incredibly powerful gift," I reminded him. "One that you all possess."

"The venom," he agreed. "Did your mother ever drink from you? Have you been touched by the venom?"

I closed my eyes and wrung my fingers together. "Only once," I admitted. "When I caught a fever and was very, very ill. My mother couldn't afford to visit a healer and did not know what else to do. She bit me, drank a bit of my blood, and my fever broke within a matter of hours. She explained very little about how the venom worked. I believe that she didn't want me to fully understand it, knowing that at some point I would grow up and face illness and injury, and I could not, for my own safety, rely on her venom to heal me. Or, even worse, seek out others as if venom was a cure. We kept pets. Cats, a dog when we could afford it. Mum trained them not to fear the bite, and she drank freely from them as she needed."

He watched me intently, leaning forward as he pressed me with more questions. "What happened at the foundling home? How did you end up there?"

"I believe Mum was very old when she took me in. She never told me how old she was. We celebrated birthdays together at the start of the new year since we never knew exactly when mine was either. All I knew was that at some point, she seemed to age very quickly. She went from beautiful and vibrant to...dying"

He nodded. "She knew she was leaving this Realm, then."

I swallowed hard, the memory of my mother's beauty as real as if she were standing beside me holding my hand. Tears wet my cheeks, but still, I continued. "My mother had no family. No friends. Why she'd been an outcast, I never knew. She brought me to a foundling home for..."

I hesitated, not because of the pain of the memory, but because this might be information even Neo didn't know.

"How can I trust you?" I asked, my voice a whisper. "If I tell you all I know, what I've experienced..."

Neo left the settee and kneeled on the cold tile floor beside me. "Tell me," he urged. "I need to know everything."

I squeezed my eyes shut and debated what to say, what to withhold. I could feel the heat of his body so near mine. His hands gripped the armrest of the chair. I squeezed the charm from my sister, the only proof I had that someone in this world had loved me. Held the only evidence that she'd ever existed tight in my hands.

"Brexia," he said, his voice gentle, the sound of my name a plea as it passed his lips. "What more is there to your story?"

Guide me, sister, I thought.

I considered what my mother might have said if she were with me now, looking down on Neo, the bitter vampire lord, and me, the helpless woman I'd become. Trapped. Powerless. Weak.

What did I really want? Did I want to give away all that I had, all that I knew, to someone who was practically a stranger to me? To this man who could cast me out with a single word?

I opened my eyes and lifted my chin. Took a breath in to steady my thoughts and confirm the decision that was forming in my mind.

Do I really want this?

I considered what I knew of this man, his scarred face, his hardened heart, his secrets and plans and family, and then I said it. I told him exactly how much my trust would cost him.

"I want you to marry me," I said, my eyes never leaving his honeyed gaze.

"I... What? I beg your pardon, but... What?" His brows lowered as he searched my face, our eyes perfectly aligned where he kneeled before me.

"I'm asking you to marry me, Lord Oderisi," I said firmly. "Make me your wife. Then I will tell you everything. On our wedding night."

He was silent for a moment, his lips parting as if the words warred with one another on his tongue. He babbled, looking confused. "I don't understand..."

I reached for his chin and held his face in my hands. "I need assurance that once I tell you what I know, you will not cast me out. Reveal my secrets. Harm those I love. Use the information against me or against others."

The reality of my demand must have started to sink in, because he stood, looking lost in thought. All softness, any genuine concern he might have displayed while I spoke of my mother disappeared. His eyes grew hard, and he stormed toward the fire, turning away from me.

"That's the most preposterous suggestion I've ever heard," he said, his voice still sounding confused, thoughtful. But then he pointed at me. "You have no more secrets. You're simply trying to manipulate me. If I marry you, you'll have rights to my property. My riches."

"Your riches?" I barked, standing from the chair and pointing right back at his chest. "Do you think I'm a fool? That I'd show up on your doorstep without the least bit of investigation into who you are?"

Of course, that had been my plan, but the gracious farrier Laura had provided an earful of information about this man and his so-called property and riches.

His rough laugh was mocking. "You're a fool if you think I'll believe you. Did you stop by the local shire-reeve? Inquire after any complaints filed against me? Seek character references and tax records? I'm finished with this conversation."

He strode toward the door, but just as he reached for the doorknob, I blurted out, "You're broke, Neo. Not so much so that you'll lose the manor, but there is no wealth to speak of here. You and your brother were left nearly penniless when your mother passed. Your brother assumed the property rights to the land in name only when you went missing for several weeks, but when you returned, all was restored to you. If you marry me, I'll be nothing more than the wife of a nearly bankrupt man."

He froze, his fingers poised to open the door, and then slowly withdrew his hand. His shoulders slumped only slightly before he turned on me, hatred in his glowing red eyes.

"Why," he hissed, "if you believe that to be true, did you first demand a job from me and now demand to become my wife? Is marrying a nearly bankrupt man going to provide that much improvement to your current circumstances?"

I waved my hand around, gesturing angrily at the fire, the fine furnishings. "You're supporting an entire household. I may not have met all the staff, but you have a crofter, someone who tends your fields and crops, do you not?" I didn't wait for him to answer. "And you generously offered your friend back in Fish Head End time to heal his knee and work for you with all his needs met. You must be earning money if you have it to spend. I may not know how you make your living, but I assure you, I can help. I can contribute. I can—"

"Enough!" Somehow the slow steps he took toward me

were even more agonizing and fearsome than the furious stomping he'd done all morning. When his face was mere inches from mine, he touched the tip of my chin with two fingers and opened his mouth. Razor-sharp fangs peeked between his lips, and his golden eyes matched the intensity of the fire, glowing the same vibrant crimson I'd seen in my mother's gaze when she was hungry, drinking, or angry. "I will never marry you. At least not for the reasons you propose."

If he thought his wild eyes and fangs were going to coerce me into cowering submission, he was a bigger fool than I'd thought.

"I don't see how you have any other choice," I whispered.

I recalled what Rain had said about how I was all Neo had spoken of since returning from Fish Head End. There was a reason he'd been taken with me enough to speak of me long after he had every reason to believe I was out of his life. Maybe, just maybe, I truly did have the upper hand in this unequal transaction.

I leaned closer to him, shoving his fingers away from my chin. I brought my lips dangerously close to his fangs. "How do you propose to ensure that I will protect your secrets? That I won't ride off into the village screaming vampire?" When I was close enough to brush my nose against his, I felt the uneasy restraint of his uneven breaths against my lips. "Marry me, Neo. And we'll both get what we want."

Every fear I'd ever had disappeared as I looked into his blood-red eyes, as I watched him take in my face not with contempt, not with distrust, but with something like respect. His fangs retracted and his eyes softened back into liquid gold. "What are your terms?" he demanded.

Terms... I'd not considered terms when I proposed he marry me, but now, I racked my brain for what I wanted. What I needed.

"A contract," I said. "Enforceable and binding by law."

He laughed. "Really? You intend to...what? Take a bit of parchment to the shire-reeve and say my vampire husband violated this term right here. You're a fool, Brex, and this entire idea grows more tiresome the longer you go on about it."

I walked over to the planks of wood he'd so carelessly thrown against the wall earlier. I picked up the length of split log and held it out to him. "A tally stick," I said. "We'll carve the terms into the stick, and we'll split it down the middle. If either one of us defaults on the terms, we'll have a binding, enforceable agreement."

I held the wood in my hands, almost not believing that I was negotiating the terms of my marriage with a tree branch in my hands. But did it really matter how, as long as it accomplished my goal? This would never be a love match. This would not make me part of a true family. A marriage to Neo would provide shelter, an income, and a guarantee that what I knew would not be used to harm the one person I truly did love—my sister.

I dropped into the armchair, the length of wood in my lap. "I want to learn a trade," I said. "Something that I can rely on to support myself once you...divorce me," I said softly. "You'll need to pay for the guild fees, if I'm to join a guild, and if I learn privately, you'll need to provide written testimony about my work ethic and abilities before I leave."

Neo stood silent, immobile, staring past me as I spoke. His face gave nothing away, so I pressed on.

"I need a place to live and a small income, which I will work to earn while I'm learning a trade. I will never be an untouchable mistress of the manor. I want to learn everything. Your work, how you earn your livelihood. I want that job your spoke of and the salary appropriate for the skill required of it."

Still, he said nothing. Didn't move, didn't even blink.

I pressed on. "Sara," I said. "Her care must be included in what you'll provide. I have a small debt at the farrier already for her shoes and—"

"Enough," he said, his voice suspiciously devoid of emotion. "I expect you plan on eating three meals and bathing, but that bit of wood isn't large enough to itemize every morsel of food and bit of clothing you might cost me."

"Cost you?" I shook my head. "No, Neo. I won't cost you anything. I'll bring more to this arrangement over time than your morsels of food and pennies of salary. You'll come out the better for the deal than me, I'm certain."

I grew a tiny bit sad as I considered all I'd be giving up but shoved aside the emotions as I realized the true value of what I was negotiating. "After you divorce me, which I would ask you not do for at least one year, I will leave Omrora, go to the far ends of the Realm. You'll never hear from me again. I won't seek a portion of your estate, nor will I demand rights to your property."

I understood but did not say that I'd be right back where I started. Alone. No home. No family. But I would have skills, and if the gods were kind, I'd have my sister back. I'd make a new life someplace where no one would know a respectable gentleman had married and quickly divorced me.

"And how exactly is this arrangement supposed to guarantee me anything? What benefit will this marriage bring me?"

I couldn't help but shake my head at that question. If I were a woman who had more confidence in her powers of flirtation, I might have toyed with him. Seduced him, or teased him. But I couldn't. Couldn't play a role that was contrary to everything within me. I could lie when the occasion justified it—as I had when I'd insisted I hadn't stolen his eating blade. Somehow trying to broker an agreement using my body as bait... I just couldn't. I wouldn't know how to even if I had a foolish hope that might work.

"I won't require you to pretend," I said softly, looking at my fists again. "You need not play the role of a...loving...spouse. This will be an arrangement built on trust. This the price of my fidelity. You'll be guaranteed a partner and a confidant. For as long as you can tolerate me."

He was quiet for long moments. Long, unnerving moments when he paced the room, tugging his fingers through his hair. As I watched his long, muscular legs and stiff back as he covered the length of the tile floor, I realized perhaps my demand was premature. Baseless. I knew that vampires existed, and that I knew both he and Rain were blood-drinkers. He could kill me, and that dangerous secret would no longer be a threat to him or his family. He could simply send me away and trust that if I attempted to use the information against him, I might, in fact, incur the wrath of common people upon myself. Speaking the truth to anyone, regardless of what side of the truth one was on, could be deadly.

"Brex?" Neo stood before me, his puzzled honey-gold eyes looking me over from top to toe.

I didn't answer, just lifted my face to his, braced and ready for whatever he'd decided. My life might end. My future might collapse. No matter the outcome, I would face it with courage. With dignity. My lips pressed together, I waited.

"We marry tonight." He reached for the wood that was in my hands and walked to the fireplace. He tipped back the iron grate and tossed the scrap into the fire. "We'll not carve a piece of wood to seal our agreement. My sister-in-law is a scrivener. I'll have her draw up a proper marriage contract. Can you read?"

My hands were shaking, but I held myself firm. "Yes, very well, actually." Knowing that my body, mind, and soul were in his hands, that my future was no longer just mine, I had to ask. "And your terms?"

"Only one." He met me at the chair and again kneeled before me, facing me at eye level. "Do nothing to bring dishonor upon yourself, me, or my family."

I narrowed my eyes at him and crossed my arms over my chest. "What specifically does that mean? What do you mean for me to do or to avoid? I don't want to be found guilty for something we disagree might bring dishonor."

"Those are my terms," he said, his voice deep and inflected with deep emotion that I could not fully understand. "Do you accept, Brexia Eloise?"

I had no idea what he might consider dishonorable behavior. Stealing, perhaps? But if his family's current enterprise was raiding or theft, how could I debase his name by joining him in his work? There was no need to worry that I would violate our marital intimacy, since I assumed he did not expect to share a marriage bed with me. Heat rose to my cheeks, and I wondered if perhaps I should add more terms. Clarify what he expected of me once I became his wife... The very idea was both enthralling and horrifying. Exciting and somehow terrifying all at once. No, I could not ask. I'd find out soon enough what was expected of the wife of Lord Oderisi. I'd be better off not knowing ahead of time.

But there was one thing I needed to know. One thing I could not abide, and I simply could not accept if it were true. "Neo," I said, trying to keep any hint of fear from my voice. "Are you a cruel man?"

His honey-gold eyes fluttered shut, and his brows furrowed as if he were deeply, deeply troubled by the question. He appeared to be in physical pain. Then he opened his eyes and extended his hand to me. I looked at the strong fingers dusted with dark hair and, without meeting his eyes, slipped my hand in his.

Heat flooded my body as I looked at our hands. I'd never held hands with someone like this before. The contact was delicious, sweet, and exciting, but I reminded myself it meant nothing to him. I would be little more than an employee, honor bound in name and by vow to this man for a period of one year. Anything that took place between us was simply honoring the commitment we'd made. Girlish fantasies of romance, family, even love, had no place in this marriage. Or in my life. No matter how my heart pounded in my chest and my fingers seemed content to stay locked with his.

He brought my hand to his lips and pressed a kiss against the back of my hand. "I am cruel," he admitted. "I am damaged and angry. There is space for revenge in my heart and very little else. I'm a man with one mission in life, and that mission is brutal. You should expect nothing but disappointment from my personality and misery in my mood. But I will never, ever turn the darkness in me against an innocent. Not a horse, not a pet... Not you." He kissed my hand again. "Never against you."

That was reassurance enough for me.

"Let's call in your sister-in-law," I said. "I accept. I will marry you. And would beg you to do it tonight."

The only one who seemed uncomfortable with the announcement of our plans to marry was, to my surprise, Gia. As Neo called the household together, she sat in the velvet armchair apart from the rest of the family, her eyes fixed on the floor.

Odile looked surprised but then laughed as though she'd heard the most enchanting joke. "This is unexpected, but how very exciting!"

Rain looked smugly at his brother, shaking his head. "And you both enter into this willingly?" he asked, a protective hand on the back of the settee, where I sat holding tight to the charm around my neck.

"Yes," I confirmed quickly, while Neo simply nodded.

"It makes sense, sir," Antonia said, her voice somber. "The deepest of secrets can only be protected by the most intimate unions. Marriage and family above all else. I look forward to welcoming the new lady of the manor to the family."

I didn't think ours would be an intimate union, but we would certainly protect each other's secrets. I thanked Antonia formally, wishing I could throw myself in the woman's arms and hug her but not at all feeling that would be appropriate behavior. While I'd said I wouldn't be the distant mistress of the manor, I knew I had a lot to learn about being a lady. A wife. By the gods, I had so, so much to learn.

So much so that I decided if I were to make a grievous error, now would be the time to do so. Forgiveness might be offered a bit more generously now than later. I cast my worries aside and approached Antonia with my hands clasped together, my eyes lowered. "I could not be more grateful to have two such as you and your husband to guide me through this. I know nothing of manor life and expect I will be a most disappointing lady." I put my hands on her shoulders and squeezed gently.

Antonia laughed, a carefree sound from deep in her belly. "Girl!" she exclaimed. "You've already far surpassed my expectations for you." She gave me a conspiratorial wink and threw her arms around me, giving me a moment's hug before releasing me. "Beg your pardon. I should say, my lady."

After the household had been informed, and once the shock began to wear off, the excitement over planning a small feast began. Odile went off to search the manor for something suitable for me to wear. Rain excused himself with a slap of his brother's shoulder and a few low, whispered murmurs. Dale and Antonia set about the preparations.

Gia stood from the chair, but Neo stopped her. "We have a request, sister."

I noticed immediately that he'd said we, as if he were already treating he and I as a bonded unit. An us. *We.* Part of me felt uncomfortable with the newness of the term, with the way the word suggested there was more than just myself and Neoruzzi Oderisi, two nearly total strangers despite everything that had happened since Fish Head End. But that word, that *we*, somehow stitched us together, like the embroidered threads which flowered in wreaths on the luxurious pillow. Apart, we were petal and stem, but now we would come together to form a new whole.

Gia waited, quietly studying her brother-in-law's face as he spoke.

"A marriage contract," he said. "May we impose upon you to write the terms and witness our signatures?"

Gia's lower lip trembled, and she looked at Neo with raw concern on her face. "You really mean to do this?" she asked. "Marriage?"

He nodded, and I mirrored the action when her eyes met mine.

"And this is something you truly both enter into willingly?" she asked.

"Again, yes," Neo said curtly, his tone sharpening. I could see what he'd meant when he spoke of his sour mood and lack of patience.

"Gia," I said, "is there something on a professional level that gives you pause? Are you concerned about the validity of the agreement or signing as witness? Because I assure you, I—"

"No, it's... It's not that." She shook her head. "I'm happy to write up the terms for you. I just..." She wrung her hands together and finally sighed. "When I married Rain, I had nothing. No one but Odile to stand as witness. No parents, no well-wishers. Certainly no friends, unless of course, you count Flynn. But what we did have was love. Deep and joyful love." She addressed her words to me, not at her brother-in-law. "I wish for every bride to have that."

I rested a hand lightly on Gia's shoulder. "Thank you," I said. "For caring so much about a stranger. I assure you, I have no people, nor do I have any love to look forward to. There is no one waiting for me back where I came from. This marriage is a..." The words caught in my throat. I didn't know what to say, but the reality of what I was about to do was beginning to sink in.

"It's an agreement," Neo supplied, but I couldn't help noticing how he didn't look at me as he said it. "Please, Gia. We're all in agreement. Let's not delay."

I glared at him, annoyed that would so quickly dismiss his sister-in-law's concerns, but Gia seemed unperturbed by his manner. Perhaps she was just used to the cantankerous, abrasive vampire. She left the sitting room to gather ink and parchment.

For long seconds, the fire crackling and the heavy sounds of Neo's breathing as he leaned against the window blocked out all my thoughts, leaving plenty of space for my fears. I thought of my sister, of what she might think if she heard I was to be married. Would she refuse to celebrate, knowing that this marriage was one of convenience? Born of circumstance and secret, not love? Or would she applaud the opportunities such a union might bring?

Try as I might, I could not conjure any memory, could not hear my sister's voice. A vague, shadowy image of her face fluttered across my mind, and I closed my eyes and gripped the charm at my neck. *Send me your love, Gini,* I prayed, *from wherever you are. Would that you were at my side now.*

Gia returned and quickly drew up the contract, which conveyed to me on the eve of our wedding exactly what I'd requested. Neo stood over the scribe's shoulders, guiding her as she penned what he and I had so quickly agreed upon.

"And your terms, Neo?" Gia waited, the quill poised over the inkwell, waiting for his answer.

"That is all," he said curtly.

She looked at him, her face no doubt looking as puzzled as mine.

"That is all," he repeated, more sharply. He pointed to the parchment. "Signature?"

Gia handed him the quill, which he dipped into the horn of ink. He signed his name in long, unhurried strokes, as if the gravity of this undertaking deserved a somber, elegant hand. Then he handed the quill to me, and I added my name beside his. As was the custom of the Realm of Tutovl, it was done. Without a word or a glance or any further ceremony, by mutual vow and agreement, we were married. Gia signed the document, witnessing the commitment we'd made and then quickly wrote up a second, far simpler version. That one did not include the full terms of the marriage. All the shire-reeve required to certify our marriage as valid and binding was the date, a second set of our signatures, and the witness's signature.

After assuring us that she would submit the document to the shire-reeve on her next trip to the village, Gia turned to me.

"Lady Oderisi," she said, gifting me a sincere but small smile. "Welcome to the family."

I was in shock, truly. Not only because something as significant as a marriage could be accomplished so simply, but also that Neo had not bothered to make his terms a permanent part of the contract.

"Thank you," I said, unsure what had truly just happened.

Gia, now my sister-in-law, left the longer version of the contract with us and took the simpler away with her. Then, she left us.

Me and my husband.

THE REST of the day passed quickly. Odile insisted on dressing me for the evening meal, as well as styling my hair. Gia sat with us, still adorned in her day breeches and tunic, and watched as

Odile fussed over me like a treasured friend. Not someone she'd known a single day. I bathed and then retired to Odile's bedroom, where I sat gingerly on her bed, brushing out my hair so it would dry by the heat of the fire.

Odile laid out several dresses that she thought would fit me and made a lovely crown of flowers and leaves she'd picked from the Oderisi grounds.

"You're a wonder, sister," Gia said softly. "Healer, designer of hairstyles, wardrober."

I was in shock, truly, at the generosity of Odile. She chattered at me as though she was delighted to spend time with me. Her innocence and energy was infectious, and I found myself grateful for the sisters' company.

Gia, while kind, was more reserved. "I'd best change into something more festive," she said, brushing her hands on her thighs. Her long hair was tied back in braids, and she had a trace of ink still staining her fingertips from writing up the marriage contract.

"Gia, before you go... Do you think you might teach me something in the coming days? I was hoping to learn to make breeches." I nodded at the day dress I'd discarded before bathing, which now looked so ripe, I didn't think I'd be able to wear it ever again. At least not until I'd washed it thoroughly. Maybe twice.

"I'd love to teach you." Gia grinned and looked much more relaxed as she nodded. "I hate dresses. Hate them! Thankfully, the clothes I prefer suit my occupation."

She retreated to the rooms she shared with Rain to ready herself for dinner, while Odile took over brushing my hair.

"Can I ask about your charm?" she asked, carefully pulling the brush through my waist-length hair.

"Of course," I said, closing my eyes and luxuriating in the absolute bliss of having my hair brushed. I'd not been tended to this way since...since my mother was alive. The relaxing strokes against my scalp, Odile's soft voice, and the warmth of the fire nearly put me to sleep. "It was a gift," I explained, trying to keep my relaxed lids open. "I was close to a girl at the foundling home. I called her my sister, but... She was just another foundling. Like me. She left this under my pillow the day she left the home."

"What a precious treasure." Odile smoothed my hair with her hands and opened a small vial of scented oil. She dribbled the fragrant contents on my scalp and massaged the oil through my hair, making me smell of lavender and cedar.

"Mmm," I sighed, falling into an even deeper state of relaxation. "That smells wonderful."

"It's a love potion," she confessed, a giggle in her voice. "The tonic smells of lavender and cedar, but the secret ingredient is sea holly. I dry it and grind it then infuse it in oil. I strain the leafy bits, which color the oil a vibrant blue, and then add just a few drops to the lavender and cedar."

"Love potion?" I echoed. "Well, it must work, because I think I'm falling in love with this hairbrush."

"Not really," she laughed and twisted the last of the oil on her fingers around the ends of my hair, twirling the light-blonde strands into soft curls. "I don't dabble in magic, so there's no enchantment there. But I can say many of my heart-broken clients found their true mates after using a bit of this. It certainly can't hurt. May it soften the heart of that brute you married since you're stuck with him now." She gave me a smile to assure me she was teasing me and then helped me into her dress. The garment fit almost perfectly since both Odile and I were both tall and nearly the same weight. She set the crown of flowers on my head and announced that I was ready.

"You're beautiful!" she exclaimed, clasping her hands

together. "A vision, Brex. Just lovely. Exactly as a bride should be on her wedding night."

"You know that Neo doesn't love me," I said somberly. This wasn't a wedding night. This was simply the first night of my marriage to Neoruzzi Oderisi.

"No matter the circumstance, this is a night to celebrate and remember," she insisted. "A night of joy and optimism for what might come. I'm jealous, if you must know." She ran the brush through her own hair and quickly rushed on to explain. "Not that you're marrying Neo." She blurted out an awkward laugh. "I pray the gods help you manage that man. He's... Well, I'll just say that I know he has a good heart. It's just buried deep beneath a lot of—"

"Manure?" I asked.

Odile crowed with laughter and shook her head. "I was going to say pain." She grew serious as she adjusted the hem of my dress to cover my humble shoes, which now looked absolutely awful to my eyes. One bath and one fine dress, and already I was developing the sensibilities of a lady.

"Neo was nearly lost, several times in fact," she admitted. "When he was imprisoned, his keeper was one of his kind. One who knew exactly how to inflict the most brutal torture. How to bring him close to death and then drag him back. There is love and goodness and so much promise in that man," she assured me. "But none of us have yet been able to free him from the bonds of memory." She touched my cheek with a hand. "I hope to learn all about your memories too someday, sister," she said sweetly. "For now, be gentle with Neo. I believe the hardest materials are sometimes made, not created as such. But time and care can wear away even walls of stone."

Even without her pretty words, Odile, with her hair styled and wearing a lovely pale-orange colored dress, was a truly stunning woman. Beautiful in a way I'd never even considered I might be. But in her dress, with my hair styled and fragrant, I felt overwhelmed with gratitude. Overwhelmed with hope. Neo might never love me, but I would play the part of the lady of this manor. In time. It was all still so new, it hardly felt real.

Before we left her room and headed to the wedding feast, Odile stopped, twisting her lips into a scowl. "Come," she said. "You simply cannot wear those shoes!"

I breathed a sigh of relief when she pulled my road-broken shoes from my feet and handed me a pair of very simple, very clean brown leather shoes. The toes were slightly elongated and pointy, and the reinforced heel made a soft but satisfying clack on the stone floor as I walked.

"Here. Try this." She knelt on the floor and lifted the hem of my dress then stuffed a bit of clean rags into the toes of the shoes. "Better?" she asked. "My feet are just a bit longer than yours, but this should do for one night."

I tried walking with the rags in, and to my surprise, the shoes felt comfortable. "They are perfect," I said.

Odile opened the door to her bedroom and waved me out. Before I could leave the sanctuary of her quarters, I stopped and looked at the floor.

"May I hug you?" I asked quietly. "I have no other way to thank you for your many, many kindnesses."

She said not a word but pulled me into a generous hug before releasing me and smoothing my crown once more. "You are a vision," she said. "Neo has no idea what's in store for him."

What I was soon to discover was how much my new husband had in store for me on our wedding night.

I'd been impressed by the cart full of food Antonia had prepared upon my arrival last night, but the table set for our wedding feast was unlike anything I'd ever in my entire life beheld. Dozens of slim candles of different heights were set on a circular pillar made of stones, each flicking with soft, warm light. Small wooden dishes held floral arrangements of native grasses and clustered green blooms of garden angelica surrounding clippings of Dragon's Blood Sedum from the manor grounds. Tiny blood oranges with their pretty mottled skins were scattered along the length of an embroidered table runner. A cask of honeymead was open, and Antonia was calling out to Dale to begin dinner service as soon as the groom arrived.

Odile and I were the first to arrive, which was fine by me. I spent a few minutes in awe, trailing my hands along the surface of the dining table, the planks so smooth under my fingers they might have been coated with wax. I counted six chairs; one at either end of the table, the rest paired neatly on either side.

I reverently held the charm around my neck and spent a moment in prayer, my thoughts drifting to my mother. Emotion bloomed in my chest as I wondered how she would feel today, knowing that her child was married. Stable, secure—for now. I wondered if she too would mourn the love that was lacking between Neo and me, or if she, like Odile would put her trust in whatever the marriage bond delivered.

My thoughts were interrupted by the skidding of feet and a loudly blurted, "By the gods!"

I turned to the source of the voice and met the eyes of the apprentice Flynn. His face was flushed, his hair flopping over his eyes. He brushed the strands back and nodded at me.

"Miss Eloise, you are the most beautiful woman I've ever seen. I... I..."

"She is Lady Oderisi now, boy. That beautiful woman is my wife." Neo's voice boomed from behind me. I had no time to thank Flynn for his compliment before losing my breath at Neo's words.

"Your wife? Lady?" Flynn continued to stare at me, his mouth gaping open. "I need somebody to catch me up..."

I nodded demurely, completely unused to not only this kind of attention, but to compliments in general. "Thank you?" I said, my voice lifting as though I'd asked a question.

"You. Are. Welcome." Flynn's dramatic response relaxed me, and I giggled, while Odile put a hand on his shoulder and steered him toward a wash basin.

"Clean up, Flynnie," she urged. "We'll be eating soon, and your hands look like you just shoed a horse."

"I kind of did," he said, shrugging, but let himself be led away.

Gia and Rain came into the room then, holding hands and trading loving glances. Neo clamped his brother on the shoulder, embracing him in a hug. Rain again whispered something under his breath to Neo, who grunted in response. Then Gia kissed her brother-in-law's cheek.

"May the gods favor your union with love, safety, prosperity, and peace," she said. "I wish you every happiness."

Neo's eyes flitted to mine at the blessing, but he said nothing. Just stared, those brooding, honey-gold eyes revealing nothing.

Rain and Gia greeted me warmly, both of them commenting on the lovely fit of Odile's dress. I complimented Gia's gown, a simple natural-colored fabric with a scoop neck and modest train. The sleeves were flared in the shape of a bell, and around her waist was a wide gathered belt in a rich green color, embroidered like the pillow with flower garlands and studded with very small, sparkly stones.

"You are a vision," I said, clasping her hands in mine.

"Maybe I should ask you to teach me to dress like this, rather than in pants."

Gia squeezed my hands back, grinning as she murmured, "Nothing compares to a good pair of breeches. You'll see."

Rain waited until Gia and I had finished chatting to take my hand. He kissed the back of it and then held mine in both of his. "Most men would look at a woman who married their brother after one day of knowing him and threaten her. Warn her not to hurt him, not to steal from him."

Rain shook his head.

"I'm not going to warn you against hurting him. There's nothing anyone can do to damage my dear brother more than has already been done. Quite the opposite. I'm praying you're the one who will finally set him free from all that."

He released my hand and gave me a slight bow. "Welcome to the family, sister."

Overcome with emotion, I could not speak. I bent slightly to bow to him, thankful Odile's crown of flowers didn't fly from my head as I did so.

"By the gods!" Antonia breezed into the room with Dale pushing a much larger butler's cart right at her heels. She came right for me, her hands outstretched for mine. I held her hands, a genuine smile on my face at the sight of the caring older woman. "You could not be more perfect," she said, her voice a reverent whisper. "Your eyes are like midnight, your hair like the rays of purest sunlight." She bit her lip, tears in her eyes. "You're a vision, sweet girl. May every blessing of Forráheim be yours. Now and forevermore."

I bowed my head in thanks, blinking back tears.

"Take yer seats," Dale called out. "There'll be plenty of time for boo-hooing after the soup."

I watched Rain pull out a chair for Gia, as I looked uncertainly about the table. Before I could choose the wrong seat, I felt a hand at my elbow.

"Lady Oderisi."

I felt the heat of his body behind my back, the almost tender grip of his fingers against the sleeve of my dress. I peeked up at him, this man, my husband, and lost the ability to think, to speak, to breathe at his raw beauty. Neo was a furious god of a man. His glossy black hair, perfectly smooth and free, looked like waves of the darkest sea at night. His full, scar-marked lips bowed as he appraised me, looking me over from crown of flowers to the tips of my borrowed shoes.

"You look beautiful," he said tightly, as if complimenting me caused him discomfort. "You'll sit at the head of the table, opposite me, from now on." He led me to a chair, pulled it out for me, and waited while I gathered my skirts and sat.

I could hardly pull my eyes from this man. My husband. I'd seen him in fine clothing, but this—what he wore tonight was elegant, regal, and yet somehow also sensual. His vibrant blue doublet was heavily stitched with a pattern of symbols in gold and red thread. The cap sleeves at the shoulders emphasized the girth of his arms, and the belt around the waist of the garment was of the softest brown leather studded with embellishments that looked as if they were fashioned of pure gold. His eyes blazed with molten fire as my gaze raked along the length of the tight fabric encasing his muscular legs. He looked like he would fight me, or fight for me, whichever the circumstance demanded.

He bent low, his voice caressing my ear. "I mentioned to Antonia you were not a fan of fish head soup."

He nodded at me, a twinkle in his eyes, and then strode to the opposite end of the table and took his seat. Antonia wheeled the cart from seat to seat, filling each bowl with a fragrant, decidedly not fish head soup while Dale circled the table the opposite direction, filling the cups. When each of us had been served, Neo stood from his chair.

"Antonia, would you please pour two more? I'd like you and Dale to join us in a toast."

Antonia pulled two more cups from the lower shelf on her butler's cart. "I expected you might, sir," she said, smiling fondly at him.

Neo waited for Dale to pour himself and his wife honeymead and then held his mug aloft. "To Antonia and Dale," he said, "may your long years of love be everlasting. To Rain and Gia, may your new love grow stronger with each passing season. To Odile, may your love continue to pour blessings upon this family. To you, Flynn, the very life and breath of loyal friendship." His eyes met mine across the table, and my stomach lurched behind my pretty gown. "And to my wife, Brexia Eloise, Lady Oderisi. May the vows we exchanged be the beginning of a fruitful union."

He tipped his cup to me, and I sipped my mead, my hand trembling so hard I feared I would spill on Odile's pretty gown. The sweet, slightly spicy drink relaxed me enough that I stopped shaking. But I still pressed my fingers to the charm around my neck for solace. Then suddenly, I felt compelled to say something. Whether it was my new role as the lady of this manor, or simply the nudging of spirit, I stood from my chair.

"May I?" I asked the question but did not wait for approval. I stared into the honeyed contents of my mug as I spoke, letting my heart lead me. "I simply wanted to give a prayer of thanks," I began. "To the Oderisi family, those near, those who have passed, and those long forgotten to time, who lived on this land and who built this home which I feel fortunate to call mine. For now." I flicked a glance at Neo as I said that, but his face was stony. Unreadable. "And to my family, wherever they are and whatever they were. Most especially, my mother and sister."

Tears threatened to spill down my cheeks, but I swallowed hard against the feelings of longing and love and loss as I pictured my mother's face.

"And to my husband." I longed to say something beautiful, inspiring, but looking at his stony face, all I could hope was that he didn't find me lacking and cast me out too soon. "And new beginnings." I lifted my mug in the air and waited. Neo was the first to stand. His brother and Gia followed and then finally Odile and Flynn as well. We tipped our cups and sipped our drinks.

Once Neo sat, the family began talking, soft conversation and laughter punctuating course after course of delicious food. I sipped the thick pea soup, trying not to stare at Neo, whose eyes seemed to follow my every move. I snuck a glance at him while Antonia served roasted boar with herbs, stifling a smile as he used his eating blade to pierce the slices of tender meat. He seemed almost triumphant that the knife was back in his possession. While I tried to sample wine-soaked pears and dessert of lemon posset with biscuits, my mouth felt dry and my hands clammy.

Every morsel I tried was delicious, every sip of the honeymead an intoxicating treat. While I was famished, my nerves wouldn't permit more than a few bites of each. My body wasn't used to such decadent food, and my mind couldn't think of a single word to contribute to the conversation. I watched these people, so at ease with one another, as one on the outside looking in, not as one seated at the very same table. Antonia seemed to understand my anxieties and served me small portions and did not comment as she brought the next course before even the last had been cleared from my trencher.

Finally, the meal concluded, and Flynn clapped his hands and rubbed them together loudly. "Ladies and gentlemen," he said dramatically, pushing his chair back from the table, "I had no idea when Rain invited me to this feast that we would be celebrating young love!"

Neo's hands clenched into fists on the table, while Flynn pulled a wooden flute from a pocket. "Now, if I may," the boy said, "some of you may know that I've carried for many years a flame of devotion for a performer, a brilliant, beautiful bard whose words and voice and body—"

"*Flynn.*" The single word from Neo had the boy hurrying through his monologue.

"Yes, well, she inspired me to learn many things. Poetry. Dance. Music! Allow me to play a few notes on this happy and so very unexpected occasion."

Flynn began playing a light tune that had Dale clapping his hands and Rain tapping his foot. I smiled, the drinks loosening my nerves. After the first song had completed, I immediately burst into applause.

"Flynn! That was wonderful!"

Every eye in the room was on me, as I realized these were the first words I'd spoken since we'd sat down to dinner.

Flynn looked elated, his cheeks so red and his eyes so bright, I thought he'd nearly burst with pride. "Allow me to play another, milady."

The second song he played was softer, slower. A romantic melody that fit the mood of a celebration of marriage. Rain rook Gia's hand and led her by the fire, where together they clasped hands and danced.

"Neo!" Odile waved a hand toward the man at the head of the table. "Dance with your bride!"

He lifted a single thick brow and leaned back in his chair. I was certain he would refuse. After all, I was hardly his bride. I was his partner, the keeper of secrets. As I worried over his reaction to the suggestion, he rose from his chair, walked past his brother and sister-in-law, and stopped beside me. He said nothing. Just extended his hand with the most vulnerable, uncertain look on his face. As if I might refuse my husband our first dance.

I swallowed, a nervous thrill making me uncertain that my knees could lift me from the chair. I rested my hand in his, and he held it firmly, holding back my chair. Then he took both hands and pulled me close to his chest, moving his enormous frame in light, easy steps. Together we danced to Flynn's sweet, gentle tune. As we whirled through the dining room, the firelight cast shadows on Neo's face. His thick stubble moved as he smiled at me. *Smiled.* His eyes softened and the edge of anger that seemed to sharpen his every mood blunted a bit. Maybe it was the meal or the wine, but he moved a hand to guide my waist, and I thought I felt him touch the ends of my curls where they fell against the back of the dress.

All too soon, the song ended. He released his hold on my waist and hand but stood in place, scant inches away. My heart raced, my chest lifting with uncomfortable breaths at his closeness. The warmth of the fire mixed with the heat of Neo's broad chest, so close I'd have to look up to see his face. I cleared my throat nervously and clapped again, mostly so I had something to do with my hands.

Flynn was about to play again, when a knock at the door interrupted the festivities. The dancing disrupted, Gia and Rain fell into quiet conversation while Neo and I stood, locked in an intensely charged silence. I stroked the charm around my neck, worrying over the interest my husband seemed to have in staring at me. Thankfully, Antonia returned a few moments later to share that Odile had been called back to the village to attend a child with a bellyache.

"My thanks to you all," Flynn said with a dramatic bow. "I must be off for home. I have a mother and many siblings who will hunt me down with torches if I'm not tucked into bed before the vengersax hour. Odile, I'll be happy to ride with you into the village, if you'd like."

Flynn and Odile left as they had the night before when I first arrived. While Antonia and Dale cleared the table, Rain and Gia bid the rest of us goodnight.

Neo was sitting at the head of the table, his long legs outstretched as he stared into the fire. I did the same, having no idea what else I should be doing. How a woman should act on her wedding night. Where I would go, what I would wear. With Odile gone, I had no way of giving her back this dress. I hoped that Antonia would assist me, but then I reminded myself I was lady of this manor now. Of course she would help me, wouldn't she? I assumed I only had to ask.

"If you'll excuse me," I said, avoiding Neo's gaze, "I'd like to find Antonia. See if she'll help ready me for bed."

"Don't you think that's your husband's duty?" The question hung heavy on the air, so much implied by the sensual curl of his lips as he asked.

"If you wish to take the rags out of these shoes, I'll not stop you," I fired back, more out of fear than anything else.

"Come," he said, standing and stalking toward the stairs. "I'll take you to our room."

"Our room," I echoed, the words feeling like wood in my mouth.

Those full, scarred lips twisted into a grimace. "We've only so many rooms, Brex. If you prefer to sleep in the sitting room, I suppose we can discuss that. But not until your part of the bargain has been fulfilled. You vowed to tell me your secrets on our wedding night. And I intend to hear them."

I followed him up the winding stone staircase that led to the second floor of the manor. At the far end of the hallway, he pushed open an ornately carved door.

"I'll have a key made for you," he said, holding the door

open for me. As I passed by him, he planted a hand on my shoulder and stopped me. "Brexia, this is very important. In this house, we lock our doors. Every night. No exceptions."

So I had been locked in the sitting room last night... "Why?" I asked.

"I'll explain when the time is right," he said dismissively. "For now, you must swear to me. Keep this door locked if you're inside. Especially if you plan to sleep. No exceptions. Do you understand?"

I nodded, not understanding at all, and walked into the large room. There was no fire lit, so the room was dark and very cold. Just a few candles burned within iron lamps, illuminating a very large, luxurious-looking bed. On the bed I could see some clothes neatly laid out. I stopped just inside the doorway and froze.

"You'll need to change out of that dress."

It wasn't a question. I nodded and walked toward the bed, hoping that the items there were bedclothes of some sort that Gia or Odile had left. What I found was puzzling.

"What's this?" I asked.

Neo began unfastening his doublet, a devilish grin on his face. "Something for you to change into," he explained. "You wanted to be part of the family business. I have work to do tonight, and you're coming with me. But if the goblin guild-master sees you in that dress, this will be the first and last night you'll be my wife."

EIGHT

On the ride though the chilly night to the goblin sanctum, Neo assured me we would be completely safe. Contrary to the common people's myths, goblins didn't steal women or eat children. Apparently, the goblin guildmaster had an eye for human women with generous curves and was a notorious flirt. Neo shook his head with obvious warmth and affection.

"Most of the visitors to the sanctum come through one of very few trusted emissaries, like me," he explained, the sliver of moonlight above us casting a dark shadow over his hooded face. "Consider this another unequal transaction. The fact that you're not blindfolded and in the back of Flynn's cart means..." He gave me a cryptic look, part warning and partly warm. I almost thought he was enjoying having me along until he growled, "Just don't make me regret bringing you here."

I had no intention of making him regret anything. At least not yet.

We made the trip riding fairly slowly, each of us holding lamps in one hand and our reins in the other, the light the only protection between us and a vengersax attack. We'd ridden in silence more than a quarter hour's distance from the manor, the opposite direction of the village, until we reached a small clearing.

"Something is wrong." Neo slowed his mare near a dense, low shrub and held his iron-encased lantern higher in the night air.

His words were quite the understatement. Nothing about this night seemed right. Instead of doing what newlyweds should do after the celebration and feast ended, my new husband and I were riding to meet a goblin under cover of dark.

I brought my horse, Sara, to a stop beside his mare, Sedda. "What is it?" I asked, straining to see through the darkness.

Neo turned slightly and lifted a gloved finger to his lips, and my blood turned cold. The night was young, but the chill on the air raised a foggy mist that blanketed the terrain ahead. I cursed the decadent meal I'd eaten earlier, my stomach tightening in anticipation. Fear and confusion blanketed my thoughts.

What if he's brought me here to kill me?

He wouldn't... Surely couldn't, could he? If Neo planned to drag me far from the manor and be done with me, would he have gone through the trouble of inking the marriage contract? Putting on the feast and the celebration...the toasts... I'd been lured into believing that he truly wanted to secure my fidelity with a contract, but now, with only a slice of moon overhead to light the path and his gloomy presence shadowing the already dark night, I was genuinely afraid.

Neo had armed himself with a short sword, but he was hardly dressed for murder. He'd given me a small dagger, something scarcely more useful than an eating blade, which I'd fastened beneath my cloak. The clean pair of breeches and tunic of Dale's I wore were ill-fitting and hardly battle-ready. The clothes were clean, but if there was a fight ahead, Neo would have every advantage.

He directed his horse to reverse course, and we rode a short distance back the way we'd come. Then, he leapt from his horse and motioned for me to join him. He held my torch while I jumped down and then handed it back to me. His eyes blazed red, and fangs parted his lips.

"Shhhh," he said. "Listen."

"What?" I whispered, fear coating my limbs and making me tremble. "Is it vengersax?"

"Blood." His nostrils flared, and his eyes faintly glowed crimson. "I smell it. Spilled at most a night ago, and there's a lot of it. Listen. Do you hear that?"

I shook my head. I heard nothing but the faint rustle of the breeze through long grass. I couldn't make out the dark trunks of trees, so I suspected we were near water. A pond, maybe? It was too early in the night for wood frogs to sing or the chittering of bark beetles.

"No, I hear nothing," I said weakly, frustrated with my human hearing. I knew Neo's senses were stronger, better adapted than mine by nature, but I didn't like it.

"Corpse rats," he grumbled. "I can hear them rooting."

A sour flavor filled my mouth. I had no idea what the sanctum of the goblin guildmaster might look like, but if there were corpse rats in abundance, that was evidence of death. An abundance of it.

"Where is your dagger?" he asked, his voice abrupt.

I tapped my hip, and he turned his red eyes on me. "I'm going to leave you with the horses and go ahead on foot. Keep your torch lit. We're especially vulnerable to attacks from the air in this clearing." He swore softly under his breath as he handed me his mare's reins. "Wait for me here. But if anything happens—and I mean anything—ride Sedda. She knows the way home. Lead Sara back. Do not leave her here. Travel as quickly as you can, as safely you can. Whatever you do, do not let that torch go out. Do you understand? If that torch dies, you'll die. All three of you."

"What could happen? Why would I need to leave you? Where are you going?" My mind buzzed with questions, but at least I began to trust my husband a bit more. It was unlikely he'd brought me here to murder me if he was providing me an escape plan.

"I'm going inside Vlareq's sanctum." He handed me his torch while he removed his cloak, revealing a coat and leggings of leather scale mail. He tossed the cloak over Sedda's back and tugged a length of leather lacing from his traveling pouch. He tied back his hair with the leather, adjusted the fitting on his scabbard, then took back the torch.

"I want to go with you," I said. "How will I know if you're safe?"

"You won't know," he barked. "Which is why I gave you clear instructions. Wait for me no more than a quarter hour. After that, leave and do not delay. Do you understand?"

"Neo, I can't leave you here. By the gods, what if—"

"Brex!" His harsh bark interrupted my concern. "Give me your word. You must do this. It's far too dangerous. I'll not put myself in harm's way unnecessarily, but I cannot leave without knowing what's become of my allies. If they are in trouble..."

"So you'll walk into trouble alone, then?" My teeth began chattering, a combination of the damp chill and nerves. "Why can't I follow behind? Bring the horses? That way if there's trouble, we'll escape. Ride back together."

The red in his eyes dimmed, and in the flickering torchlight, the honey-gold warmth returned. "I will *not* put you in harm's way. This was supposed to be an easy run to pick up a mask Vlareq made. A chance to show off my beautiful bride. No risk, no danger." With a gloved hand, he lifted my chin and touched my nose with the tip of his. "I regret now bringing you along.

This is not the wedding night I'd planned. Promise me," he growled, his breath sweet against my face, "you will do what you must to keep yourself safe."

Heat bloomed in my chest, and I lifted my face, my nose nudging his. But I refused to make a promise I had no intention of keeping. That may not have been grounds for divorce, but I would not risk bringing dishonor upon myself by lying before I'd been married even a single day.

"Keep your weapon close." He unsheathed his short sword. "And the torch—"

"I know, I know," I assured him. "Go. And may the gods guide you."

He took off running, the torch flickering through the dense iron cover. He was surprisingly quiet and quick, even in his leather armor, but not too quick for me to catch up to him.

"Shhh," I urged the horses, not that they would speak or reveal my plan to Neo. I secured the reins as best I could to the thick stem of a low-growing shrub. "Ouch!" I pricked myself on a thorny shoot but thought that might be a good thing. The horses wouldn't nibble at the greenery and loosen their positions. At least that was my hope as I knelt and felt the soil. It was rich and damp, which told me quite a bit about where we were. I stuck the end of my torch into the ground. Using both hands, I sunk the handle deep into the earth.

"Gods willing, this will stay lit." The breeze was gentle, not likely to blow out the sturdy candle, but I whispered a prayer and touched my sister's charm through my tunic and cloak before unsheathing my dagger. Then I stroked Sara and Sedda and whispered goodbye. "Stay safe, girls."

Then I took off after the diminishing light of Neo's torch.

The farther I ran, the more wet the ground became. My thin leather boots sank into the mud, and I nearly slipped and fell on my behind trying to keep pace with him, but I stayed focused on following Neo's light. My heart hammered in my chest, but I kept my hood up, my chin lowered, and my eyes on that spark of light ahead. I hoped his torch would be enough to keep the vengersax away from both of us. The thought that I was truly exposed in the dark, sweating, and likely smelling better than my wedding feast to a hungry, flesh-eating bird put a fire in my steps, and I ran all the faster.

Neo tracked through the wettest of the muck until finally the soil dried out. By the time I caught up to him, he was on his hands and knees, angling the torch to examine what looked to me like nothing more than a patch of overgrown ground.

I stayed a few feet back, thinking I was hidden, but as soon as Neo pulled up a door hatch that appeared to be carved right into the earth, he turned to face me.

"I told you to stay with the horses!" His whisper was furious. *"Brex, you're endangering all of our lives!"*

"I won't let you run into danger alone!" I fired back. "I'm not leaving you, so you may as well tell me what's ahead." The dagger was firm in my hand, and my eyes fixed on the door in the ground. "What, by the gods, is that?"

"Below this door is Vlareq's sanctum—the outpost where he conducts business with the few outsiders the goblins trust."

In all that I had seen back in Byrlad, I'd never actually met a goblin. What I had heard of them, however, made the idea of crawling into their subterranean lair feel like walking down into the depths of Ástleysi, the underworld. The Realm of chaos and evil. I shivered again, this time so violently, Neo clamped a hand on my shoulder.

"Ready your dagger," Neo instructed, "and stay close. And by the gods, Brex, if I say run, you *run*."

I nodded, then watched as Neo crawled beneath the small wooden door. He descended a few shallow stairs, perfectly sized to goblin feet, and held the door open for me while I climbed past him, stepping below ground and into the unknown. An overwhelming stench assaulted my nose as soon as I took the first few stairs, a combination of sickness and the metallic tang of blood that nearly brought my entire wedding dinner back up. I swallowed the saliva that filled my mouth and tugged at my cloak so my mouth and nose were covered.

"Stay close," Neo whispered, passing me on the stairs, his torch in one hand, the short sword drawn in the other.

I did, following him down the narrow stone staircase, my hands clenched and clammy. My shoulders tensed painfully as I kept my steps light, my tummy roiling with the need to be sick. Whatever had happened down here, it had been bad. Before we reached the end of the staircase, Neo stopped suddenly. I collided with his back, nearly knocking him forward. His feet were firmly planted at an angle on the tiny stairs, his broad shoulders stopping me from toppling past him.

He said nothing, just shushed me. The torch illuminated the shadows under his honey-gold eyes. The crinkles around them as he squinted in the dark revealed how truly worried he was. I rested a hand on the back of his scale mail, the smooth leather cool under my skin. I brushed the hair he'd tied back, and I withdrew it quickly, not wishing to distract him or cause him to fall. And not wishing to distract myself from the task ahead. Especially not with my husband's enchanting beauty.

"Neo." I kept my voice low, feeling the packed dirt wall as I followed him step after terrifying step. Whatever was at the bottom of the steps stunk. I suspected the tiny scratching noises I heard were corpse rats making quick work of whatever was there.

"Shhh," he urged. "Stay close. Stay quiet."

He broke his own rule when he held up the torch and cast a ray of light over the body at the bottom of the stairs. Neo gasped and leapt onto a swarming mass of rats, stabbing at them with his sword and stomping on the ground to scatter the ravenous rodents.

"No, no, no," Neo gritted out between clenched teeth. "Brex, help me. Come here."

I took the rest of the stairs quickly, stopping fast on the last step. I could see in the glow of the torch the mangled remains of a goblin dressed in mail, a spear cracked in half still clenched in a lifeless hand. His skin was pale orange and the tips of his ears were pointy, just like the legends described. I couldn't, thank the gods, see the man's face, but the way his feet with their elongated, claw-like nails were positioned at unnatural angles, I suspected this death was no accident.

Neo handed me his torch, which I held high enough that the flame illuminated the grotesque spectacle ahead. His voice broke. "Gimbra is...*was*...a dune goblin. Two hundred years old, thousands of miles from his birthplace. He served his guild well."

"Come," he whispered, extending his hand to me. "Try not to look."

I replaced the dagger in my scabbard and took his hand, holding the torch securely in the other. He held on tightly to my hand as I stepped over the body of the dead goblin, his bristly graying brown hair matted with bloody tangles. My mouth watering at the horrific smell. I squeezed my eyes shut to clear the tears that formed there and whispered a prayer for the poor soul.

Once I'd stepped past the pool of nearly dry blood, sending an angry kick after the few remaining corpse rats, Neo released my hand and met my eyes.

Be careful, he mouthed, reclaiming the torch from my hold.

I nodded and pulled out my dagger again, unsure what, if anything, I would do with it if a swarm of rats followed us. I realized as I followed him down a narrow tunnel that the solitary guard at the entrance was likely only one of many goblins down here in the sanctum. How many more, and what had happened, we would only know by pressing onward. While the tunnel was narrow, it was tall enough for a man of Neo's height to walk without stooping. That meant we were likely at least eight or ten feet underground. Maybe deeper.

I followed Neo's back, the torch illuminating the path ahead only so much. I tried not to look past his massive form but couldn't help myself as the path, scarcely wide enough for two to walk side by side, widened to reveal an intricately designed wooden door, fortified with iron fittings. The door was ajar, its lock coated in a powdery black dust. Neo ran a gloved fingertip along the residue, sniffed it, then whispered, "Magic."

I closed my eyes and shook my head. If magic had been used down here... There might be no goblins left alive. Neo must have believed the same thing. He shoved the door open and rushed into the sanctum, the torch casting light on every rat. And there were hundreds.

Goblin bodies littered the floor of the sanctum, their blood drying in pools or splashed in grotesque-looking shapes across the walls. The creatures here had died horrible, violent deaths. Their bellies cut open, their hands cut off, and in the case of one in particular, an even more nightmarish fate. A blood-red glow illuminated the ceiling and the walls. A terrifying, creeping canopy that looked exactly like the blood moss that grew on the Oderisi land. I wondered if that's where the blood moss had come from. That would explain why I'd not seen it elsewhere in the realm. Moss spores tracked from Neo's shoes to his home? I knew little of the study of plants, but at least since I'd seen the moss already, I wasn't horrified by the sickly red light that cast a haunting hue over the devastation before us.

"Vlareq..." Neo sank to his knees, swatting at rats and ignoring the sticky, blackening blood that seeped into his leather mail. He dropped his sword on the ground and looked helplessly behind him. I was right there, taking the torch to unburden his hands.

Neo knelt before the head that had been separated so brutally from its body. Long black hair covered a cruelly severed neck, the eyes of the goblin still open, blood red, and lifeless. His mouth was locked in what looked like an eternal snarl, the nostrils of its hooked nose permanently flared.

I longed to rest a hand on Neo's shoulder, to utter soothing words, but I had none. I did not know the depths of my husband's friendship with this goblin, but the grief in his sunken shoulders tore my heart to ribbons. I was growing used to the stench and as my eyes adjusted to the darkness, I noticed lamps affixed to the walls and assumed there had to be some sort of ventilation system if the goblins could breathe down here. I carefully stepped past the headless body to light as many as I could find, anxious to drive away the ghastly red glow with some true light. I followed the line of the wall, lighting lamps and kicking at corpse rats, trying not to look upon the faces of the many who'd been slain.

"Gods, no." Neo's broken whispers brought tears to my eyes as I lit the last lamp.

An artist illustrating the demons and devils of Ástleysi could not have imagined a more nightmarish scene. Fully illuminated, the sanctum was now clearly a tomb. By my quick count, dozens of goblins lay dead, but also animals, beasts I'd never seen before, had been hacked to bits or cut into pieces.

I walked up to one of them, holding the torch close to look at the creature's face.

"Those are megadrile moles," Neo said, his voice shattered. "The goblins ride them through the tunnels, use them to help dig and burrow."

The large animal had the segmented, pinkish body of the

common earthworm, with a barbed tail. Its four legs bore claws like that of a mole, long and sharp with a slightly scooped shape. Perfect for digging tunnels. I reached down to touch one outfitted with a small custom-made saddle but recoiled at the cold, slimy body. That's when the tears began to fall. I willed myself to stay silent, letting tears stream down my face as Neo stood, holding the head of his friend in his hands.

"H-He..." The tiniest voice croaked from someplace in the sanctum.

Neo surged to his feet, his sword clenched in a fist. "Who's there!" he demanded, his voice echoing with rage.

"Here! Neo, here!" I saw movement, a slight shift coming from a dark mound of clothes and bodies and hair.

I ran to the source of the sound, holding the torch high.

"Who are you, friend? What's your name?" I stomped my foot, scattering a few tenacious corpse rats feasting near the survivor, then dropped to my knees.

"El..." The voice was labored, and I wished that I had gloves. But I would not let my bare hands stop me from rooting through the dead to free the trapped one.

"Go on," I urged as Neo joined me, carefully moving aside the bodies that had been thrown or tossed atop the survivor.

"Elgit." The word came out in a single, pained grunt.

"Elgit," Neo echoed. "I am Neoruzzi Oderisi. You know me as friend of Vlareq, ally of your kin. What happened?"

I considered reaching for the traveling pouch tied around my waist, to offer the survivor some water from my cask, but Neo stopped me with a hand on my shoulder. He squeezed gently, trying to send a message that I did not understand.

Neo knelt to get a closer look at the man's extensive injuries. I could see now why he'd discouraged the water. The goblin's belly was cut clean open, blood and viscera soiling his tunic.

Though his gray lips were so dry they looked cracked, they

barely moved as they goblin whispered one coherent word. *"Haeloc."*

Neo leapt as if he'd been stung. "Where? Here!" His voice was so loud, I could see the dying body flinch against the sound.

Neo drew his sword, his eyes flaming red, his fangs fully elongated.

"I will take his head and burn every hair one by one. Where is he? Where!"

I stuck the end of Neo's torch into the soil as I'd done with mine outside by the horses. Once my hands were free, I knelt beside the shuddering goblin and pulled my cloak from around my shoulders. "Here," I said, bunching the garment and setting it behind his head like a pillow. My mind was racing toward one direction, but I could tell Neo's went the opposite.

"We need Odile," I said, my stare pulling Neo's gaze to me.

He shook his head, his fiery eyes and thick brows boring into me. "Where is Haeloc? Was he here!"

There was a weak groan from the goblin, so I squatted as low as I could and reached for his tiny hand. His claw-like grip was so, so weak. My pulse danced a frantic beat in my wrists as I summoned my courage. This being was dying. Suffering greatly. If we couldn't get Odile here, or get him back to Odile, we could at least make his final moments less horrific.

Elgit groaned, using his remaining strength to look at me. The corners of his mouth curved a bit, and I knew he was thankful for the cloak. I wrapped both my hands around one of his, the flesh clammy and cold. The touch of the nearly dead. I wanted to reach beneath my tunic, find my charm, and stroke it for comfort. I wouldn't, though. I dared not release the fading goblin's hands.

My warmth seeped into his flesh, and he seemed better able to speak, his fingers jerking as if he was clinging to every bit of warmth from me. I would not deprive him of that small comfort, and as he groaned a whisper, I pressed his hand.

"Came...for Haeloc..."

"Who?" Neo demanded. "Someone came looking for Haeloc here? Why? What do you know? Tell me, man, and I will avenge your brothers, your guildmaster, and every beast that's been slaughtered in this sanctum!"

I wanted to tell Neo to calm down, that exciting the goblin might only lead to his deterioration, but the small being seemed to regain a bit of purpose, a bit of spirit.

"Vlareq... Fangs..."

That seemed to tell Neo everything he needed to know. He clenched his hands together and roared, a soul-rending sound that startled me into a full-body shiver. The goblin on the ground didn't react. Didn't move. His dry-looking tongue lolled between his slack lips.

"Stay with him," Neo demanded. "I'll make sure there are no other survivors."

I nodded, but I was fairly certain there was no one else left. I had little experience with the dead, but the absence of breath or sound, the absence of tears in this mess of misery suggested to me that none but this poor, wrecked Elgit had escaped fatal injury.

Neo wandered every inch of the sanctum, inspecting the walls, opening drawers of desks that had been overturned. It looked as though this had been a workspace for trades of all sorts. The goblins whose bodies littered the floor were all dressed for craft. Aprons covered their clothes. Many wore gloves that reached their bent elbows and hats that held back their hair. Money sacks had been emptied and discarded. Mugs of ale and buckets of water crushed as though stomped under the boots of giants. Which, compared to the goblins, even an average-sized man was.

Elgit gurgled, the word sounding like it was being spoken through water.

"Neo!" I called through the sanctum, fearful this creature was dying.

But even my panicked cry could not distract Neo from whatever he had found. He stood over an upended wooden workbench, holding a mask in his hands. The impression of a woman's face was still visible, despite the goblin dagger that pierced the space between the eyes.

"This...This was our business here tonight." His voice was bitter, the glint in his red eyes hard. He sheathed his sword and took the mask between both hands, slowly pulling the dagger from between the eyes of the girl.

"That mask?" I asked.

Neo nodded. "The goblins make death masks for the living. Their mud is infused with a serum only they can create. It's unlike anything the common folk have. Allows them to create a perfect seal over the nostrils and eyes. I've seen no other creature craft such a perfect death mask on a living person, not even using enchantment."

I stroked the back of Elgit's hand, noting that his temperature seemed to be improving. He was warmer, even if all I felt was my own transferred heat. Holding his small hands in mine felt less like holding the fingers of a corpse, which made the task feel that much easier. "Why would a living person want a death mask?"

"Such a mask would be convincing proof if one sought to fake their own death," he said simply.

The sadness in his voice clutched my already aching heart. "Why would someone fake their death?" I asked. Of course, I could imagine many, many reasons. Had I the means or the opportunity, I might have sought one myself before escaping the foundling home the way that I did. How much sooner might I have found my freedom with an object such as this?

As my eyes traveled the features of the mask, I could not believe the mask was not alive. The curve of the lips and the perfect detail of her eyes and lashes gave the impression that any moment the mask would open its eyes and speak.

"My client was a girl," Neo said bitterly. "Destined for an unwanted marriage because she has means and land. I brokered the deal with the goblins. Brought her here in Flynn's cart, her eyes and head covered so she would not know the way or the means by which the mask was being made. Vlareq's craftsmen charged her an unreasonably high price for this. I was to collect my own high price from the girl after picking it up and delivering it to her."

While I tucked away that bit of information about how my husband made his money, my heart went out to the girl whose problems were the opposite of mine but no less difficult. And the solution she'd sought was now useless.

"What will she do now?" I asked. "Can the mask be repaired?"

He held the damaged item in his hands and spoke to it as though he were addressing the girl herself. "I will find a way. There are other goblin camps. Vlareq and I have a long history of trust, though." He sighed. "*Had.* It seems those I may truly trust grow fewer day by day."

While Neo walked past bodies, looking for clues or evidence or what, I did not know, I whispered to my charge.

"Would you like some water?"

No matter what Neo thought, there was a chance this creature would live, and I would do anything within my reach to help him.

The goblin did not respond, his breathing heavy and his eyes closed.

"We need to go, Brex. Now." Neo held out a hand to help me up, but I refused.

"I don't think I can carry him," I said.

"Carry him?" Neo shook his head. "No."

I glared at him. "You can't possibly mean to leave him."

"Brex." His eyes had lost their crimson glow, but even if they had been red, I would not have seen it. He tilted his chin and knelt beside the goblin. He laid a hand on the barely moving chest and whispered a prayer. "His soul is destined for Forráheim now, Brex. We cannot stop that journey."

I reluctantly released Elgit's hand and rose to my feet. The torch I'd stuck in the ground flickered with my sudden movements.

"You cannot be serious. If that were me lying there, or your brother, would you whisper your prayers and leave him to pass into Forráheim alone?"

He stared at me, his scarred lips a tight, thin line.

"Would you!" I demanded.

"What would you have me do? If we're caught with a goblin, Brex... By the gods. Do you have any idea what would become of us? How quickly we'd be drawn and quartered by the common people? That's if they even waited until they found two horses! We'd be staked alive and strung up faster than we could say the word goblin!"

"We will not be discovered," I seethed. "No one has to know he's a goblin. Look." I pointed to my cloak. "Wrap him in it. Carry him like a child."

"That will never work!" Neo pinched his brows between two fingers. "He is dying, Brex. If we'd never come tonight, if we'd spent our wedding night like man and wife should..." He trailed off, his hands clenched into fists, the goblin dagger still in one hand. "Elgit would have made the journey alone. We cannot intervene with destiny."

"But he's not alone," I insisted. "And people intervene with destiny every day! Just last week you did not know that I even existed, and now..."

He closed his eyes but appeared unpersuaded.

"You dare to speak to me of dishonor!" I exclaimed, reminding him of the one term he'd cared enough but to demand, but not to ink into our marriage contract. "Do as you will. I will not leave him. Go, if you must. Abandon us both here, and be certain to tell your family the truth about my demise."

"How do you expect to do this!" Neo demanded. "Do you know the pain we'll cause him? The suffering he'll endure just by being moved? The ride on horseback alone might finish him."

I started walking through the mess of the sanctum, lifting anything that wasn't a body, looking for wine, ale, anything. "We can give him something to ease the pain," I said, panic edging my words. "There must be something here that will help him!"

A pair of strong hands on my shoulders stopped me from rooting through the stinking, bloody mess.

"*Stop*." Neo turned me to face him, peering down at me. "Why are you so fixed on the impossible? Odile cannot save him. The gods will not spare him. Not with an injury this severe. The kindest path is to say a final prayer and leave him to the journey."

"No!" I nearly screamed, wriggling to free myself from his grip. "No one should die alone. Ever. I will not leave him!"

Neo studied me as I returned to Elgit's form and hovered a hand over his shoulder.

"We're going to get you help," I vowed, my tears wetting the poor goblin's gray cheeks. "We will not leave you."

Neo kneeled beside me, this time resting a hand gently on

my shoulder. "Who was it?" he asked. "Your mother? Did she leave you at the foundling home and then..."

I nodded, suppressing full-body sobs. I would not let my mind return there. I would not indulge memory and grief when the room was full of lives that had been viciously cut short. And I would not fall apart while this vampire lord stood and watched.

"She died alone," I admitted. "You asked me to do nothing to dishonor you, myself, or your family." I strained to keep my words clear, my voice steady. "Is there anything more honorable than risking our own safety on even the slightest possibility that we might save a life?"

Neo didn't bother to reply. He sighed but knelt beside me. He peered into the silent goblin's face and gently moved my cloak from behind Elgit's head. "Grab the torch," he said, "and keep hold of these." He handed me the goblin dagger and the death mask. "You'll need to lead the way."

He covered Elgit with my cloak like a blanket, tucked his arms gingerly under the goblin's knees, and lifted the limp body into his arms. The goblin wailed like an infant at the movement, but he quieted once Neo settled him.

"Take the hood and the rest of the garment," he instructed, "wrap him so his face cannot be seen. We cannot risk even a hint of his body being seen by anyone who dares be on the road."

I set the mask and dagger down and stuck the torch back into the ground. I gently wrapped Elgit's face beneath the cloak and tucked his hands on his bleeding belly so his skin and claws would not immediately mark him as not one of the common folk. Then I grabbed everything and pointed toward the torches that were still lit. "Should I extinguish them?" I asked.

"No time." Neo motioned for me to lead the way up the stairs. "They'll burn out. And if not, let the place burn. That's a kinder fate for these bodies than what the corpse rats have planned."

I dashed up the narrow stairs, lighting the way while Neo cautiously took each step with Elgit in his arms. I put my shoulder into the hatch door and shoved with my all my strength, but it took three tries before I could budge the heavy wood. Even then I had a tough time balancing the torch, the other items, and keeping the door open.

"Let me move past," Neo instructed, "and slam that closed behind us. Rustle the leaves and twigs to cover the door as we found it, but don't spend too long. I'll head for the horses."

He wedged his way past me, the bundle in his arms unnervingly still. Just after Neo cleared the hatch door, he picked up his pace, walking quickly toward the horses. I tried to carefully close the heavy door, but with my arms full, the torch slipped from my grasp and tumbled all the way back down the stairs. I was suddenly bathed in darkness.

It was night. We were in a clearing where the vengersax, winged daggers, roamed the skies, and Neo was carrying a bleeding goblin, its flesh and sweat sending waves of scent through the dark. I scrambled to scatter some twigs and leaves on the closed hatch door then searched the horizon for the tiny torch still burning bright by the horses.

"Neo," I cried out, "run!"

NINE

The ride back to the Oderisi manor was more exhausting and chilling than my darkest nightmares on the longest of nights. While the gods must have kept the vengersax securely in their nests, they seemed to have completely abandoned Elgit. Neo insisted on holding the goblin on the slow, arduous journey. I rode beside Neo, Sara too new to me and to the manor to lead the way back. I hated to admit it, but my arm grew weary of holding the torch, the muscles tight and trembling. If we hadn't needed it for protection, I was certain I would have dropped it a dozen times. But every sound from Neo braced my resolve to hold the light high and keep the dangers of the air away.

Elgit remained silent, but every step Sedda took seemed to cause Neo more and more distress. Whether it was simply the physical strain of holding Elgit's bleeding body steady or the emotional drain of what we'd seen, I did not ask. Every time I looked at him, curious and concerned, he clamped his lips shut and stared straight ahead.

When we finally arrived at the manor, the relief I felt that the ride was over was short-lived. I left my horse with Neo and threw my body against the front door, pounding with what was left of my strength and praying that Antonia and Dale were awake. When the butler, her hair mussed and eyes sleepy, did finally open the door, her alarm at my state was clear.

"We have an injured...being," I cried, too concerned that we might be overheard to admit what Elgit was. "He's near death! Neo's holding him."

Antonia wasted not a step, frantically ringing for Dale and rushing him off to rouse the household.

As soon as I knew help was on the way, I ran back to Neo. Every muscle in his jaw was locked in grim determination. His hair was slick with sweat, his arms locked beneath Elgit's legs and back. His face bore smudges of dirt from our subterranean descent, and if I wasn't mistaken, fresh tears tracked thin paths through the smudges on his face.

Rain ran out to meet us first. Getting Elgit from Neo's arms was heart-wrenching. Dale brought a sturdy wooden box from inside the house and set it beside the horse. Rain climbed onto the box so that his arms were nearly level with his brother's.

"Careful, now," Rain said. "Hand him to me."

Neo didn't speak, didn't move. I didn't know if he was reluctant to release the goblin or if fatigue and exertion had ruined his limbs so he simply couldn't.

"Neo," Rain urged, "you'll cause him more injury and distress if you try to dismount without aid. I have no idea how you got onto that horse with him in the first place."

I hardly believed he'd been able to do it. I'd been running so fast toward the horses, all I could see was Neo jostle the goblin from two arms to one, grab the reins, and mount the horse before I even arrived to pick up the torch. If his fear had spiked like mine, I would not have been surprised to see him leap onto the horse fueled by terror alone.

But now, Rain had to coax his brother to release his precious cargo.

"There, easy... I've got him. You can let go." Rain stood on the box with Elgit in his arms, a nauseated grimace on Rain's face. "Did you bite him, brother?" Rain asked. "Even the smallest bit of venom might..."

Elgit was still wrapped in the cloak, his injuries as well as his face still masked. Neo climbed down from his horse, a low groan the only evidence that he was indeed sore and tired. He stood with his arms outstretched, as if waiting for Rain to return the bundle.

"Trust me," Neo gritted out, "he's too far gone to be helped by a bite. Much too far gone. We focused on surviving the ride."

Rain refused to hand Elgit back to Neo, instead holding fast to the silent bundle while he stepped down from the box. Dale took the horses and urged me to get inside.

"Set up in the sitting room," Antonia ordered the moment our miserable group entered the manor. "Is anyone else hurt?" She rested her cool palms on either side of my face, the pinch of her lips and the crease between her brows belying her concern. "My dear, you look..."

"I'm fine," I assured her. "Please, we must help him. His name is Elgit."

She nodded. "Come on, then."

Rain placed the motionless bundle on the settee where I'd slept last night. I pushed past him to unwrap my cloak and free the goblin from the constraints of the fabric. When the small gray face was exposed, Rain gasped and gripped his brother's shoulder. Antonia immediately began praying.

"I'll bring hot water, drinking water, and fresh blankets and rags. May the gods bring Odile back to us before we lose him."

Rain and Neo spoke quietly about what we'd found in the

sanctum while Gia, barefoot but dressed in breeches and a tunic, came running into the sitting room.

"By the gods," she breathed, a hand over her mouth as her eyes filled with tears.

The stench of Elgit's injuries and what was no doubt a horrific infection filled the room as I gently peeled my cloak away from his belly.

"I'll get something to help," Gia said. "I'm not a healer, but until Odile's back, I'll do what I can."

"Brother," Rain said somberly. "What do you make of this?"

I busied myself dragging an armchair to Elgit's side but listened intently to their conversation.

"Elgit was in and out of clarity when we found him. He mentioned Haeloc and, specifically, fangs." Neo's voice was hard, emotionless. "After Haeloc disappeared, he must have gone to the goblins seeking replacement fangs. But why?"

"Whoever extracted Haeloc's fangs may not have wanted to punish him. Perhaps they used the fangs to control him... Some sort of magic? If that's true, how would another set of fangs stop that?"

Neo rolled his neck and groaned, closing his eyes to his private pain. "I don't know. But I am certain now that Haeloc's disappearance is connected to magic. There's no other explanation for his escape from you the day you freed me. His connection to the goblins has cost them their lives. Gimbra, Vlareq... Two dozen or more of them massacred by Haeloc or someone who wanted Haeloc dead."

"That means he's back." Rain's voice hardened with hatred and possibly fear. His nostrils flared as he gritted, "I never should have doubted you, brother. We should have posted someone at Haeloc's manor the day we rescued you."

"I don't think one vampire could have accomplished what

we witnessed tonight—even with the aid of magic. Something more is behind the massacre of the goblins."

A cold chill slithered up my spine as images flashed past my eyes. What kind of monster could do such things? And why?

Rain's voice lifted as he demanded his brother leap to action. "What if Haeloc has returned to his manor this very moment?"

"We can't run all over the Realm every time we suspect Haeloc has set foot on his own property. Or that of our allies. We need a strategy. We have no idea what type of trouble Haeloc has brought down upon himself or what alliances he's made." Neo's weariness seemed to abate as another emotion replaced it: determination. "That's why I rode out to Fish Head End. To secure a permanent guard at the godforsaken place. Unfortunately, my old friend Trond had no interest in babysitting an abandoned raider's lair."

As I gripped Elgit's now-cold hand in mine, the brothers both fell silent. I assumed they were considering those larger forces, the deeper evil that could wield magic to end dozens of innocent lives—those of the goblins and their megadrile moles.

At least some of the pieces were falling into place now. Haeloc must have been the one who'd imprisoned Neo, and the job he'd sought to fill was a guardian or spy. Posting someone at Haeloc's manor in case he returned. Instead, Neo had returned from Fish Head End not with a guardian, but a thief. A thief he'd married.

Antonia and Gia's return to the sitting room halted the brothers' muted conversation. Rain and Gia together removed the filthy, blood-stained cloak from Elgit's body while I washed my hands using one of the buckets of water Antonia had brought. Then I set to work drenching rags with clean water and wiping Elgit's face and hands.

I slipped my hands beneath the gray, wrinkled flesh of his

neck while Gia dripped a tonic into his mouth. He grimaced at the taste, but his dry tongue slid back into his mouth, and he seemed to swallow it down. She peeked at the wound in his belly, the look on her face revealing how truly hopeless the situation was. Nonetheless, she covered him with a very thin, soft length of cloth and tucked a fresh blanket lightly over his belly.

"Feed him water using this." Gia handed me the small metal spoon with a tiny pouring spout she'd used to give him the tonic. "Flynn's brother made this for Odile, specifically for administering small quantities to sick people. Give him water very slowly, just a few sips at most at a time. Even if he seems to be dying of thirst, giving him too much too quickly will make him sicker."

I nodded and took the spoon, admiring the unusual design and craftsmanship.

"The tonic I gave him is only to ease the pain. I've picked up a bit from my sister over the years, but any real healing will need to wait until she sees him and can concoct something to treat the infection." Gia worried her lower lip with her teeth. "These injuries may require a surgeon," she said. "But I...I don't see how that's possible."

"Let's not get ahead of ourselves," Antonia said lightly. "Odile is the healer. She'll know, and the lot of us would just be wasting our wits standing around in the dead of night trying to come up with a plan before she's back. Let's do what we can do, and beyond that, may the gods guide us. And him."

I searched Gia's face for any information she had but wasn't willing to share. Like whether she was certain already that Elgit's injuries surpassed anything her sister could heal. "Has she ever treated one like him?" I asked. "A goblin?"

Gia shook her head. "Not that I'm aware. But bodies are bodies. Goblins may manipulate magic, but they are made of flesh and bone. If he's to be saved, Odile will know what to do."

If he was to be saved.

After offering Elgit just the tiniest bit of water, I set the spoon back on the butler's cart and reclaimed his hand.

Gia squeezed my shoulder and gave me a kind look. "Why don't you get some rest? You must be exhausted."

I shook my head. "I'd prefer to remain with him." I looked to Antonia, who was stoking the fire and ordering Dale to move furniture so that Odile would have room to move freely around the carts she'd supplied once she arrived. "May I stay here?" I asked. I'd slept here once already. I'd not miss a night in a luxurious bed that I'd never experienced. Besides, I couldn't imagine that Neo truly meant for me to share his room.

Antonia looked from me to Neo and back. "The lady of the manor should do as she desires."

Neo nodded. "Bring all the bedding from my room down here." Rain helped him strip off the filthy, heavy scale armor. I couldn't help but watch as the coat was removed, revealing nothing more than a thin shirt underneath that was likewise damp with Neo's sweat and Elgit's blood. "*Our* room," he corrected as Rain handed the intricate leatherwork to Dale. "Draw a bath in our bedroom, please, Dale."

Antonia left, going upstairs to gather what she could while Dale scurried away with the coat of armor in his hands. I was so tired, so consumed by the dying figure before me, I hadn't the energy to thank anyone. I reminded myself I was a member of this household now. I'd have time enough for that. For now, my attention returned to my charge.

While I held fast to the weak hand in mine, Neo drank a mug of water, refilled it and drank again, and then handed it to me. "Drink," he said. "I'm going to clean up. Don't weaken yourself with caregiving, or you'll be of no help to this soul."

The fact that Neo hadn't worn padded armor beneath the more decorative scales of leather made me believe he truly had not anticipated that we'd encounter any danger at the sanctum. His long hair had fallen partly free of its binding. Loose strands stuck to his face with sweat, dirt, and blood. His body was impressive, the planes of his chest sculpted and muscular. I tried not to look at his thighs, still clad in the leather leggings, but my mind did briefly wonder whether he'd fully undress right here in front of everyone. I tore my eyes from his weary body and focused on our small, fragile patient.

Neo hovered beside the settee, staring down at Elgit. He ran a hand over the man's forehead without actually touching his skin. "May the goddesses of your mountains guide you." He looked at me. "I won't be long." Then he and Rain left, closing the door firmly behind them.

Once we were alone, Gia stood beside my chair. "Do I want to know why Neo took you to a goblin sanctum on your wedding night?"

"Introducing me to the family business." I gave her a weak smile then stroked the deep crevices in the skin of Elgit's fingers. I wanted to make a joke, to tease that my new husband would prefer the site of a massacre to a night alone with me, but I simply couldn't. Couldn't laugh or smile. Could only contemplate the painful journey this creature was embarking upon. I only hoped he had the strength and the blessings of the gods to return to this Realm. I did not want to fathom the alternative. Even worse would be the attention and danger I'd bring upon the household if our charge indeed did not survive.

I tried not to consider the worst. The small hand in mine was still warm. There was still life in Elgit. I would pray that healing and care would coax that small glimmer of soul into resisting the hasty mist of death. Gia moved toward the window, staring out over the glowing hills of the Oderisi land.

My eyelids must have drooped, because the next thing that aroused me was a firm hand on my shoulder.

"Antonia has a fresh bath ready for you." Neo was dressed in a loose pair of ankle-length breeches and a waist-length tunic, his still-damp hair as smooth as a pond on a windless night.

"No, thank you." As blissful as a hot bath sounded, as long as I could stay awake, I would. I looked down at my hand, my fingers still laced with Elgit's. "I'll wait until Odile is back. I'm sorry to waste the hot water, though. I'll use it cold later. I'm well used to cold baths."

Neo kneeled beside me and rested his hand atop mine and Elgit's. "Brex, I'm not going to try to talk you out of being here for him. A bath will be a few minutes well spent. The entire household is awake. On my honor, I will retrieve you should there be any change." He gently unwound my fingers from Elgit's and then took the goblin's hand in his. "I'll stay here in your stead."

He threw a look over his shoulder at Antonia, who shuffled over.

"Come, love," she said to me. "We won't be but a few moments."

I looked down at my filthy clothing and messed hair. Gone were the pretty smells and careful finishes of the wedding feast. I bore the stains of what I'd seen tonight, not only on my heart but all over my clothing. Neo had a point. Cleaning up would be good for me, and I would be a better guardian if I was fresh and alert. Too weary to say anything more, I nodded at Neo. Something passed between us then, a look so full of meaning, I could not take the time to unravel the layers. I looked at his hand, so enormous beside the goblin's, and on impulse, I wordlessly leaned over and placed a kiss on Neo's cheek. My legs and feet felt like wood, my hand cold without the small, weak one within it. But I wanted him to know that what he was doing mattered to me. That I was grateful. Perhaps more than words could have accomplished.

I followed Antonia through the manor, up the stairs, and into Neo's room—our room—where I let the kind woman help peel away my filthy clothes.

"Your charm, milady," she said. I appreciated the more formal address while I stood in a strange room, naked and trembling with fatigue and cold. "Shall I set it aside for safe-keeping?"

I gripped the charm in my hand and shook my head. "No, thank you. It brings me comfort, and the water won't damage it."

She did not argue. Simply took my hand and helped me into the tub then stood behind me scrubbing oil into my wet hair. While she worked, I closed my eyes and finally let the tears fall. How long I'd been in the bath silently weeping I did not know. It seemed like Antonia had scarcely rinsed my hair when there was a pounding at the door. Gia let herself in, her eyes immediately finding mine.

"Come, sister," she said to me. "Hurry. Odile has returned."

CLAD in yet another outfit of clothes that did not belong to me, I did not bother covering my feet and took off running for the stairs. My hair was drenched and soaked through the light-colored tunic I wore, but I did not care. I had a hand on my charm and my heart in my throat as I entered the sitting room.

Neo was still holding Elgit's hand, but his gaze raked over my body as I bolted toward the settee. Odile was examining the nightmare under the blankets and speaking in a low voice.

"He needs a surgeon." Her words tightened like a fist around my heart. "But I know of none to be trusted with a goblin." She turned a sour frown on Neo. "Do you?" she asked. "Where are the others? Perhaps we can send for someone?"

Neo shook his head. "At least a full day's journey away on a capable horse. Likely longer. And I cannot guarantee I wouldn't be killed upon site if I went alone. Without Vlareq to make an introduction, I am not sure how I'd be received. The sanctum was an outpost. A safe place where Vlareq could conduct business without having to endure the risk of traveling back and forth on the roads between the shires and the mountains of Skickligera. Perhaps if I brought Elgit there, they would admit me or take him and treat him."

Odile shook her head. "He should not be moved. I cannot believe he survived the journey on horseback. Even a few moments of jostling should have..."

"Neo carried him. Went to great pains to hold him steady, at the cost of his own safety." The pride in my words surprised me.

"The gods indeed guided your way." She asked us to turn away and give her a bit of privacy while she moved aside Elgit's pants and shirt to assess what might be done for him. She moved quickly, her voice focused as she asked Antonia and Gia to gather rags and a certain ointment from her room. I knew where nothing was. I was a member of this household and yet a stranger. I hadn't even seen the other rooms yet, so I was essentially useless. I stayed close to the healer, worrying the charm between my fingers and trying to slow the chattering of my teeth.

"You're cold." Neo draped a blanket from the bedding Antonia had brought over my shoulders. "Stand by the fire until your hair dries."

I did as he suggested, since Odile needed space to move without me hovering. Once she had dressed the wounds and applied ointment and tonics to his belly, forehead, throat, wrists, and chest, she cleaned her hands in a fresh bucket of water and mopped her sweating brow with the back of her sleeve.

"Leave him to rest now," she urged.

"Alone?" I felt all eyes in the room on me. I'd interrupted her, and I lowered my chin politely. "I feel responsible for him. I insisted we take him from the sanctum. I feel I should stay with him. Should he wake in a strange place, possibly in great pain…"

Her smile was weakened by fatigue, but her words were warm. "You did right, sister. No creature should make the journey from this Realm alone, and in such a state of suffering. It happens, of course, but my heart would have been led as yours was. You did well." She cleared her throat. "Antonia, could I trouble you for a bit of tea? I'd like to take a bit myself and rest. I expect I'll be needed in the morning, if not for our guest here, for the child back in the village."

Antonia went to fix the tea, while Gia and Rain bid us goodnight. "Should you need us, do not hesitate," Rain said. He clapped his brother in a rough hug and then stood by the fire with me. "Let's hope the second day of your marriage is far less eventful." He nodded to me, and Gia waved goodnight.

Odile pointed to the bedding on the settee. "Who will keep watch?" she asked.

"Me," I said, but Neo's voice carried over mine as he said, "We both will."

Odile nodded. "If he shows any signs of distress, wake me." She covered her mouth as she yawned. "I have a key to this room and will let myself in when I wake to check him if you've not summoned me before then."

After Odile left, I heard the lock turn. I took my place in the armchair beside Elgit, but since Odile had anointed his hands and tucked them beneath the covers, all I could do was worry my charm and watch the gentle rise and fall of the goblin's small chest.

"It must be nearly midnight," Neo surmised, suppressing a yawn of his own. "We should rest in shifts. One at a time. If there's any change in his condition, one of us will be awake to alert Odile."

"You sleep," I told him, my eyes never leaving Elgit's wrinkled, craggy face. He looked so vulnerable, so lost. Deep in the valley a soul had to travel alone. I couldn't, just couldn't look away. Couldn't leave him. "This was my decision, bringing him here. I've disrupted your entire household. Created needless danger, simply because my heart couldn't..." I broke off and shook away the words. "Please, Neo. You sleep. Spend what's left of the night in your bed. I'll stay here and keep watch."

Neo stood beside me, peering down at the goblin through tired eyes. "We may have disagreed at first, but you were right," he said, his rich, low voice surprisingly close to my ear. "You stood by your heart. I only followed your good counsel. Please, offer no more apologies. And no sacrifices, Brex. Your husband will take you up on the offer of first sleep, but I'll wake soon to relieve you. And if I don't, you're to wake me so you don't drive yourself into illness. Are we agreed?"

"Yes," I said, my lips suddenly so dry, I desperately needed to quench my thirst. I dropped the blanket on the chair and stood to refill my mug of water.

"Brex."

I turned to him, stunned to see my husband's arms held partway open. Inviting me. Waiting for me to go to him.

I didn't hesitate but leaned into his hold and let his arms surround me, holding me so close I could feel the echo of his heart hammering in his chest. I drew a deep breath, taking in the heat of him, the scents of smoke and blood, the lavender from his bath and a brighter smell, like citrus. I laced my arms around his waist, not at all sure what to do with my hands. He buried his face against the top of my hair, the heat of his breath warm against my damp scalp. I felt his body move, the thin clothes still wet from my hair providing very little coverage.

This felt different. Despite my exhaustion, I felt every bit of my body come to life. The cold tile beneath my feet, the grip of his fingers as they slipped beneath my hair. The thin fabric that separated my breasts from his body.

Something must have shifted for him too. I felt him tense before roughly releasing me.

I stepped back and nodded at him. "Goodnight," I whispered, my nerves raw and my body fluttering with confusion. I poured myself some water with a shaky hand and then reclaimed my seat beside Elgit.

Neo strode to the bedding Antonia had piled on another settee. The well-cushioned piece of furniture was pushed far into the dark corner of the room. I could hear him sink onto it then toss and turn, adjusting the covers. And I could have sworn the last thing I heard before he fell silent were the words, "Goodnight, wife."

I'd scarcely settled into my chair when a thought occurred to me. I crept back to the far corner of the room, where Neo's breathing was not yet steady and slow.

"Neo?" I whispered.

"Hmmm?" He was awake, but only just.

"Why do you keep the inside doors locked when you sleep? Why are we locked in for the night?"

He sighed, and I heard the covers move aside. "Sit with me."

I dared not sit with him. I was so tired, if I joined him on that luxurious makeshift bed, I'd be asleep within seconds, I was certain. But a weaker part of me craved the warmth his nearness offered. If he was going to share something surprising, something terrifying—as if anything could be worse than what we'd seen tonight—I wanted to be close to him. I couldn't explain why, but after what we'd seen tonight, I felt allied with him. Bound in a much more real way than that of our contract marriage. I perched on the edge of the settee, trying not to take up too much room.

He remained in the darkness, his eyes and face hidden by pockets of shadow. "Haeloc, the name that Elgit uttered in the sanctum," he said, sounding exhausted. "He is a vampire raider. A dying vampire raider. I don't know what I was thinking going to work for him." He sighed, and I could almost picture the sag of his shoulders. My fingers itched to comfort him, but I resisted the foolish instinct and simply listened. "I went to work for him after my mother passed. As you already know, she'd spent most of the Oderisi wealth after her second partner, a wife, fell ill. The woman was human, so that was a futile endeavor from the start. But as I believe you know, love does not understand the meaning of futility."

I swallowed hard and clutched the charm from my sister in my hands.

"After my mother passed, I did what I could to cut expenses. Reduced the household staff, took up whatever work of the manor my brother and I could manage ourselves. We even sold off some of the furniture and rugs." His voice was low, tinged with shame. "But it wasn't enough to manage the crofter's salary and maintain our meager farm, support Dale and Antonia, stay current on our taxes... I started taking jobs, dangerous jobs, for pay." He breathed deeply, chuckling softly to himself. "And I surprised myself. I loved working. The risk, the reward."

"When you say working...do you mean raiding?" I asked. It wouldn't help me to understand him if I wasn't absolutely clear. "You were...stealing?"

"Not at first," he said, rustling his legs under the blankets. "At first I took dangerous work. Brokering deals between goblins and humans, for example. But then yes, eventually, my old friend Trond—the one I met in Fish Head End—told me about a man looking for someone to salvage sunken ships. The sea trolls ruin close to a third of the cogs that try to run cargo along the coastline. I thought I'd be diving, sailing. Maybe fighting trolls. So Trond made the introduction to a local lord named Rekker Haeloc. As soon as I met him, I knew I'd made a profound mistake."

I looked across the sitting room. A single lamp was burning near the ailing goblin, illuminating his small form. He was breathing and wasn't moving, so I relaxed a bit, scooting back farther until I felt the solid form of Neo's legs behind me.

"What was your mistake?" I asked.

"Haeloc was a vampire with ties to my family. Once upon a time, he'd been in love with my mother. But her heart had already been claimed by the woman she would take as her second spouse—a *human*."

I could hear the rough scratching sounds of Neo rubbing his face. He moved back on the settee, leaving a bit more room, so I moved back as well, tucking my feet beneath me and leaning my rear end against his thighs.

"Did Haeloc know you were... What was your mother's name?" I asked.

"Cherryn." The love Neo felt for his mother came through in the tenderness in his voice. "Cherryn Luisana Oderisi."

"That's lovely," I said, my eyelids growing heavy. I stifled a yawn but scooted back just a bit farther onto the settee. My arms were so tired, and I could see Elgit from here. I'd just rest myself a few short moments while Neo explained. "So did Haeloc know that you were your mother's son?"

"Worse than that," he growled. "I believe he knew I was Cherryn's son and meant to kill me. He lured me into taking the job on the pretense of wanting to help us out of our 'unfortunate circumstances.' He made it too easy, and I was fool enough to trust him. He provided a cog and a crew, but the cog was faulty. Either that, or someone on the crew was paid to sink it.

We began to take on water. I panicked, tried to repair the leak, but by the time it was clear we had to abandon ship or lose the crew, twilight had fallen."

"Sea trolls," I whispered. If vengersax ruled the night air, the sea trolls ruled the coast at night and very often wandered as far inland as they needed to. For meat.

"I made damn sure every man on that crew made it to shore," he said, his voice flinty with anger. "But the cog couldn't be saved. It sank. I dragged myself back to Haeloc, blaming myself for the loss of the ship. By the gods, I was a fool. I should have known. Should have suspected! Haeloc didn't apologize that he'd sent me out on a ship that was nowhere near seaworthy. Didn't breathe a sigh of relief that none of the men on that ship had become troll bait. No. The wretched monster tallied up the damages that I owed him. The full value of the ship. The time he'd have to pay the crew in wages. Every barrel of drinking water, every supply. He itemized everything, and not only that... He insisted I repay every penny of the value of the cargo I'd been sent to salvage."

I worried my lower lip between my teeth, dragging the tiniest corner of a blanket over my hands to warm them. "I don't understand," I said softly. "I thought you hadn't salvaged anything because the cog took on water?"

Neo barked a harsh, soft laugh. "Reality was just a distraction to Haeloc. To a desperate man in pursuit of treasure, reality was something to be shaped and formed, not something to bend to. By the time he hired me, he'd become cruel and bitter. I suspect he was dying and was doing something not unlike what my mother had done. Spending every penny he had to stay a step ahead of death."

I felt him move over to make a bit more room. While he didn't speak the invitation, I rolled onto my side, supporting my head with a pillow so I could still see Elgit.

"I refused to pay him anything but the value of the cog. Since I couldn't prove he'd damaged it intentionally to sabotage me, it seemed a reasonable compromise on the exorbitant amount he claimed. But nothing about Haeloc was reasonable. He threw me in a cell, imprisoned me in his manor. Had a henchman beat me nearly to death but left me alive long enough to let me know he'd summoned my brother. When Rain arrived, Haeloc made him a deal. Pay the full amount of what he claimed I owed him within a few short weeks, or he'd kill me. Brick me into the wall of his dungeon."

My stomach sank. "He threatened to brick you in?"

I could feel Neo nod. "Haeloc's henchman beat my brother within an inch of his life, then cast him out."

"You were imprisoned, then, by this Haeloc. The cruel man who wanted your mother but settled for you. And the same man who somehow is connected to what happened to the goblins?"

"Yes," he sighed.

I felt the warm weight of his arm over my side. I tucked myself a tiny bit closer to him, willing my eyes to stay open while I rested my body but kept watch over my charge.

"When Rain, Gia, and Odile rescued me, Haeloc disappeared. Fully vanished right before their eyes. He'd had his fangs removed at some point—either intentionally or against his will. We suspected he'd been dabbling with magic—either personally or through some mage who used his fangs to bind him. But we know not where he is. Since the day I was rescued by Rain, Gia, and Odile, as far as I know, Haeloc has never returned to his wretched manor. It's been nearly three months now, and the place is in utter disrepair. But I can't stay there in wait, ready to kill him if he returns."

"That was the job you offered your friend in Fish Head End?" I asked. It all made sense now. Of course the caretaking job would be too dangerous for me. The caretaker would not be taking care of the manor. He would be lying in wait to kill the vampire lord if he ever returned.

"It was," he said softly. "And that's why we lock our doors, even inside the house. Until Haeloc is dead, no member of the Oderisi household is safe."

"Brother, stop. I beg you to think this through. We have no idea what we're dealing with!"

I squinted through the sleep that claimed my eyes, the sound of rising voices breaking through my dreams. As soon as I stretched and rolled over, everything returned to me. The marriage contract. Rescuing Elgit. Neo's history with the vampire raider.

I shoved aside the blankets and sat up, trying to still the panic that overtook me like a sudden storm. Where was Neo? How was Elgit? And how, by the gods, had I slept so long?

The settee behind me was cold, an empty space and smashed pillows the only evidence that anyone had slept alongside me. My body warmed and my face flushed hot as I remembered the tossing and turning, and—dare I admit it— the closeness we'd shared as we slept. I remember a kiss on my forehead, my cheek against Neo's chest. A leg thrown over mine. A tangle of light and dark hair spilled over our nestling bodies. As far as a wedding night, we'd certainly not behaved as newlyweds. But we had shared a bed, falling into that uncommon intimacy of actually sleeping beside each other, intertwined for warmth and comfort.

As soon as I shook myself awake, I grabbed the charm around my neck and took a deep breath. The darkness outside the volcano glass windows suggested it was early, just before sunrise. Exactly when Neo had awakened and left, I did not know. As much as I seemed to remember how sleeping beside him felt, I had not noticed him leave me.

I set my bare feet on the cool floor, grateful that someone— Neo, most likely—had tended the fire before he left. The room was comfortably warm, and I could see the gentle movements of Elgit's chest in the orange light from the flames that flickered onto his sleeping form.

I hovered over the goblin, curious if he was feverish. I rested the back of my hand against his forehead, but not knowing what fever might feel like in a goblin, I gave up the effort and instead took hold of his hand. He moved slightly, a subtle reactive quiver in his fingers that I took as an excellent sign. He was at least no closer to death. Perhaps he'd inched a bit closer to this Realm in the hours he'd been resting—and that bit was more than enough to give me hope. I was afraid to touch his bedding or the bindings that Odile had applied, so I said a prayer over him and headed for the door.

"None of us will be safe until he is dead!" Neo's harsh voice echoed through the manor. He had the death mask in one hand and gestured with the goblin dagger that had ruined the mask in his other hand. "And didn't you, just last night, brother, passionately argue for an attack on Haeloc's Manor? Why withdraw your passion now, when the light of day and a night of rest redeems me?"

I closed the heavy door to the sitting room and hugged my arms around my body. Outside the warmth of the fire, the manor was cold, the puff of my breath as I exhaled misting in a small cloud of heat. "Good morning," I said stiffly. I looked at Rain first and then at Neo, who was not only wide awake but already dressed.

Neo's entire expression softened as he looked at me. "How is he?" he asked without prelude or greeting.

"Resting. When I held his hand, he seemed to feel it."

Neo pressed his lips together, his eyes never leaving my face. Beside him, Rain raked a hand through his sandy blond curls and sighed.

"What's wrong?" I asked, cocking my head to the side. The question sounded so childish, even as I uttered the words. The simpler question might have been what was *not* wrong. "Have I interrupted something?"

"Your timing couldn't be more perfect." Rain's indignation was tiny compared to the sudden swell of concern in my belly. "It seems we have a reversal of opinion. While I've seen the light of reason and beg further investigation, your husband now plans to ride to Haeloc's manor. Right now, this morning."

"Alone?" I asked, the swell of concern rising to a powerful wave. "To what end? Do you plan to take the man on? After what happened in the sanctum, do you think that's wise?"

"I do not make a habit of making myself a fool," Neo gritted. Gone was the warm, caring husband I'd slept beside. The bitter vampire replaced everything I was beginning to like about him.

"Is that so?" I murmured, fully aware that I was poking the beast within him.

"Caution, wife," he sneered. "Busy yourself with our guest and leave matters of revenge to me."

I combed my fingers through my sleep-mussed hair and pretended to be fascinated with the state of my tangled ends. "Matters of revenge?" I repeated. "Those are definitely not the musings of a fool."

He stormed across the quiet hall and presented the mask to

me like the horrifying token it was. "See this?" he asked, pointing the tip of the dagger at the very place it had pierced the replica of young girl's face. "I have exactly what I need to confront the monster. I don't know how he's connected to this, but I am certain he is. Not that I need more evidence to justify ridding this Realm of Haeloc." He sucked his lower lip between his teeth. "The evidence of his evildoing is all over my body."

I tried not to think of his body as I replied. "Why the rush to run there now? Are there not leads to pursue? Perhaps someone among the goblins was aware of a threat from another who might be to blame?"

Rain threw his hands in the air dramatically. "Thank you, sister! This is the point I've been trying to make. If the rumors are to be believed, the queen's spies are thick in the shires. Some say they have infiltrated the guilds and masquerade as common people—our neighbors, villagers, merchants. Lying in wait for any evidence of the use of magic, any sign that the creatures long forgotten are in fact right before the common people's faces!"

"I have more pressing concerns than the foolish pursuits of a queen whose line has long denied the truth any fool would admit!" Neo stormed up to his brother, gesturing angrily. "Do you think I don't know how dangerous this Realm is to those like us? To any who are not 'harmless' common folk? Do you think I have not asked myself a thousand times if our own family might be doomed simply because our father insisted on staying on this ancestral plot?"

Rain hung his head, the spiral curls of his hair covering his eyes. "If our mother had only sold this land after our father died. Moved to parts of the Realm where magic and misfits were not forced into hiding, were not persecuted."

My pulse thundered in my throat as I listened to this part of their story. My mother had often spoke of other places, Realms across valleys and distant seas where beings like her lived in the open. Places where my kind and hers were allied in society, in love, and in work. Places where magic was practiced openly, where memories of the good that magic could do hadn't been buried by fear and time.

That meant, too, there were also places where the inhabitants were at war. Where magic was a dark force that brought no light into the lives of creatures and commoners. Efimia, all of the known world, was ruled by the balance that had been ordained by the gods since creation. If good existed, evil was not only real, but it was equally as powerful.

My mother and I never had the chance to leave the shire of Byrlad, let alone the Realm of Tutovl, in search of safer shores. But I now realized despite our very different circumstances, the same choices may have plagued this family. This family that by marriage was mine now, too.

"Had our mother had access to magic..." Neo grunted and shook his head as a firm knock sounded at the door. "That'll be your apprentice," he barked. "Let him in, and by the gods, brother... Speak no more of the rumors of spies."

Rain pressed his brows between his thumb and finger and shook his head. "I will, brother, if you will please speak no more of storming Haeloc's manor! Listen to reason. Let's make a plan. Be methodical." He opened the door to Flynn just as Antonia dashed into the hall pushing the butler's cart.

"Mornin', Rain." Flynn stumbled through the door, his hair askew and his clothes very much rumpled. "Neo, you're looking exceptionally...awake...this morning. Salutations to you, lovely Miss Brexia, I mean, *Lady*. Lady Oderisi."

I nodded to the boy and watched as he took in my bare feet, thin breeches, and sleep-wrinkled tunic.

He widened his eyes and moved his head slowly from me to Neo to Rain. "Why do I feel like something's afoot?" he asked.

Neo shook his head. "Nothing is afoot, Flynn. At least nothing you should concern yourself with."

Flynn stepped closer and pointed to the dagger. "Where did you get *that*?" He raised a brow and ran a hand through his hair, which only made the unruly strands stand up higher. "The only person I know who can make daggers like that is my brother. But this may exceed even Syndrian's skills. Is that...enchanted?" He whispered the word and looked over one shoulder then the other, as if spies of the queen were lurking. Listening even within these stone walls for any trace of the illegal use of magic.

Neo extended the grip of the dagger toward Flynn. "Look closely," he said. "What do you make of it?"

Flynn held his hands in the air, refusing to touch the thing. "I don't know anything about magic or weapons. I didn't want to follow in my family's footsteps. I'm just a lowly apprentice thief."

"What does your family do?" I asked, crossing my arms over my chest. I noticed Neo's expression darken at my bare feet, and I curled my chilly toes.

"My father's a cutler. My brothers are cutler. My sis—"

"I believe she gets the idea, Flynn. Cutlery is the family business." Neo palmed the dagger, turning the pommel away from Flynn as Gia came down the stairs with her sister close on her heels.

Odile looked at me straight away. "How is he? How was the night?"

I flicked a slightly guilty glance at Neo. "I admit I slept deeply and didn't keep the careful watch I'd hoped. But I checked him just a moment ago, and he is breathing steadily. Seems a bit more responsive."

"Oh, thank the gods." Odile rubbed her face and sighed. "I had the strangest nightmares last night. No doubt in part because we have a dying goblin in the sitting room, but still. I am truly relieved. I'll look in on him before breakfast."

She wished Flynn a good morning and headed into the sitting room, closing the door tightly behind her.

"A...a...goblin. *Dying*. In the...sitting room..." Flynn looked as though a frog had leapt into his hand and begged for a kiss. The color drained from his face, and he tilted to one side like he might tip over.

I rushed to his side and offered him my arm. "Doesn't Flynn know about goblins?"

"He assists with much of the work we do, but some things we haven't dared share with him," Gia explained. She propped up Flynn's other side, shaking her head. "Until now, I suppose."

"The boy has a point," Rain said thoughtfully. He curled his hand into a fist and tapped his knuckles against his lips. "Perhaps Syndrian can be of assistance. We can take the dagger to him. Ask about its manufacture, finishing. Anything an expert cutler can identify might lead us closer to answers."

"We need information we don't already have," Neo insisted. "This is a goblin dagger. What else matters?"

"If it's enchanted? If its craftsmanship suggests human origin? Maybe this weapon was simply in their possession, left behind by someone local? We won't know what we don't know until we ask. And we can trust Syndrian." Rain gave his brother a look that made me curious about what relationship the cutler had to the family—other than the fact that his little brother was an apprentice thief.

"It's worth the inquiry, Neo," Gia agreed, releasing Flynn as the color returned to his freckled cheeks. "Perhaps you and Brex can visit the cutler's guild this morning. Pay a visit to the girl who is waiting for that mask and let her know it will be delayed. Rain and I have business with the shire-reeve today, but that won't take long. We'll return after to keep watch with Elgit in case Odile is called away."

"Happy to take you to my brother," Flynn said. "After I have some of Antonia's breakfast." He rubbed his hands together and licked his lips in expectation but then froze, his hands pressed together in front of his face. "And, by the gods, will someone please introduce me to this goblin?"

Rain, Gia, and Flynn went into the sitting room, leaving Neo and me alone. I stepped up to my husband and placed a hand on his arm. "I agree with you," I said quietly. "We should ride to Haeloc's manor. Perhaps after the cutler?"

Neo's lips disappeared as he clenched his jaw so hard the muscles at the corners twitched. "I will not willingly lead you into doom," he said. "We will go into the village together. That will give us time to talk. You need clothes and weapons. We'll pay a visit to the cutler. But you will not go to Haeloc's manor."

He grunted, and rather than wait for me to respond, he yanked open the sitting room door and held it open until I passed by him to join the rest of the family. As unreal as that word felt as I passed through those doors, I wondered at how much my life had changed in such short time.

I had more interesting things to ponder. Like how I was going to get past my husband to investigate Haeloc's manor for myself.

By the time I mounted Sara for the ride into the village, the sunshine was bright. The peak of my hood fell back as I lifted my face to the sky to let the gentle morning rays warm my cheeks. Woody, late-season grasses swayed with the breeze as we rode past, teasing my nose with scents of the earth. Neo's horse clomped along beside me, her rider's face a tortured mask.

I, however, felt a curious and unusual sense of peace. I had a full belly and a feeling of purpose. I let my thoughts travel freely to my past, to my sister. What I might do if I could accumulate the means to go back to the foundling home. To demand—or buy—answers. Not even Neo's mood could diminish my sense of hope.

I looked curiously at my husband. "Why haven't you insisted I fulfill my marital obligation?" Of course, I was referring to the very information he'd married me to achieve, but it was clear by the sudden startle of his body and the uneasy expression on his face that he'd assumed quite another meaning in my question. I laughed, clutching Sara's reins and shaking my head.

After a momentary look of thunderous rage, Neo softened, his lips curling playfully. "You're dangerous, Brexia."

I returned the smile, coyly shrugging one shoulder.

His grumpy intensity broken, he breathed in deeply, the cloak that flowed over his massive shoulders rising and falling. "Now hardly seems the time for a confidential conversation," he said. "But I would like to continue this in a more private place."

I met his eyes, no hint of embarrassment between us. I nodded and focused on the road and my memories. "It's so very strange," I mused, shifting the conversation away from lighter banter. "Sometimes I feel as though I cannot fully grasp my memories. I cannot see my sister's face clearly. It's like I know she is there, but her face is just out my reach. Specific memories elude me. It unsettles me."

Neo nodded. "You miss her. It's understandable that your mind grasps after that which the heart has lost."

"I pray she's all right." Frustrated that I could not picture my sister, my thoughts turned to the girl whose death mask we'd recovered. I contemplated the lengths she would have gone to just to secure a safer, happier future. "Do you ever tire of it, Neo?" I asked. "Tire of the constant struggle? For food, for fresh water. For the feeling, no matter how fleeting, of peace and safety?" I didn't wait for an answer. "I always assumed that was the foundling's burden. But I am beginning to believe that life for all of us, no matter our circumstances, is a constant battle against some form of death."

Our arrival at the farrier's ended the conversation. Neo dismounted his horse and reached a hand up to help me down. Once my feet were solidly on the ground, he snaked a hand behind my hair, his strong fingers at the back of my neck. He leaned his face beside mine, his lips grazing my ear. I sucked a breath at the immediate flow of sensation as he spoke against my ear.

"There are moments," he breathed, "that provide true rest to the weary. The hope of more of those moments... That is what makes the pains of life tolerable. Sometimes the promise of even one more beautiful moment can be enough."

There was no denying the effect his closeness had on me. And no ignoring the reminder in his words of the true rest we'd shared last night.

I closed my eyes, battling now not hunger or the needs of my physical body, but the longings of my heart. I rested my temple against his jaw and breathed the scent of his skin, clean-shaven and smooth. I pictured the tiny scars of his lips and reached for his forearm, holding him to steady my weakening limbs.

"Come," he whispered, "before we make a display of newlywed affection that draws more than just curious stares."

As I adjusted the hood over my hair and separated from him, I could see he was right. Lord Oderisi arriving in the village with a woman in his arms seemed indeed to attract more attention than was wise. I felt the unfriendly looks as sharply as if they were pebbles tossed at us in derision. Whatever Neo had done to create such a reputation in the village would clearly extend to me. No wonder the farrier had been so quick to warn me off the job I'd said I was after. And I was so much further in now.

We walked the horses to the stall where I'd been helped by Laura. As we approached, she stood straighter and nodded at me before addressing Neo.

"Lord Oderisi." Her voice was guarded but kind. "Good morning, sir. Welcome back, Miss Brexia."

"Lady Oderisi," Neo corrected without explanation. "I believe my wife was here recently and incurred a debt."

For only a moment, Laura's face looked horrified, betrayed even. But she quickly composed herself and grabbed the tally stick from the wall behind her. "Certainly, sir. If you'd like to settle the account..."

"Laura..." I handed Neo the reins to my horse and stepped forward to address the woman myself. "I'm so sorry. I hope you don't feel deceived. I—"

Her smile was cautious but held a bit of warmth. I felt a small surge of hope that she would believe me. I could not stomach her thinking I'd been intentionally untruthful.

"Not at all, milady. Your business is your own to share as you see fit. I find myself a bit embarrassed that perhaps I spoke out of turn, and I..."

Ah, so that was it.

"No," I said firmly. "You've been nothing less than a friend to me. An honest, considerate friend. I am in your debt for that, as well as for the services you provided to my sweet Sara." I took the farrier's half of the tally stick and handed it back to her. "We'll not be settling the account today. We have other business—"

"I will handle it." Neo reached for the sack strapped under his cloak, but my hand instinctively followed his.

I held his hand where it rested on his purse, his skin fiery beneath mine. "Husband," I said, a note of warning in my voice. "I'll return to pay the debt with my own means. I only meant to reassure the farrier that her trust in a stranger was well-placed and that she will indeed be paid soon."

"*Wife*," Neo said, withdrawing his hand from his cloak and slipping both hands around my waist. "What I have is yours whether we spend the coins today or in three months' time. Let's settle our debt while we're here, shall we?"

"I'll, uh, give you a moment." Laura scurried behind the wall that led back to the stables, leaving us alone.

My hips pressed to Neo's, I had no choice but to look into his face. "What are you doing?" I whispered. "I told you, I want to work and earn my way."

"As you will," he assured me. "But if we want people to believe we are married, we must play the part, no?"

I laced my hands around his hips, enjoying far too much the bond blossoming between us. "I suppose we must," I breathed.

Once we separated, Laura returned. She came around the counter and looked Sara over. "What a remarkable recovery. Her wounds are almost fully healed."

"Between my sister-in-law's care and that of my wife, Sara could ask for no better." Neo was quick to redirect the conversation and asked to review the figures on the tally stick. He set more than enough coins to satisfy my debt on the counter. "Thank you, Laura, for giving aid to my wife when she had nothing but her honor to offer."

Laura flushed and extended her hand for my half of the tally stick. I didn't want to forget how deeply indebted I'd felt to the woman for her kindness. This stick was a token of friendship in some ways. And friendship was not something I was used to being given.

"Brex," Neo reminded me. "Flynn will be waiting for us."

I nodded and handed Laura back the length of wood that would bring my account to zero. No debt. Nothing owed. At least nothing that could be measured in coin. My chest tightened with an inexplicable sense of gratitude. "Thank you," I said in a hushed voice, my eyes bright. The words hardly seemed sufficient to convey the depth of my feelings, but to say more would only make the transaction more significant than it probably was.

I felt Neo's hand on my shoulder, and I turned away from the counter.

"I look forward to your next visit, milady. And sir." Laura's words seemed purposefully directed at me, and I looked back at her with a friendly smile.

"As do I," I said.

Neo and I led our horses into the square. "I probably should have asked what she told you about me *before* I paid your debt," he teased, a smirk curling the corner of his lips.

I shook my head, matching his grin, and followed him to a large shop that was already bustling with activity.

"Over here! I'll take your horses!" Flynn was standing outside Serlo's Cutlery, motioning for us to follow him. "Don't go in the front," he warned. "My father doesn't approve of me working with the Oderisi family." He looked at me and dramatically rolled his eyes. "Nothin' personal, mind you. Doesn't approve of my brother meeting with nonpaying clients. Doesn't approve of much, truth be told."

"We don't mean to cause trouble for you, Flynn." Neo helped the boy tie off the horses behind the shop.

"Pssshhhht." Flynn waved a dismissive hand. "I'm always in some sort of trouble. But everyone knows I'm my dad's favorite.

He won't stay mad for long." He motioned toward the rear door. "Come on. Syndrian's working in the office. You'll have a bit of privacy. I'll go up front and pester my father so he doesn't grow curious."

Flynn pounded on the rear door, and it flew open almost instantly.

"By the gods, boy." A man nearly as tall and massive as Neo filled the doorway. The sides of his head were shaved, and his shoulder-length hair was held back by several lengths of leather. "Is this what you call subtle?"

The cutler shook his head and held the door open for us.

"Go on, now." He nudged Flynn on the shoulder, a loving look in his eyes despite the grumpy set of his dark brows. "Keep our father busy."

Neo and I joined the man in his office while Flynn ran back around to the front of the shop. Syndrian crossed his arms over his chest and nodded at Neo. "Lord Oderisi." Then he looked at me. "Miss."

Neo extended a hand to the man and introduced me. "Syndrian, this is my wife, Brexia."

Syndrian uncrossed his arms and shook Neo's hand, then turned to me. "Milady, my apologies. I'd not heard that there'd been a wedding." His sour face turned surprisingly appealing when he relaxed into a smile. "Perhaps my young brother is not the failure at thieving I suspected he'd be. At least he's proven he can keep his mouth shut once in a while."

At the word thieving, Neo's visibly stiffened. "I was not aware that Flynn had shared the nature of the...work...he..."

Syndrian waved a hand. "Speak freely, and if it's all the same to you, informally. My brother is incapable of keeping anything confidential for very long. He needed an ally in the family. Someone who understands your line of work and can assist—or cover for him—when needed." Syndrian tapped the front of his leather apron. "Let's just say, I dabble from time to time in the less savory side of business, if opportunity presents. Consider myself an ally to your cause, whatever that cause may be."

Neo didn't seem comforted by that, but we didn't have much choice. How much Syndrian knew, I was uncertain. But was determined to find out.

"We stumbled upon a weapon," I explained, not waiting for Neo, "in our work. Can you tell us anything about it? Where it was made, perhaps?"

Neo pulled the dagger from a scabbard inside his cloak but hesitated before setting it down. "We require absolute discretion. Not only about the visit itself, but about...this."

I shook my head and grabbed the dagger from his hands. "Flynn wouldn't have brought us here if he didn't believe we could trust Syndrian." I offered the man the weapon, but like his brother had earlier, he declined to touch it. I set it on the bare wooden desk.

The man inspected the dagger from a distance. As his well-schooled eyes studied it, he appeared to grow less suspicious and more fascinated. "I don't believe it's enchanted," he said, his voice low. "May I touch it now?"

I nodded and Neo waved him on, so he carefully picked up the grip and turned the thing every direction, inspecting the way the light hit the blade, the details on the pommel.

"This craftsmanship," he said, his voice echoing with wonder. "I've not seen anything like this. How did you come upon it? Where?" he asked.

Neo shook his head. "It may be safer that you remain ignorant of the details," he said. "I mean no disrespect by that."

"Just knowing such a blade exists is dangerous in these parts," he agreed, running his fingertip reverently across the blade. "I assume it's goblin-made?"

Neo and I traded a look.

"You hardly seem afraid. Not of the blade itself, and certainly not of its maker, if it is indeed as you've suggested," Neo said.

"Fear." Syndrian grimaced. "Useless emotion. I avoid it when I can. Which isn't always, but when it comes to fine tools such as this? I feel nothing but admiration."

"Admiration?" I echoed, thoroughly confused. The sleek, light dagger with its intricately shaped hilt was finely made and far from common, but I saw nothing that would arouse admiration. Especially in one as skilled as even the average cutler in weaponry, and from what I understood, Syndrian was far above average as far as this trade was concerned.

"Listen." The cutler laid the dagger flat in his palm, bobbing his arm lightly up and down. He nodded in satisfaction. "There's something inside the hilt," he said.

"Inside? Open it," Neo demanded, leaning over the desk. "Can you? Without destroying it?"

"Wait." I took hold of his arm. "What if it's a trap? Filled with poison? Perhaps we shouldn't..."

But by the time I let the words fade from my lips, Syndrian was already unraveling the complicated leatherwork that wound its way up the grip. "Certainly could contain poison, but I don't think there's a mechanism to release it. Unlikely to be a trap. This is a no more than a trickster's tool, designed to transport and conceal. Hiding cargo inside an otherwise functional weapon." He worked intently, a look of pure fascination on his face. He muttered to himself as he loosened the plaits of leather with deft fingers. "Well-made dagger... Blade extends the length of the grip, but... Aha!"

Once he'd unraveled the tightly wound leather, it was clear the pommel could be unscrewed from the hilt. He started to twist it but then looked at Neo for approval.

"May I?" he asked. "There may be no putting back whatever's inside."

"Stand behind me," Neo demanded, stepping between the desk and me.

"Syndrian said it couldn't be a trap. Come, now." I moved past him to get a close look as the cutler separated the pommel from the weapon.

He gasped in admiration as he peeked inside the partially hollowed out hilt. He tipped the handle, and two long, yellowing bits of something—bone, perhaps—dropped onto the desk.

"By the gods..." Neo lunged forward and grabbed the items in his hand before I could make out what they were. "Syndrian... I...I apologize. Bringing this to you was a grave error. We've exposed you to risk that I did not intend." He turned to me. "We must leave."

"Neo, wait!" I grabbed his arm, but it was Syndrian's words that stopped him.

"I may be one of the few common people who don't spook easily," he said, nodding to Neo. "That's why Flynn knew he could bring you here."

Neo's fist tightened protectively around whatever he had in his hand. "You know, then? What these are? And why they matter to me?"

Syndrian didn't respond. Instead, he dug into the deep front pocket of his leather apron and pulled out a tiny key. He stuck the key inside a lock hidden in the front of the desk, releasing the top, which swung open on silent hinges.

"Come," he said.

We walked around to meet him behind the desk, my eyes wild with wonder at the treasures inside. Hidden beneath the locked surface of the desk was an assortment of instruments and tools the likes of which I'd never seen before.

"These are only what I keep here at the guild shop," he admitted. "My father is nosy and quarrelsome but thankfully doesn't care to indulge my interest in making custom tools. I craft them on my own time. There's a place in Kyruna where I can trade freely. Meet with clients."

"Freely?" Neo echoed.

They spoke of a place called Knuckles & Bones, a pub on the outskirts of a neighboring shire, while I stared with wonder at the instruments neatly laid out inside the desk.

"You made these?" I asked, unable to keep the awe from my voice. I'd never seen such intricate handiwork, such an impressive assortment of wonders.

The huge cutler's face reddened as he nodded at my praise. "That'll remove arrows." Syndrian pointed to one particular instrument, then lowered his voice. "Even those of elvish origin, not that we've seen any of those in these parts for at least a thousand years."

I grimaced, knowing there would be no point in making a tool that would never need to be used. "And this?" I asked.

"Dental tongs," he said. "Strong enough to tear out any tooth *and* its roots." He scrubbed the back of his hand along the stubble above his ear. "Even a tooth long and strong as a fang."

Fangs. Panic tightened around my throat like a clawed hand as I looked at Neo's fist. "Are those…"

"I believe so," he said. "Haeloc's."

Haeloc's fangs. Inside a goblin-made dagger left in the sanctum. But why? For what purpose? Did that mean that whoever did such a thing left the fangs as a message? For whom?

Neo and I had a lot more to sort out than simply my secrets.

"As I said, I'm not like most common folk. The things forgotten for generations are like the volcanoes that created our land. Truth lives eternally beneath the surface. And eventually, no matter how buried, the truth will erupt. I maintain a steady business thanks to things better left forgotten." Syndrian reassembled the dagger as he added, "I believe vampires exist. Just like I believe in a lot of things that are forbidden. Goblin craftsmen and the magic they wield, just to name a few. But I keep my nose in my business and leave others to theirs," he said, meeting Neo's eyes.

Whether Syndrian was trying to convey that he neither knew nor cared if Neo was himself a vampire, I wasn't certain. I added that to the growing list of things my husband and I would need to discuss. In private.

"Syndrian." I pointed to something inside the desk. "Can you tell me about these?"

His grin was unexpected, wide and sincere, his perfect teeth softening the hard planes of his face. "Those are brand-new," he said. "Not a commission. Made 'em for myself but don't have a need for 'em just yet. Double edged, spear point. Set of four identical throwing knives." He slipped a finger through the wide ring at the end of one and held it out for me to inspect.

"Are they for sale?" I asked.

He opened a drawer in the desk and pulled out a length of supple brown leather with beautifully sewn fittings and sheaths shaped to hold the four matched blades. Syndrian raised his dark brows and looked from me to Neo. "I assume you'll need me to resize the leg harness?"

ELEVEN

Meeting with Syndrian only seemed to make Neo more agitated. After we left Serlo's Cutlery, Neo had a change of heart. Instead of going ourselves, he sent Flynn off to deliver a message to the girl who'd purchased the death mask.

"I don't know her family name. Refer to her as Lady Pali." Neo gave the boy directions to a cottage on the opposite end of the shire. He clamped a hand on the boy's collar. "Please, Flynn, for once in your young life, say as little as possible. Simply let her know I've been delayed and will be in touch. That's all. No jokes, no chatter, not a single unnecessary word. The lady is winsome, so be prepared. No flirtation, no romancing. This is a matter of the utmost discretion. Do you understand?"

I unwound Sara's reins from the stall behind the cutlery and mounted my horse while Flynn looked at Neo like he'd been gifted an entire purse of gold.

"I'm going alone?" he breathed. "My first real quest? I'm... I'm... You trust me?" he babbled, practically falling over himself with excitement.

"Let's be clear. I do *not* trust you," Neo growled, "but I have more pressing concerns. Circumstances leave me no choice. And this not a quest. This is an errand. You're simply a messenger."

"I trust you, Flynn," I said, smiling down at him from my lovely horse.

Neo raised a dark eyebrow at me and continued scolding his apprentice. "Repeat after me. I will say as little as possible to the woman."

"Neo, sir, Lord Oderisi, I swear to you, on the soul of..."

Neo closed his eyes and crossed his arms over his chest, huffing furious breaths between his full lips.

"Yes, sir. I will say as little as possible." Flynn stood upright and lifted his chin. "I can do this, sir. I will not let you down."

Neo opened his eyes and uncrossed his arms. "Good," he started, but Flynn was already rambling on.

"Maybe if I do this well, Rain will let me go on a graveyard run with him? Do you think? Would you ask him? By the gods, I've been wanting to—"

Neo didn't even have to blink before Flynn clamped a hand over his own mouth. Mumbling through his fingers, he began backing away. "Right. Understood. I've got this. And I'm going... I'm off, sir!"

"Flynn!" Neo called after him before he could scurry too far. "Thank you for arranging the meeting with your brother. This was an exceptionally useful morning. You did well. Keep up the good work. And keep your mouth—"

"Shut, I've got it, sir. Absolutely. Completely got it. Yes, yes, will do." Flynn's crooked grin and wild hair left quite the impression as he scampered off.

Neo breathed a loud, weary sigh as he mounted Sedda. He rested a large hand on her neck and closed his eyes as if seeking some type of comfort from the beast. Then he nodded at me. "Shall we visit the market?"

I raised my brows at him. "Shall we talk about your brother and what he does in graveyards?"

Neo surprised me by laughing. "I don't know if you'd believe me if I told you."

"That seems to be the theme of our marriage so far." I gave him another smile, but this one felt more tender, more intimate. Teasing and laughter somehow connected me to Neo more than sleeping beside him had. I could only wonder what more might happen in the coming year to make this marriage feel...real.

We rode into the square and purchased fabric so I could make more clothes and picked up some bread and cheese at the market.

"I know you're not exactly a fan of fish," Neo teased, his hand grazing mine as we walked between the stalls.

I shook my head. "I meant no offense to fish head soup! When you're nearly starving and you plan to help yourself to someone else's dinner, which would you choose? Broth or meat?"

The weight of Neo's hand on the back of my hood sent shivers of delight up and down my spine. His fingers curled protectively against my neck through my cloak. "You will never starve again, Brex."

I peeked up at him, the golden intensity in his eyes nearly dizzying. The thundering of my heart in my chest made it impossible to deny that something, something more than necessity, more than obligation was growing between us. I licked my lips, unsure what to say, how to respond. The look in Neo's eyes made me certain I did not have to thank him. Did not have to explain or say more. I dared to believe he felt the same way.

We strolled side by side in silence until I noticed a stall that piqued my interest. "Your crofter raises animals for food, yes? Do you know if we need any *different* foods than what Antonia normally prepares for our ailing houseguest?" I looked over the unusual jars of preserved foods, wondering about the delights inside.

Neo looked confused for a moment but then nodded. "The meat our family eats will be sufficient for everyone in our household. He will be all right, if he's able to eat. I believe chicken is a dish of choice, which we have."

The square was crowded and busy. Stray dogs dashed between our feet, barking and stealing bits of dropped food. Children cried as they tugged on their parents' legs. Between the chatter and bartering between vendors and shoppers, it was easy to get lost in a feeling that this was a normal day. That my brand new husband and I were not talking about the dietary needs of a goblin.

I was, though, relieved to hear that Elgit ate the same things that Antonia would put on our table. If we had to source frogs or crickets or some other difficult to find material to feed him as he healed, well, I supposed that's what we would have had to do. This simply eliminated one more worry about the poor soul whose life I felt in some ways rested in my hands.

Walking beside Neo this way, shopping for things, discussing matters of the home... It felt too real and at the same time unreal. I hated to drive the calmer, more playful Neo away, but somehow his anger felt far less dangerous than his affection. In spite of what I knew the question would do to him, I asked it. "Any more thought to making a quest of our own today?"

The change I expected came, but even more quickly than I'd thought.

"No," he barked. "And not with you. Never with you."

I immediately regretted saying anything that brought storms back to his countenance. But I would have to manage all kinds of weather if I was to be married to this man for a year. I adjusted the fabric we'd purchased in a pouch over my shoulder and slipped my free hand into Neo's.

"I'm sorry what I asked angered you," I said, boldly lacing my fingers through his. "Can you tell me why? If I'm to be your wife, I'd like to know everything. Be a part of everything."

As if the very weather mirrored the changes between us, dense clouds gathered overhead, momentarily cloaking the sun in shadow. I felt Neo's hand stiffen, his fingers tense, and his entire body beside me went rigid.

"Do not think I'll be easily manipulated by your beauty. You dishonor yourself with the attempt." Contempt coated his words. The change in him struck me with the force of an arrow. He yanked his hand from mine. "Let's return to the manor. We have no further business here."

I stood still in place, my feet reacting to the shock and shame that flooded my system. I'd not meant to manipulate him... I'd simply misread him, misread the lighter feelings between us. I'd only thought the closeness we were sharing meant something. But his abrupt dismissal set my mind to rights. We were man and wife by contract. We might play the happy couple in the village, but there was no joy in this union for Neo. I'd been a fool to indulge myself in thinking otherwise. I swallowed hot tears and ducked my head deeper into my hood. He'd hurt me, embarrassed me, but I would not give him the satisfaction of seeing how sharply his abrupt turn of mood stung.

I held my chin high, trying to suppress the feelings that felt so raw, I was certain everyone in Omrora could see them. I felt hollow inside, like a tally stick that had been carved with a debt but which in and of itself held no value to anyone. With the hand he'd refused, I grabbed the charm around my neck. For once, the token didn't soothe me.

WE RODE BACK to the manor in painful silence. Neo kept pace ahead of me, never looking back to ensure Sara and I followed. Maybe at points he did check on me, but if he did, I would not have seen. I couldn't—wouldn't—look at him. I tried to understand his reaction to me, the lack of trust, the feeling that I'd attempted to manipulate him. He did mention my beauty, which truly came as a shock to me. But if he did find me beautiful, how would I—a foundling, a thief—know that?

Even if I did have the knowledge, using it to my advantage simply wasn't possible. I wouldn't know how to do that even if I had the inclination. My whole life I'd been able to think or talk my way through difficult situations. Charm? Seduction? Laughable concepts. And certainly nothing I'd ever used to my advantage. I'd have more skill with my brand-new throwing knives than any feminine vitality I may have had.

After just a few short days basking in the warmth of belonging, tentative and new as it was, I felt as out of place and unwanted as I had on the worst day at the foundling home. The still-darkening sky matched my gloomy mood.

A smattering of raindrops teased my cheeks as we neared the manor, but breaking through my indulgent grief was the same man who'd caused it.

"By the gods, what now?" Neo held up a hand to alert me and drew Sedda to a stop. He turned, his face a radiant mask of rage, cursing under his breath. "Brexia, stay here."

I had no time to respond. I saw what he must have seen, and the melancholy in my heart transformed into soul-clenching fear. The front gate of the manor was not only open, but it had been torn from its hinge. The iron rested at an impossible angle, half on the ground, half of its bent metal sticking haphazardly in the air.

Neo tossed Sedda's reins to me and took off for the manor, drawing his short sword as he ran. I leapt from Sara's back, my hands shaking so hard I could hardly knot the reins of the horses. They'd be safer secured here, farther away from whatever was happening at the manor. I reached for my new leg harness and tightened my fingers around the wide ring of one of my throwing knives. I pulled it from its fitting and raced up the path after Neo.

He was frozen on the wide stone steps on the manor, his short sword drawn. With the heavy cloud cover and no sun to illuminate the pretty angles of the plant, the Dragon's Blood Sedum coated the grounds, it red color dull and ominous as dried blood. My lips trembled and I whispered a prayer to the gods as the rain began to fall in angry, violent sheets. Neo shook his head, his drenched hair scattering raindrops and soaking through the padded armor he wore beneath his cloak. He met my eyes only briefly before pointing at the front door. That, too, hung wide open, like a mouth frozen open in mid-scream. The door didn't appear damaged, though. Whatever was inside had been let in.

My stomach lurched as I pictured Antonia, surprised not by some ailing visitor, but a wicked presence. My heart sank for vulnerable Elgit and the rest of the household, helplessly at the mercy of some dark power. I lowered my face and strained my ears for any sound, any clues, but there were no cries, no sounds of violence. Nothing to hint at what had happened or was still happening.

Neo bent his knees and with silent steps approached the eerily open door. I followed, sweat collecting at my hairline as I swallowed against the dryness in my mouth. I felt something, sensed it, perhaps. Magic. Someone or something magic was definitely inside. A sudden feeling of dizziness almost knocked me from my feet, but then I heard it—the screams—and every bit of vitality in my body surged forward. I followed Neo into the manor and raced to Antonia, collapsed outside the sitting room on the floor, a small trickle of blood seeping from a gash in her forehead. Her eyes were closed and she breathed heavily, but thankfully, she was alive. Dale was at the opposite end of the hall, his body angled awkwardly on the stairs as if he'd been thrown or blown by a powerful force. Neo's body went rigid, and his eyes glowed brilliant crimson as he took them in.

"Check them," he whispered, just as another scream pierced the air.

I ran toward Dale as fast as I could. He gurgled a sound, a few droplets of blood staining the stone steps behind his head.

"Dale," I whispered, holding his dry, wrinkled hand. "It's Brex. Can you hear me?"

He fluttered his eyes open and panted. "Lady," he sighed. I didn't know if he was addressing me or asking after a lady, telling me a lady was here, but I didn't want to tire him further with talking.

"Shhh," I urged. "Be still. Don't move. I'll be back for you. Don't move, please. Stay right here."

"Magic," he whispered, holding a violently shaking hand out to me.

"I know," I said, taking his hand and gently setting it on his chest. "I'll be back. Everything is going to be okay."

His heavy breathing was steady and clear, so I ran to Antonia. She was conscious, blinking, and fighting to get up the moment she saw me.

"Please don't move," I begged her. Inside the sitting room, I heard more screams, and I squeezed her hand. "I have to help. I'll be back. Don't move."

A thunderclap overhead and the heavy pounding of rain on the roof momentarily muffled the cries coming from the sitting room, but then we heard it. Heard her.

"Stop! By the gods, stop!" Odile screamed. "Please, let her go!"

Neo lifted a boot and, without uttering a sound, kicked the sitting room door. It wasn't locked, and the wood gave an audible crack as it slammed open with such force it hit the wall and splintered.

I ran mindlessly, one throwing knife gripped in my fingers. I had no idea how to throw them, but I'd stab anything or anyone hurting this family. I'd use my bare hands if I had to. But nothing could have prepared me for the scene before me.

Inside the sitting room, the fire had gone out. A vile chill raised the hair on my arms, and the sounds of rain crashing against the roof made the dark room feel all the more menacing. The furniture was overturned, pillows torn open, ribbons of shredded fabric and stuffing littering the floor. The only part of the room that was intact was the settee where Elgit slept. Odile was with him, covering his small form with hers and weeping, her thin fingers gripping the settee as she tried to protect the goblin without any regard for herself. The relief I felt that he was still alive was shattered by what I saw next.

Gia was the one screaming, a nightmarish cry of pain and fear, but I could not see what tormented her. Nothing held her captive, yet she held her arms out where she stood against a wall, motionless and rigid as if she were bound there. But she was not. She was free but couldn't seem to move and howled as if tortured by something only she could see. Rain was similarly trapped, limbs splayed against the wall, his powerful arms fixed in place. Unlike Gia, Rain was silent, his mouth open. His red eyes and elongated fangs were frozen, transfixed. His suffering appeared no less great than Gia's, as silent tears leaked from the corners of his eyes.

Neo was spinning like a funnel cloud through the room,

slashing and stabbing his sword at nothing and everything at once, his massive arms slicing through the air.

"It's an illusionist!" Neo screamed. "Run, Brex! Get to safety!"

An illusionist.

I immediately fisted my knife in front of my face, the blade pointed away from me. If there was mage, a sorcerer of some kind in the room, he was controlling Rain and Gia with magic... But since Neo was free and I felt unaffected, it wasn't powerful enough to control all of us at the same time.

"It's a woman," Odile cried, trying to explain. "She disappeared when you kicked down the door. Vanished! I can't see her, but she's here. She's still here!"

"You'll tire, and then I'll have your godforsaken head!" Neo swore, his voice seething with fury. His eyes blazed with murderous fire. He grunted and swung his arms, stabbing his sword and wildly slashing every inch of the air in the room, trying to strike the invisible enemy.

Holding my knife in front of my face, I closed the mostly intact doors behind me, trapping all of us inside. If she was here but had cast a spell that prevented us from seeing her, at least I could keep her from escaping. Or we would know exactly where she was if she tried to leave this room. I knew magic like this. Had grown up with it. I could taste its metallic funk in my mouth, and it made me furious. Enraged. I hardly knew the bounds of my own emotions as I fully took in what was being done to these people. This family.

"Stoooooop!" I screamed at the top of my lungs, the single word scraping past my throat with such force that I swear for a moment I saw a flicker in the room.

"Neo, there!" I pointed, and he lunged, but just as soon as it happened, it was over. The shadow of the woman's form disappeared again.

Odile, her red face drenched with tears, her shoulders powerfully shaken by sobs, pointed too. "I saw it! She's there! She was right there!"

Neo's movements reached a frenzied pace, and I screamed and screamed, my teeth bared, my mouth hanging open as saliva flew from between my lips. The only way to overpower this kind of magic was to break the concentration of the mage, forcing her to focus on so many threats at once that she couldn't maintain her illusion of invisibility.

But that momentary glimpse of her gone, she renewed her magic, meeting my rage with her own. She increased the force she used to control Gia and Rain. Gia's eyes rolled back in her head, and her lips began to turn blue.

"Gia!" I cried, but no matter what, I would not move away from the door, would not give her access to escape.

While Gia trembled, locked in her silent restraints, Neo lunged forward and must have struck something. Both Gia and Rain suddenly dropped to the floor, released from their invisible bonds. Odile left Elgit, dashing to her sister and lifting her floppy limbs from the hard tile. "Sister," she cried, and in that moment, something inside me turned dark. Cold.

I felt tendrils of invisible power, its energy turned not on Gia and Rain, but on me. Icy vines snaked around my throat, its razor-sharp thorns pricking into my neck. An unseen force slammed me back against the door and tried to shove me aside, but I grabbed the doorknob and would not let go.

I saw purple behind my closed eyes. My throat was raw, scraped from screaming, collapsing from the invisible power that sought to strangle the life from me.

It's not real, I told myself. *It's an illusion. She's making me believe something that isn't really happening to my body. Keep breathing.*

I fought hard, squeezing my eyes shut to focus all my

concentration on resisting the illusion. But instead of fighting it, behind my closed lids, images of home taunted me. My real home, my mother, weakened my heart and my resolve to fight. Grief and loss and memory curled around my head, luring me to look deeper, to walk toward the mist of memory.

I will die if I give in.

I wrenched my eyes open and gasped, dropping my throwing knife as I released the doorknob to claw at my throat. There was nothing to claw away, but I still couldn't breathe, couldn't bring enough air into my lungs. My mother's face disappeared from my mind, and I could make out through the choking terror the faces of Gia. Rain. Neo.

But my mind and body couldn't connect, couldn't work together to drive away the vines that closed a fatal coil around my throat. I fought against myself, wrestling and twisting against the power that tried to suffocate me while slamming my rear end back against the door to prevent her from escaping.

"Don't...let...it...out," I wheezed, my eyes rolling back in my head. I couldn't focus on Neo, couldn't see anything. It was like someone had picked me up by the throat and was turning me upside down and around, trying to toss my body like an out of place broom away from the door.

I was losing the fight. I couldn't hear anymore, couldn't keep my eyes open for more than a few seconds. Blinking took so much effort, but I knew I couldn't let her escape. With the last bit of strength I could muster, I stretched my arms wide and pressed myself flat against the door. She'd have to get past me to get out. She still had a corporal form, still had a body, even if I couldn't see it. She was hidden in plain sight, just like the thorns around my neck were only real in my mind. The effect they had on me was real, but that was her true power. Making me believe something that only she controlled.

I would not give in, and coughed, gagging as I tried to beg Neo. "*Hurry...*"

Rain staggered to his feet, grabbed a poker from the fireplace, and followed his brother. His fangs out and his eyes ablaze, Rain spun through the room, whipping the poker high and low, side to side, hoping to strike the unseen enemy. Neo's eyes locked on mine just as I felt my knees weaken. I was exhausted and struggling for air, but if the mage escaped, we'd never find her. She might even remain in the manor, controlling us with an illusion which would allow her to remain invisible until she chose to reveal herself. Or until we were all dead.

"Get her," I whimpered, closing one eye, hoping that it would be easier to control just one. My muscles burned with my effort, my arms weakening as the entire room turned shadowy and dark. I desperately searched for Neo's face, trying to draw any strength I could from his powerful presence. I'd never seen him like this, even though what I was doing could hardly be called seeing him. Glossy panels of hair flew as he stabbed the air, his eyes brilliant crimson, his lips parted in a predatory snarl. I squinted and listened, straining to stay awake even if I was uselessly weak. If I closed both eyes, if I gave in to the fatigue...

"Die!" Neo shrieked, surging toward my wrecked body.

She must have been close to me, concentrating all her power on me alone, because suddenly, it stopped. I collapsed on the floor, free of the invisible bonds. I grabbed my neck on instinct and gasped hungrily for air, looking up as Neo's blade made contact with something neither of us could see. A small shriek pierced the air, and a stream of blood stained the tip of his blade. I looked up, exhausted but unharmed, just in time to see Neo about to plunge his sword toward the mage's back.

"No... No..." I stumbled to my feet and slammed my back against the door. My hands behind me, I fumbled for the doorknob, unable to believe what I was seeing. The room began to spin, but this time, I was certain it was not the effect of magic. This was no illusion. The mage before me was real. I knew her. I knew her face. And it was as real as it had been every day of every year I'd lived in the foundling home.

"Neo!" I screamed at the top of my lungs, my throat chafed raw. "Stop!"

I twisted the knob and threw open the sitting room door. Gray light from the hall streamed into the sitting room, and I became vaguely aware of Odile comforting Gia. Elgit on the settee. Neo and Rain before me, poised to kill.

The door open, the figure disappeared again. Neo lurched toward the space where she'd stood and stabbed his sword into the air. I heard a sickening groan, and fresh blood fell in the hall as the invader fled the manor, past the prone forms of Antonia and Dale, and out the front door, leaving a trail of crimson droplets behind her.

Rain stumbled past me, armed with nothing but a poker, and watched the blood mark the path of the mage's escape from the manor.

"Why!" Neo charged at me, his sword drawn. "How could you let her escape! She could have killed us all. She still might!"

I dropped onto the floor and rested my hands against my knees. I hung my head, the charm around my neck dangling forward ominously from its leather cord. "Kill me," I said quietly. "I understand if it's what you must do."

"I should end you here," he seethed, "but first I must know why." Neo grabbed the back of my shirt and roughly pulled me to my feet. "What do you know! Tell me what that was!"

An acrid taste filled my mouth as I held back the need to be sick. My eyes burned, and my tongue felt heavy and dry. I was still on all fours, unable to stand, unwilling to try. My shaking hands could hardly support my weight. I wept violently as I tried to explain.

What I'd seen would change my reality forever. My past, my present. My future. Tears choked my words as I looked into my husband's furious face. Any hope I might have had died in my chest, my freedom a flower clipped from its stem and left to wither in the sun.

"That mage was my sister." I coughed, gagging as I forced the words out. Shame and confusion compressed my chest, making it almost as hard to breathe as the illusion had. I lifted my chin to see Neo's blood-red eyes close, his fangs retract, and his sword lower as he considered my words. "That was Gini."

TWELVE

Neo sheathed his sword and turned away from me in disgust. "Get up," he barked. "The only place you're welcome now is the cellar. You'll be locked up where you can't hurt anyone until we decide your fate."

"Neo, wait." Odile released the arms she had wrapped around her sister and tiptoed through the wrecked sitting room, avoiding the blood spilled on the dark tile.

"This is not the time for compassion! She must be dealt with as the danger she is," he growled. "This woman has brought doom to our door!"

"That's my point exactly." Odile lowered herself to the floor, getting down on hands and knees. Her probing voice was gentle, curious. "You met this girl just days ago, and she's not been out of your sight since she arrived here. She's had no contact with anyone that we know of, so how did the mage find us?"

Odile rested a hand on my shoulder. Her question was kind, as if she hadn't immediately leapt to Neo's conclusion. That I had *intentionally* brought danger to their door. That I somehow was behind the mage who came here wreaking destruction on the manor. I didn't blame his sense of caution, but it made far more sense that I was the one in danger—not them. There was no reason they would have been targeted by my sister if I was not here.

I leaned back on my heels and covered my face with my hands, not caring to wipe the snot and tears away. I couldn't think. Couldn't process what I'd seen, why this was happening. My heart ached with questions that erupted from deep within me. Why? How? I didn't understand, and if I couldn't provide answers to them, Neo would be done with me. Send me to the cellar, and then what? Brick me into the wall? Leave me to die?

I shook my head, my voice breaking with grief and regret. "I am so, so sorry. I...truly don't understand."

"Was that really your sister?" Odile asked. "Could that have been another illusion? A trick she played on your mind to convince you to let her past?"

I shook my head, immediately rejecting the idea. I sniffed hard, my swollen eyes and runny nose making it nearly impossible to speak clearly. "My sister's magic doesn't work that way. She can only cast illusions that make you believe something is real. Minor mind control. That's all she can do. She cannot create the appearance in the physical world of something that doesn't exist. She can make you think you cannot see her, but that's far easier than taking someone's own memories or treasured thoughts and creating something inside their mind with them."

"You're sure?" Odile dug into her sleeve and withdrew a length of clean cloth and handed it to me to wipe my face. "Maybe she manipulated your thoughts so you believed the woman you saw was your sister?"

Gia looked badly shaken, but she agreed. "When the woman arrived, she looked exactly as she did when she left. I would have no idea what Brex's sister looked like. If she was trying to control me, or scare me, there are plenty of other things she could have shown me."

"If she meant to deceive the entire household, she would arrive looking like exactly what Brex expected. Don't be fools!" Neo's nostrils flared as he shouted, his eyes hard and unfeeling.

"Yes, that makes sense, but..." Fresh tears sprung to Gia's eyes, as if even in explaining it, she was reliving the pain and fear. "The entire time I was bound, I saw *nothing*. Only felt the sensations, and my body reacted as if it were all real. It was all the more terrifying because I could not see anything to fight against. It was as though my enemy was my own mind."

I blew my nose miserably and nodded. That sounded exactly like Gini's magic.

"You're certain?" Odile asked, her eyes staring into mine. "You do not believe that was someone else, someone who maintained the illusion of looking like your sister, while at the same time controlling both Rain and Gia?"

I shook my head. "I suppose it is possible, but...who would it be? I don't know anyone else who would want to appear to me in Gini's guise." I bit my lip hard to stop myself from crying again. This type of betrayal was senseless. Why would my sister come here to hurt people I cared for? And how, by the gods, how did she find me? "I believe that was truly her. I believe she did this to all of you. I just do not understand why. I simply *cannot* understand."

"She did this to you too," Gia pointed out. She was more guarded than Odile, but she seemed shaken, not nearly as suspicious of me as Neo.

He knelt beside Odile and me, fury in his drawn brows. "Answer me this. How did she know where to find you? Who knows you're here!"

"I don't know," I said, growing more hopeless under his scrutiny. I looked at him, my words weak and pathetic, even to myself. I wasn't certain if the roles were reversed if I'd believe the words coming out of my mouth. "Not a soul in the Realm knows I'm here. I've told no one. Spoken to no one. I had no idea whether Gini was even still alive. That was the whole reason I sought you out in Fish Head End, demanded your job. I wanted to return to the foundling home and buy the information I needed to find her. To be reunited with her. I thought she... I thought she truly loved me."

My mouth was so dry it was difficult to speak. The pain in my throat had faded, but I felt the shadowy tendrils of magic as if the vines were still wrapped around my neck. I swallowed what little saliva I could and pressed a hand to the front of my throat.

Neo's eyes followed my every move. The way I licked my parched lips, my trembling hand as I reached for my charm. I could no longer count on the precious little comfort it might bring, but the habit felt natural to me now.

There was no compassion in his stony gaze as he snarled a question. "What is this? What is that token you hold so dear?"

I clenched the stone between my fingers. "A gift," I whispered. "From my sister."

"It's enchanted." As Neo said the words, Odile seemed to be struck by the same realization.

"Tracking magic?" she asked, looking puzzled. "Would that fall within the skills of an illusionist?"

"I'm not sure." Neo's voice and expression softened only slightly, as if he began to realize that perhaps this was not my fault. Or if it was, I certainly hadn't brought this upon them intentionally. "Give me that charm."

He held his hand out, and for a moment, everything inside me screamed to run. To keep the one small token I had that was proof that anyone had ever loved me. That anyone had ever cared. Yes, I knew that my mother had adored me, had given up so much of her own comfort and stability to be my mother for the short time she was able to, but this...this was different. The charm had soothed me, guided me. It had been a gift. The only one anyone had ever given me.

Even as I resisted relinquishing my treasure, I realized I had to. If in fact it was enchanted, whether or not my sister had intended for me to have it, it was dangerous. With it, *I* was dangerous to the people I cared most about.

"I will leave," I vowed, unable to yet remove the charm where it rested gently against my skin. "That's the only solution now. I will go back where I came from. To the life they wanted for me there."

Odile startled me by stroking the damp strands of my hair that fell along my back. "Even if you did leave, that mage knows how to find the rest of us. She's used magic, Brex, which is illegal. Dangerous. We know the queen has spies living and working among the common folk. Just waiting for the smallest sign. I know this." The healer's face looked pale, the shadows under her eyes deep and dark. Mirrors of the many horrors she'd no doubt seen. "That mage came for something, and she left without whatever that was. It's safe to assume she'll be back for what she wants, whether or not you're here."

"What if what she wants is me?" I wept hard, my shoulders shaking and my stomach turning over in confusion. I felt an inexplicable pull toward home, the foundling home. As if everything within me was urging me back. I couldn't stay here. I tried to stand. "I have to leave. I'm... I'm so sorry, but I have to leave."

"Wait, Brex, please." Odile stopped me gently with a firm hand on my arm. "Let me inspect the token. If you still are determined to leave, I'll return it to you."

"I make no such promises," Neo seethed, but Odile shook her head at him.

"Neo, I don't believe the girl is at fault for this! By the gods, keep your threats to yourself. At least until we know she's deserving of them." She glared at him, clearly impatient.

I would have appreciated her defense of me if I wasn't being asked to do the one thing I wished not to do. The one thing that pained me unlike any other. Let go of everything I had. The only thing I had.

Crying like a child robbed of her only toy, I laced my fingers through the leather and slipped the charm from around my neck. My hands shaking and palms clammy, I held the stone out to Odile. She took it graciously, nodding in encouragement.

"Good girl," she said. She looked it over, turning it front to back. She licked her fingertip and tapped the stone, even sniffed it.

"What do you make of it?" Neo muttered, sounding impatient.

"I'm unschooled in enchanted objects." Her pretty face looked puzzled. "I don't know what to think. But I do believe if Brex intends to stay here, we should destroy it." Apology hung heavy in her words, and I sobbed all the harder at the mere idea of the permanent loss of the gift. "If you truly intend to leave, I will return it to you. But Brex, I do not believe you'll be safe until we understand the power of this token."

I sat back on my heels and stared at the tile floor. Shapes whirled before my eyes, and dizziness stole my ability to tell up from down. "Whoa." I squeezed my eyes closed and covered my face with my hand to shut out the shapes and movement. Suddenly, I heard sounds more clearly. The muted voices of Dale and Antonia, weak with pain and fatigue. The light melody of the late-autumn rain striking the roof. I smelled the sweat and heat from Neo's body, the smoke that clung to his hair. I could have sworn that I heard Elgit's breathing.

"Something is wrong," I sputtered, closing my eyes against

the dizzying rush of images flashing through my mind. "I don't know what's happening."

I splayed my palms on the cool floor to steady me, but that didn't help. I was falling, disappearing, dying. Maybe all three at once, I could not tell.

"What is it?" I could hear Neo's concerned question, but I couldn't see him. I felt a strong hand on my arm, but I shook it off, falling deeper and deeper down a well that only had space for me. My thoughts. My memories.

I saw in flashes everything I'd lived through. My mother, her stunning face holding nothing but affection as she held me close. The hollows in her cheeks and the dullness of her eyes before she brought me to the foundling home. I could see our cottage, a fire crackling in the familiar stone hearth. My mother's aged cooking pot bubbling with humble vegetable stew. Then, the long journey through tall grasses and dense trees as we traveled through Byrlad. My shoulders and back bent with fatigue.

The foundling home, so much larger than anything I'd ever seen, its door wide open. The owner, the woman in charge, holding her hand out. Not in welcome. Expecting to be paid. My mother passed her everything. Every last coin. The few items of clothing I owned. Even her only cooking pot. My mother tiptoed backward, inching away in the sunlit afternoon. The sun reflecting on her flowing tears as she left without even saying goodbye. Without one last kiss.

The face of the woman who'd taken me in, the mage who ran the foundling home, was foggy, a cloud obscuring her features. I felt a hand on my forehead and heard Odile's voice from very far away. My body was moving, being moved, but my mind was focused on the face behind those clouds.

"Gini?" I whispered the words through parched lips.

But it wasn't Gini, was it? Gini was my sister. Who was the

house mother? What was she? My heart thundered in my chest, an irregular beat that was at once too fast and too slow. Heat flooded my limbs, and yet I trembled in terrible cold. I was so confused. So angry. So afraid.

"The enchantment is releasing her." Odile's words filtered through the haze of memory. "She'll be all right. Don't touch her, Neo. Let her be."

In my mind, I followed the woman into the foundling home, her brazen laugh mocking and harsh. The dank room with a cot that would be my new home. My forever home.

I was introduced to the other children. The shapeshifters, the vampires... Orphans of so many species, all like my mother, long forgotten or long denied as real. We were all homeless, motherless, a family forced together without a single common bond. And among them, I was the only human.

Then the nightmares began. Longing for my mother. The inconsolable grief of knowing she was truly gone. I rocked back and forth, weeping into a hay-stuffed pillow. I pictured my mother's fangs, the apologies she sang as she sipped from our cat. I tasted blood and salt as finally, the sun rose on the fourth day of my confinement.

"Neo, don't touch her! She'll come back!" Odile's words were watery, distant.

My present reality, the floor beneath my back, the rain falling outside the manor, disappeared as I returned to that fourth day. I should have been blood-sick. I should have been weak and thirsty. A woman whose face I still could not see brought me a rat. It scampered into the corner of a small wooden trap, its fluffy fur filthy with broken bits of grass and hay. I didn't want to pet it, didn't want to touch its sleek fur and tiny nose.

"Drink," the voice urged. "It's your time, girl. Drink, or die of lack. Your choice. I've been paid either way."

My mouth watered, sour saliva spilling past my lips. I dribbled down the front of my dress, certain I'd be sick. The rat's tail was so thick, like a cord of rope. I didn't want to touch it, but I snaked my fingers through the slats of the cage in greeting. I would not hurt it, but it knew no better, well-trained in what was to come and making its feelings about the matter clear. It lunged wildly, seeking escape, and I dropped the entire cage. The wood fractured, and the tiny thing squeaked at the possibility of freedom. But she, the woman, slapped me, my name ringing in my ears like a curse.

"Find your own prey to drink, if you won't accept mine. Die if that's what you want. No one here will weep for you."

I was alone again. The room went dark. The woman snatched the rat and left me to die of blood-thirst. But I didn't. I wouldn't. Two days later, when I should have been hollow and fragile, one foot hovering in Forráheim, the Realm of the soul, she returned.

"You cannot be... This cannot... Unless..."

I understood then. She did not know she'd welcomed a common person into her sanctuary. I was not like my mother. She had been deceived. My mother had paid handsomely for my care, but in leaving me with others of her kind, my powerless mother had done the one thing she believed she could do to ensure my survival without her. She handed me to those who shared the terrible power of my secrets.

But my mother could not have known, surely, that the woman whose care she delivered me into wanted nothing more than a few extra half-pennies in her purse. She cursed my mother's soul, swore at me. Slapped me again and again. Until finally, wicked laughter grated my ears.

"You're worth little to me alive, but even less dead. Get up. You're now mine to keep. Mine to control. Mine."

My eyes snapped open, and I shook so hard my teeth

cracked against each other. I broke into an icy sweat, rivulets of moisture tickling my neck and face. I was lying on my back in the sitting room, Odile's anxious face above mine, Neo's beside her. His stony expression revealing only anger.

"Burn that godforsaken thing," I whispered, pointing to the token. And then everything went dark.

I drifted in and out of consciousness after that, aware vaguely of being carried up the stone steps of the manor. I was too exhausted, wrung out like a decades-old cleaning rag, to care. I flitted in and out of dream, memory, and reality. Blankets covered me, and I grew too hot, kicked them away. Water was held to my lips, and if I sipped, I knew not how I managed to swallow.

When I finally opened my eyes, I recognized Neo's quarters. I was in his bed, awkwardly tossed across the entire thing, legs and arms splayed, a bare foot poking from beneath layers of blankets. Tendrils of fire flared from the hearth, its lulling flicker competing with the gentle patter of rain against the windows. I blinked rapidly, feeling lighter and more alert than I had in a very long time. I reached for the charm around my neck, but to my relief, it was gone. My fingers only momentarily missed their worry stone, but I clenched them into a fist as I recalled the reality. That "gift" had been controlling me. Manipulating my memories. Altering my world so that I could not be truly free.

"I want her dead," I whispered to the dark, silent form hovering in a corner. "I will kill her with my own hands."

Neo stepped into the light cast by the fire. His chest and feet were bare. He wore only a thin pair of breeches tied loosely around his hips. "Those are hardly the first words I expected to hear out of your mouth, but somehow, I'm also not at all surprised. The loss of enchantment suits you." He smirked and sat on the bed beside me, every muscle and ridge in his back shifting with the movement. He reached a hand out, and I accepted his offering.

He laced his fingers through mine, mirroring the gentle, intimate move I'd tried and so horribly failed at earlier this morning. He held mine firmly, studying my fingers and stroking the skin of each digit with his free hand.

"How are Dale and Antonia?" I asked softly, breathing in the clean, rain-scented fragrance of his room.

"They are quite well." Neo nodded. "My brother and I were due to drink. Our venom has healed the damage done by the mage. I expect Antonia is already on her way up with a meal she expects you to awaken and eat. I told her not to haul water for a bath until she'd rested, but Flynn is downstairs, so I expect once you're up and about, we'll have quite a parade of visitors."

"Flynn... How did the girl with the death mask take the news?" Although my mind felt crystal clear, my heart was weary. I might yet be cast out from this place or would leave of my own will. But that did not mean I would stop caring about the people I'd already grown so fond of. I looked at Neo, searching the sharp planes of his face.

"She was understanding." He lifted my hand to his face and breathed a kiss against my skin. "We have time to sort that out."

Liquid fire traveled up my arm at his tenderness. My breath shuddered and my body warmed, but I would not let a single sign of affection distract me.

"And what of Elgit?" I asked.

"You've been up here two short hours," he said. "Not days. The goblin's condition is the same. Odile has taken over his watch while Rain and Gia have set about repairing the damage to the manor. The storm has kept away any from the village who might need her healing. No small favor from the gods."

I sighed and closed my eyes, holding fast to Neo's hand. "Gini was never my sister," I said, still lost to disbelief of that realization. "She was the house mother, owner of the place where she raised foundlings. Orphaned beings not like the common folk. Vampires, shapeshifters. So many species, all destined by their birth to hide." I flared my nostrils and glared at him. "She profited from my mother's innocence. From her mistake."

I explained to him how my mother believed she was leaving me with others like her, others who would protect me as one of their own. "What she didn't realize is that being human made me disposable." I'd cried so much today, I hardly had the ability to form tears. My eyes stung, but I carried on, my voice clear. "Gini claimed me as hers. I worked, cleaned, accepted abuse and poor treatment. I had nowhere else to go, and if I did in fact try to leave..." I shrugged. "I had no skills. No money. No horse."

Neo's grip on my hand tightened, his jaw clenched as he listened.

"I often wondered why she didn't just kill me. But I truly believed that over time, she grew used to my company. I worked hard, cared for the children." I smiled. "Maybe that's why I couldn't leave Elgit to die. He reminded me not only of my mother, who I know died alone, but all the children I nursed through loneliness and sickness year after year. They were my family. My siblings. Even though I was nothing like them."

"What happened?" Neo asked, moving closer to me on the bed. I shoved aside the blankets so he could tuck in beside me. "Why did you leave Byrlad?"

"One of the foundlings killed a man," I sighed. "Gini and I argued at times, but I kept my anger to myself. I felt it was a more potent weapon if she was unaware that I had it. But denying what you are, what you feel... That's only possible for so long. And for some of the foundlings..."

Neo lifted an arm, and I tucked closer to his side. His arm was heavy behind my shoulders, but the weight of him was a soothing balm. I leaned my head back against his hard bicep as he asked, "Killed a man?"

"I hardly know the details. All I know is something was changing for Gini. She'd been feeding all of the children less, and I grew as much as I could in the garden, tried to bargain hard in the market to buy more with less, but it was just never enough." I shook my head and lifted my chin, my eyes hard. "Ordinarily, Gini treated the foundlings fairly well, preferring to let the useless human feel pain, if there was suffering to be had. But there was one girl, one foundling who seemed to believe that Gini was pure evil." My voice cracked as I imagined the dewy skin and silken eyelashes of the pretty young thing. "A foundling vampire. She gave Gini a lot of trouble, and that only made Gini treat her differently, worse than the other children. To keep her weak, she only let her drink every third day, provided only tiny field mice—not even the large rats and cats she offered to the other children."

Neo released my hand and brushed my hair away from my face, watching me as I spoke. "She was blood-starving the girl," he surmised.

I nodded. "A merchant happened by the foundling home. Knew nothing of what the place truly was. I met with him, tried to send him away, but I believe since he was alone, Gini thought she could manipulate him. Steal from him." I rested my head against the firm plane of Neo's chest. I closed my eyes and whispered my story against his skin. "She invited him in, perhaps to barter. Perhaps her plan all along was..." I sighed. "I know not. While she entertained him with tea, she sent me to ransack the goods in his cart."

"When I returned, the man was dead and the girl—Valkiva—wouldn't speak of what had happened. All I know for certain is what Gini told me. Perhaps she killed the merchant and blamed it on Valkiva in exchange for something? I don't know. I only knew that had to be the last night I could spend there. If I wanted any sort of life, I had to try to find a way to freedom."

The rain outside the windows of the bedroom began to ease up, leaving the sky gray and foreboding.

"That was an agonizing decision, though. I'd been the one to show true care to those children. I felt like I was abandoning them, not seeking something for myself."

Neo held a lock of my hair between his fingers, twisting the strands tenderly. Then he set the curl back against my shoulder, his fingers skimming my arm. I wanted to get this out, to release the fear and shame I'd carried over leaving. I wrung my hands together as I spoke, twisting the end of the soft blanket between my fingers.

"While Gini disposed of the merchant's body, I slipped into her treasury and stole several half and quarter-pennies. Enough that she might not notice the loss, and certainly not enough to damage her ability to feed and care for the other foundlings. But I must not have been as clever a thief as I thought I was. The next morning, before the others were awake, Valkiva crept into my room. She climbed in bed with me, hugged me, and gave me that necklace. Told me the charm was to protect me, to thank me for keeping Gini's secret."

I'd put the necklace on and stroked the charm for good luck. Its smooth, rocky surface and natural hole in the center felt so good beneath my fingers. Just like the layers of tightly bound fabric felt now in my hands. Neo pried the wrecked material from my fingers with an understanding smile. I'd grown so used to reaching for something to bring me comfort. I knew it was a habit I'd need to quickly break. I folded my hands on my lap and faced him as he asked questions.

Neo used one hand to hold my chin as I talked, exploring my eyebrows, my cheeks, the long plane of my nose with the other hand. "A hag stone?"

I shrugged, my eyes closed so he could continue to explore my face, his sensuous, caring touch unlike anything I'd ever felt. Ribbons of delight warred in my chest with the grief I felt sharing all of this with him. "I've never heard of such a stone. Never considered that Gini might have controlled me with enchanted objects. Perhaps she controlled me while I was in her care. All those years! How can I trust my own mind, my heart, knowing the power she had over me? I thought I was the keeper of all their secrets," I whispered bitterly. "What a fool I was."

"Brexia." My name rumbled deep within his chest, his heartbeat a rhythm I could listen to for all time. "You could not have known."

I lowered my face and snuggled against him while I described the sunrise the morning I left the home. The watery blue sky clotted with clouds. I walked several miles from the wilds of Byrlad, heading northeast along the coast. I reached Fish Head End before the market even opened. I checked the public posting to find the office of the shire-reeve. I was hoping to find a job or transport out of the shire, far away from any place Gini would find me.

"That's when I met you." I looked up into his eyes, praying he would see the truth in my words. "I did not know the charm was enchanted. I should have, Neo. I should have known that Gini was behind it. Once I left Byrlad, it was like my memories of the place shifted. I couldn't remember the face of the sister I believed I had. But there was never a sister. I never found that charm under my pillow. All the memories of my mother were perfectly intact, but Gini was controlling what I remembered about the home."

"She wished to lure you back," he said. "The charm was enchanted so she was able to track you, and she controlled your memories and reasons for wanting to return to Byrlad so that when she found you, you would return willingly."

He laughed, his arms tightened around me. My stomach fluttered, and a curious heat seeped through my core. I was still fully dressed in the clothes I'd worn to the market, but I rubbed my bare toes against the tops of his feet.

"She did not expect that you'd find a completely new life before she could find you."

"Now that she has," I said gently, "I must go back."

Neo startled. Intertwined as we were, I felt the movement in my body.

"Why? Do you wish to resume a life of service to her? A life without skills and hope? Without love?"

His words made my eyes flutter shut, closing out any hopes or dreams I might have had for myself. For my freedom.

"None of you will be safe until I return," I reminded him. "She wants me. I know not what ends will satisfy her thirst for vengeance. I cannot remain here and put your family, your home at risk. She knows where I am, and if she feels that the enchantment is broken, she will be back. She may not be far even now."

"What would you choose?" he asked. "You were orphaned by those who shared your blood. Lost to a mother destined for death. Kept by a mage who only wanted to use your gifts. Your kindness. Your intelligence. She knew nothing of your beauty or your heart. Your strength."

He trailed a finger along my lower lip, making it impossible to think, let alone speak.

"Brexia," he growled, lowering his nose to mine. His breath tickled my lips. "What would you choose for your life?"

I swallowed hard, transfixed by the tiny scars that mapped his lips. This close to him, I could see so clearly the pain he'd suffered, the healing that had scarcely released him from those injuries. Those tiny scars, this close to me, told his most intimate secrets. I licked my lips. "I have never had the luxury of choice," I whispered.

"Earlier today." He wove his hand through the long panels of my hair, tugging lightly so my face lifted to his. "When you held my hand as though you cared for me... All I could think was what a fool I was. To think that I could conduct a marriage as a business transaction. Perhaps with any other woman, I could avoid complications. Avoid feelings. Pairing a human with one like me..." He trailed off, a sadness overtaking the warmth of his words.

"Your mother?" I asked. It had never occurred to me that I might remind Neo of his mother losing her second spouse—a human.

He nodded. "You say you've never had the luxury of choice. But I have," he said. "And I choose you. Stay with me. Be my wife. Not because you signed a contract. Because you desire it."

"Wh...why?" I could hardly get the question out. My heart raced in my chest, and the blood rang loudly in my ears.

"Together," he whispered, teasing my lower lip with a featherlight touch from his, "we will avenge Elgit and his goblin brothers. We will find and finish Rekker Haeloc. And we will free you once and for all from every tie that binds you to grief."

My lips parted, and I lifted a finger to touch the fracture in his lower lip.

"Choose me, Brexia, because I choose you." He lowered his face to mine and claimed my lips in a tender, gentle kiss.

Fear fled my body as something new, something beautiful

and complex and perfect, replaced it. Lost in the feel of his lips on mine, I opened my mouth to his, admitting the probing sweep of his tongue. He tasted sweet like honey but earthy like the most fragrant moss after a rain. Stars lit the darkness behind my closed lids, and I raked my fingers up his neck and through his hair.

He groaned and strained toward me, holding my face in his hands.

"You are so unexpected," he breathed. "My perfect thieving bride," he said, a smile curling his lips.

"Not without reason," I murmured between kisses. Having just a taste of kissing him, I wanted more. So much more. "Doing something wrong to accomplish a greater good."

"Spoken like a true thief."

I ran a hand from his finely stubbled neck to his chest, then lowered my head to kiss every bit of skin I could reach. The hollow of his throat, his chin.

He gasped for air and, raking his hands through my hair, tugged my face back to his. "Tell me," he demanded, sucking my lower lip into his mouth. We kissed, desire and understanding flowing between us, for once unstopped by circumstance. Our tongues danced until I was breathless, but even then I wanted more. Of this. Of him. "Tell me," he repeated. "What do you choose?"

My lids heavy with lust and my heart alive with something more, something that someday I might call love, I said, "I choose you, husband. As long as you promise I will be the one to kill Gini."

CHAPTER

THIRTEEN

"If you're going to kill her, first you must find her." Rain's voice shattered our tender moment with the abruptness of an iron pot dropped against a wooden table.

Neo and I separated reluctantly while Antonia pushed a cart laden with cheese, fruit, and a pot of steaming tea into the bedroom. Rain hovered close by her, urging the woman to move slowly and mind her head. They both seemed oblivious to what they'd interrupted.

I was reluctant to move my hands from where they'd roamed, but I did, curling my fingers together in my lap above the blankets. Neo glared at his brother while I self-consciously licked the taste of my husband's kisses from my lips.

"Thank you, dear. I'm feeling quite well enough now to manage." Antonia patted Rain's arm. "I assure you, I'm more than recovered from the morning's excitement."

"I don't believe the excitement has passed us by just yet. We have a problem," Rain said. He moved gracefully like his brother, but there was something lighter about the younger Oderisi. His light stride was loose, free, as if he didn't hold the weight of dark memory between his shoulders—like Neo did. Rain strode to the window and peered through the thick glass.

Even from several feet away, I could hear the wind still blowing, sending branches dancing across the blood-red sedum and bending leaf-heavy tree branches.

"This weather has done us no favors, brother." Rain shoved a hand through his curls and huffed a frustrated breath. "The mage's blood has been washed away."

Neo kicked his feet out of bed and strode to the window, tugging the loose waist of his breeches over his well-defined hip muscles. As he walked toward the window, I saw for the first time the scars marring his muscular back. The tiny, intricate marks read like runes recording the horrors he'd been through.

He put a hand on Rain's shoulder and peered past him. "No luck scouting her?"

Rain shook his head, his long sandy curls still damp. "I tried. Followed the droplets in the direction of the stable, but there was simply nothing to track. The animals are all calm, so I don't believe she's hiding there."

"And the damage to the manor?" Neo rolled his shoulders and neck then walked to the cart and grabbed a slice of green apple. "Do you know how an illusionist managed to destroy our gate?" He looked back at me for answers.

I squinted as I tried to remember any time that Gini had used magic to manipulate physical objects. She could damage humans and even animals by convincing the mind that it was being hurt, like she'd done to Gia, Rain, and me. The injuries her magic caused were very, very real. But I couldn't recall whether she'd ever been able to bend metal or splinter wood with her mind. "I don't know," I admitted. "Although there is much about her power I may not know. How she came by the hag stone, how it was enchanted..."

"She must be developing her powers, or working with some

other forbidden force," he mused. "I fear she may have hidden some of what she's capable from even you. After all the years you lived with her, her last hope of controlling you would be with power you weren't aware existed, and therefore couldn't defend against."

"Gia was able to get the front gate removed from the fence itself, but we'll need a craftsman to repair it." Rain explained that the sitting room door was damaged but still intact and functional. Since it could still be locked, there was no need to move Elgit upstairs to one of the other vacant rooms.

Antonia handed me a mug of hot tea, and I took it, but set it on the bedside table. I held her hands tightly in mine. "I am so, so sorry for what happened to you," I said. "To Dale..."

"Shhh, milady." Her dark eyes sparkled. "We have the best healer in the Realm under this roof. Not to mention the gentlemen of the manor whose *special gifts* fixed us right up." She pointed to her arm, which I assumed was where she and Dale had been bitten by Rain and Neo. "You know, I may be old, but I didn't go down without a fight. I got a good swing or two in when I realized that mage was not a sick villager seeking aid."

"You did?" My eyes widened. I released her hands and reached for the fragrant tea. The aromas of herbs and sweet honey met my nose as I blew on the steaming cup.

She chuckled and pointed to her forehead. "Who do you think started the fight? She finished it, but by the gods, I let that woman know she was not coming into this manor without meeting some resistance." She leaned over the bed and tucked my blankets around my legs. "If there's a mage to track, I'll watch Lady Brexia. Dale will stand by our ailing guest, and we will manage. We'll never give up our home and our family without fighting with all we've got."

"Thank you, but no. I cannot stay here and rest when Gini is out there. When any in this house are still at risk." I scooted to the edge of the bed and got up. I was still fully dressed, but the leg harness with my throwing knives had been removed. "This is one fight I plan to start *and* finish myself."

Antonia nodded at Neo. "You married well," she said, her face flush with affection. Not just for him. For me, as well. Leaving the cart behind, she slipped from the room and pulled the door closed behind her.

Neo began dressing, pulling a clean, waist-length tunic over his bare chest. "I don't expect the mage is far," he surmised. "She's injured, but possibly not so badly that she'd be unable to make the journey back to Byrlad. Did you find a horse?"

Rain shook his head. "That doesn't mean she didn't arrive by one. She may have stabled it in the village and approached the manor on foot."

"Well, she'll need to find shelter by sunset." Neo tugged the tunic over his defined shoulders and tied his hair back with a length of leather. "Unless she can manipulate the minds of a flock of vengersax."

"I don't know if she'll be aware they're out here." I spotted my harness on a simple oak desk and fastened it around my thigh. One of the throwing knives was missing, likely still in the sitting room where I'd dropped it. "We have dangerous creatures in Byrlad, but we're closer to the coast. Vengersax rarely nest there. Too much open space."

"Vengersax don't particularly like pecking the eyes of sea trolls. They prefer easier dinners. Ones that don't fight back." Rain helped his brother into a clean coat of leather armor. "Perhaps that will work to our advantage. If we can lure her out after dark..."

Neo shook his head. "Think that through, brother. The torches we'd need to keep our eyes in our own heads would drive the blasted birds away." His honey-gold eyes bored into mine. "You know this mage. Does she have any other weaknesses we can exploit? We know she's not strong enough to manipulate more than a few minds at once."

I nodded, distractedly chewing on my lower lip. I believed I knew how to get to Gini, but I knew Neo would not like my idea. Would try to stop me if he even suspected what I was planning. I kept my thoughts to myself and reminded him of what he already knew. "If she is fully engaging her magic, she can probably only restrain two people at once, as she did with Gia and Rain. If there are more, she'll need to overtake them like she did Dale and Antonia. Injure them or physically restrain them so her mind is free to concentrate."

Rain paced the room while his brother pulled on leather leggings. "This is good," he said. "Thank you, Brex. That means we simply need numbers. I'm going to wager she will come back. She came all this way for you. She probably will assume that you discovered the charm she used to track you. She won't risk you destroying it. Or worse, sending it off on a dog or a horse someplace far away from where you actually are. I believe the only course is for her to return to attempt to get what she came for. But this time, we'll be prepared. With a strong, coordinated effort to resist her."

"We must find her before dark," Neo surmised. "We cannot stay awake all night as part of some living shield. She must be found before our household sleeps. We'll be too vulnerable."

I didn't remind Neo and Rain of this fact, but I was painfully aware that Gini had seen Elgit. That meant she knew we had a vulnerable, long-forgotten being in this house. That made me feel even more confident that she would return to the manor. She would come back for me and, likely, for Elgit. He would fetch an enormous purse in the darker places of the Realm. And while he was still so weak, she would not even need to exhaust her magic to overpower him. Which was all the more reason that I knew I must commit to my own plan.

As my husband and his brother readied themselves, I indulged in a long look at Neo. The hands, so strong and powerful, that had caressed my hair. The sharp contours of his chest and back, the corded muscles in his shoulders round and firm like the shinty ball the foundlings played with. His hair, more luxurious than any dress I'd ever seen, soft and beautiful as it fell around him like a nobleman's cape. My body hummed with warmth at the mere memory of his lips on mine, his arms holding me close to his chest.

I tried not to regret the altogether too brief time we'd had together. For a few soul-changing moments, I'd been a married woman. A woman who someone had chosen—even if this had never been a partnership forged by emotion. Despite the contract and the terms, the memories of the last few days were far happier and had been filled with more love than all the years since I lost my mother.

It would be an insult to the gods to seek more, despite the tightening of my despairing heart. It would hurt. But I could not allow more harm to come upon this household. The pain that I would feel if the Oderisi family suffered anything more because of me... That would cut me far more deeply than making the difficult choice to protect them. Even though that meant losing them.

I would have to be strong and accept the only duty I was truly meant for. In so doing, I could live alone comforted by the knowledge that I'd sacrificed what I could to rid the Oderisi family from any threats. Well, at least those that I'd brought down upon them.

I knew what I had to do and just how to do it.

"Is Flynn still here?" Neo asked his brother.

"The boy can't be convinced to leave," Rain said. "I tried to send him home to his mother to get some rest, but he refused."

"Good. For once the boy's strong-headedness is an asset." He pointed to Rain. "Arm Gia and Odile. If it's safe to move to Elgit to the cellar or upstairs to one of the rooms, we'll have the boy keep watch over the goblin. If he cannot be moved, we'll barricade Antonia, Dale, and Elgit in the sitting room. Every one of us must be ready for the mage when she returns."

"How will we lure her?" Rain asked, looking nervously at me. "I'm not certain I can abide putting anyone in this family in harm's path."

I smiled weakly. Neither could I.

"I suppose the only way to lure her back is to replace the hag stone." My fingers itched to clutch the token, as if the magic still had some pull on my body.

"When you do, she'll know exactly where you are. She'll regain control of your memories. Your mind, Brexia." Neo walked up to me and slipped his hands beneath my hair. He cupped my head in his hands and leaned close to me. "Are you willing to do that?"

Tendrils of sadness wove through my chest, clutching my heart more tightly than Gini's thorny vines had choked my throat.

"Wife, answer me honestly. Are you afraid?"

The diminishing firelight in the bedroom reflected off the handsome, tortured face of Neoruzzi Oderisi as I shook my head, breathing in the sweet fragrance of his breath one last time. "No, husband," I whispered. "I feel no fear. I am committed to what must be done."

"I will let no harm come to you." His kiss was soft, his lips etching a promise against mine that meant more to me than all the words in the marriage contract. "Relieve Odile in the sitting room," he murmured, sounding as reluctant as I was to end the kiss. "Watch over Elgit while we arm and dress the sisters."

I nodded, the soft, melodic song that played in my soul when he touched me waning into whispers. "I will."

Together, we walked hand in hand down the stone stairs, Rain close at our heels. Rain went off to prepare Antonia and Dale while Neo stood outside the closed sitting room door.

"Brexia. Wait."

My hand was on the knob, frozen in place at the sound of his voice.

He moved close behind me and wrapped his arms around my waist. He whispered against my ear. "You freely choose this?"

If I'd had any tears left, I might have shed them then. But I could not. Would not.

"Yes," I said, my voice clear and steady.

I turned my back to the door and reached for him. This kiss was insistent, demanding. Scarcely a candle's flame compared to the wildfire that was beginning to burn between us. I opened my mouth to him, covering his plush, broken lips with mine, committing the taste and touch and feel of him to memory. His hands roamed my hips, tugging me impossibly closer until Gia's soft cough behind us reminded us there was no time for passion. Not now. Never again.

"I'll allow no harm befall you," he promised, as he slowly pulled his hands from my body. "You will be safe."

"I make the same vow to you," I said. Swallowing hard, I released him. For good. "I'll send out Odile."

He opened the door. After I went inside the sitting room, he closed it softly behind me, sealing the promises and hope of the last few days away forever. I looked over the room where my quest for a job, for a husband, for stability had begun just a few short days ago and dizzying pangs of love and longing struck my chest. I pinched my nose, the sting of tears threatening to undo every plan I'd made.

I freely chose this, I reminded myself. Even if the choice would not deliver what I so desperately wanted, I took comfort in the fact that at least the decision had been mine. This moment, where I was, and what I planned to do was the result of the only power I'd ever had.

I would wield and not waste it.

I got to work, searching for and finding my throwing knife on a table that had been set back onto its legs. I slipped the blade into the vacant fitting on my thigh. "Odile?"

She looked like she'd fallen asleep leaning back in the velvet armchair. "Oh!" She sat upright and immediately leaned forward to check on Elgit. "He looks surprisingly good," she said, her voice groggy. "His temperature remains steady. That's a very positive sign. His body is working hard to heal itself. He may just pull through."

I was so very relieved. "Odile, I owe you my thanks," I said, extending my hands. She took mine in hers. "You spoke up for me. Believed in me when the easier course would have been blame."

"Well, I believe in you, Brex." She lifted my hands to her lips and kissed the back of each hand. "The easier course is rarely the right one," she said sweetly. "I know that too well. My sister and I are no strangers to isolation, to persecution." She flitted her eyes down toward our hands.

I remembered the trouble Neo had mentioned that Gia and Odile had had with vampires.

"My father was a crofter," she said quietly. "He managed the farmland and livestock, as well as the farm staff that lived and worked on Haeloc's vast estate many, many years ago."

"Haeloc?" I widened my eyes, shocked at the connection. "You have a connection to him as well?"

She nodded. "My family lived in the crofter's residence until... Well, when I was a very young girl, just four years old, I fell off a horse in Lord Haeloc's stable. He was there, saw the accident, and bit me. Treated me with his venom so I would not suffer. But he did not gift me health without exacting a deep price."

She released my hands as Gia opened the door and peeked in.

"I'll be a moment, sister." Odile continued her story. "When my mother fell ill many years later, my father begged Haeloc to bite her so that he might heal her. Haeloc refused, and my father went mad with despair. Ran into the village begging for someone to bite my mother and save her. He was drawn and quartered by the common folk right before our eyes. My sister, such a young, innocent girl, watched as our father was executed without so much as a trial. Our mother died a few days later, and we were cast out of the crofter's residence. For years Gia and I worked to pay punishing fines imposed by the shire-reeve for our parents' crimes. Even to this day, I'm prohibited from charging fees or collecting any gifts for my healing work."

"Prohibited?" I echoed.

She nodded. "The shire-reeve considers healers necessary but untrustworthy. Inclined to magic and alchemy." She sighed. "No faith in those things they do not understand. Like bodies and herbs and what truly heals. Listening and compassion have cured more patients than any tonic, at least in my practice."

"By the gods," I gasped. I could not imagine surviving what these two had seen. "How do you have such kind, open hearts? After all you've been through?"

Gia called to her sister. "We must ready ourselves."

Odile released my hands and quietly gave up her seat to me. "I've seen so much pain, so much loss. Life loses its beauty when a soul hardens itself. And I refuse to give my soul over to the likes of Haeloc or that mage. Or any who might harm me. My soul is my most precious possession, and only I can protect it. Staying kind, staying open... That was a choice," she said. "One I've never once regretted."

I watched while the sisters closed the door behind them, their soft chatter dissipating as they headed upstairs to change into armor.

As soon as I was alone, I searched the room. The mess had been swept up, likely by Dale, the shredded fabric and feathers from the wrecked pillows now gone. The furniture had all been set upright, and I spotted my favorite embroidered pillow on a small table. It had escaped destruction, but only barely. Antonia's expert fingers could no doubt repair it.

I walked up to it, touching the beautiful needlework. Then I took a knife from my harness and without a moment's hesitation, cut off a length of the fabric detailed with the happiest-looking blooms. I tucked the scrap beneath my harness, between the leather and the fabric of my beeches where it would not fall out when I reached for a knife.

May this remind me what is real, I prayed. *May I never forget.*

I walked back to Elgit and kneeled beside the settee. I stroked his hair away from his forehead and watched his chest rise and fall as he slept. Odile was right. His skin felt warmer and softer than it had yesterday. Less dry, less hot. More like the skin of a living creature, not one whose spirit was already leaving behind its flesh dwelling.

I laced my hand through the goblin's and whispered against the wrinkled fingers. "Be well and strong, dear Elgit. You have friends awaiting your recovery. And you will always have a friend in Byrlad."

I rested his hand gently back beneath the covers and walked up to the fireplace. Retrieving the poker that Rain had used as a weapon against Gini, I prodded the crackling logs, scattering the embers until I found what I sought. Using the hook end of the poker, I fished the hag stone from the ash with a sad smile.

Things never burned the way people thought they would.

The leather cord had shrunk in the flames, but even charred, it was still intact enough to secure the charm against my skin. I slipped it over my head, closing my eyes.

Come and find me, sister.

Then I opened the door to the sitting room, stepped into the hall, and closed it quietly behind me. With a final look about the entryway of the place that had just begun to feel like home, I opened the front door and quietly slipped outside. I was gentle with the door so the sound of the latch wouldn't alert anyone to my movements. I walked swiftly toward the stable and greeted my sweet Sara. Odile's dog, Joi, who I'd not yet seen but had heard liked to roam the stables, woofed a tiny warning.

"Sshhh, girl," I said, dropping to my knees to pet her. Odile had told me the dog had lost most of her vision but that she was still as vibrant and full of joy as ever—living up to her name. I vigorously petted her ears.

"Lady Brex?" Flynn came round a wall and picked up the medium-sized elderly pup. "Can I help?"

I shook my head, surprised to see the boy here but glad for a chance to ensure he stayed inside where it was safe.

"Would you set Joi in a stall where she won't be injured?" I asked. "And when you're through, Neo needs you inside. He wants your help with the goblin."

Flynn needed no further motivation. He secured Joi in a stall away from my horse. Then, chattering on delightedly about finally being given the kind of quest he desired, he raced back to the manor.

Once he was far enough away, I mounted Sara, checked my harness for the remnant of the embroidered pillow, and secured my knives. For the last time, I clutched the charm around my neck, stroking the stone with my fingertips. I'd made my choice. The one that was necessary to protect these good people, regardless of the cost to my soul. I prodded Sara to a gallop and took off.

~

SARA'S RECOVERY made leaving Omrora far easier than our arrival to the shire had been. Now that she was well-fed and rested, we traveled the road to Byrlad with ease.

After we put sufficient distance between the Oderisi manor and the road, I slowed her to a canter, my thoughts jumbled and twisted. I panted and gripped the reins, trying to tiptoe through my memories. Since putting the charm over my neck, I'd grown terrified that Gini might take control over my mind. She'd already manipulated my memories. Surely she could alter or even hide my most precious thoughts completely. Make it so I would never remember Neo's face or the intensity of his tortured gold eyes.

The more I worried, the more determined I became to lose nothing, to give up none of the memories of happiness I'd had. I squinted against the sting of tears as I thought of my mother, the journey she'd made and the unlikely circumstances of my return to this place. I would not forget her. Would not let Gini take everything I held dear.

The closer we rode to Byrlad, the more my thoughts turned to what Gini might do. I was certain that she would punish me. But how? What ends would satisfy her hunger for vengeance?

Every shadow behind every tree and every snap of every twig jolted me in the saddle. As the sun traveled its path in the sky, I stole looks in every direction, alert and anxious. Was she following me? Ahead or behind? Alongside me, her control keeping me oblivious to her presence?

Gini is so angry. So very, very angry.

I rubbed my eyebrows and resisted the urge to close my eyes to the thoughts that crowded my mind. Something felt wrong. My thoughts were coming in jarring bursts, as if Gini's rage had taken possession of my mind.

I am still in here, I reassured myself. *I am still Brexia Eloise. My mind is mine. She cannot steal it from me entirely.*

But as I rounded the path that led through a clearing of the conifer, I knew my time was close. I slowed Sara to a walk and straightened my shoulders. Ahead were the fall gardens, the rows of leafy greens and root vegetables looking trim and well-harvested. I knew the knots and cracks in the bark of every tree that lined the path. The colors of every wildflower dotting the land, their delicate petals curled in against the growing cold. This place was familiar, but not beloved. This was where I'd lived, but so much less a home than where I'd stayed the last few nights.

Yet here was where I belonged. If for no other reason than to spare my true home from plunder, from pain.

"Let's go, girl. This is your home now." I climbed down from Sara's back and led her up the long path. But the sounds of wailing sent me into a run toward the peg fixed to the front of the modest straw and wattle house. I tied Sara with shaking hands as I heard the agonizing peals of baby Fina screaming.

"Valkiva! Tabby!" I shouted as I shook the front door. "It's Brex! I'm back! Please, please open up!" I shook with all my strength, only to have it open a moment later.

A nearly bald child, his face somber and stony, met my eyes. "You're back."

I bent to pick up the unexpressive little boy and hugged him to my chest. "Ivo." I breathed deeply and squeezed my eyes shut but then set the four-year-old back on his feet. "Where is Valkiva? Where are the others? Where's Gini?"

Ivo slammed the door behind me while Valkiva, small and furious, stormed toward me. "She left us, Brex." Kiva took several steps before breaking into a run. She threw her scrawny body against my waist and clung to me. "She's gone. We have no idea if she is coming back. The baby hasn't eaten since yesterday. I tried. I..."

I knelt down and gripped the girl's shoulders. The dark pools of her eyes reflected wisdom and pain back at me. "I am here now," I reassured her. "And I will not leave you again." I stood and took her hand. "Come. Take me to Fina. I'll get her fed and changed."

As I walked through the familiar rooms, all four of the children of walking age surrounded me, hugging me and weeping with relief.

"We thought you'd left us forever," Remy cried. "Where did you go, Brex?"

"It's a long story," I told her, kissing the top of her head. I stooped to pick Fina from the cradle where she kicked and screamed. "There, there, now. Sweet little Fina." The toddler immediately dropped her sweaty, tear-stained cheek against my shoulder. I patted her back, rocking her and shushing her as she hung limp in my arms.

A wave of guilt washed over me at what the kids had been through in my absence. I'd taken a portion of their stability when I left. That was a debt I intended to repay. "You're all right," I cooed, carrying the baby Fina through a dark corridor. Half the lamps were unlit, leaving large areas of the foundling home bathed in darkness.

"Come, children. Quick, now." I hurried into my former room, relieved to see both of the dresses I'd left behind exactly where I'd abandoned them. "Tabby, my sweet, take the baby and the others into the kitchen. I'll be right along to make everyone a big, fat meal. Can you do that?"

I handed Fina to Tabby and watched the nine-year-old shepherd the kids out of my tiny bedroom. "Kiva, stay a moment?" My hair was exposed, but my cloak was still on. At twelve, Valkiva was more than old enough to see what I was going to show her. And after what she'd experienced with Gini and the merchant, she needed to see this.

I motioned for Valkiva to close my door while I tugged off the traveling cloak and tossed it onto the bed. Beneath the cloak, the four throwing knives sparkled in their sheath. I worried for just a moment that Gini might be someplace inside my mind already, but I shook my head and reminded myself she could not change my thoughts. She could only form illusions. Nothing more.

Valkiva's eyes widened as I tugged a dress over my head, leaving the breeches on and the knives in place.

"How long has she been gone?" I asked. "Tell me as precisely as you can."

Kiva watched as I laced the ties of the dress and tucked the sleeves of my tunic into the dress so it would not be obvious I was wearing other clothes beneath it.

"She left yesterday afternoon. She told us she was going to the market, but she never came back." Kiva's lip trembled as she recounted the story. "When night fell, it got so dark. The others were so hungry and so scared."

I nodded. My chest tightened as I considered where Gini had been all that time. Had she watched the Oderisi manor? Had she seen Neo and me leave for the goblin sanctum on our wedding night? I shrugged the sickening thoughts away and focused on the present concern. "I believe Gini will come back. She may try to hurt me, Kiva."

The little girl's eyes glittered, and she flared her nostrils. "Like she hurt that merchant." Her small fists were tight at her sides, and I took her by the shoulders.

"I hope she does not, Kiva, but if she does…" I lifted her little chin to meet my eyes. "I have weapons. The knives under my dress. Use them to protect yourself and the other children, if you need to. Do you understand me?"

Valkiva nodded.

"When she returns, she may be very, very angry at me and will likely punish me. Whatever happens, protect yourself and the other children. Do not put yourself in harm's way. I do not believe she will kill me, but only you know what she's truly capable of. I want you to be prepared." I hugged the girl to my chest. "I have a horse outside. If you need to flee, take as many children as you can and run."

Valkiva shook her head, her thin arms tight around me. "I will not leave you, Brex. We love you. None of us cried for Gini while we were alone. But we've cried for you since you left."

A sharp pang of guilt twisted inside my heart, and I gasped against the shock of it. "I…I know, sweet girl. I love you all, too. Each of you. That's why I want you to be prepared to save the others. Now come. We must get the children fed and behave as normally as possible. If Gini returns, we must act as though everything is all right, yes?"

Valkiva gripped my hand in hers, the strength in that tiny grip surprising me. But I was also relieved. This little one was stronger than I gave her credit for.

"Come, come," I called, hurrying into the kitchen.

When Gini did arrive home, the children were all fed. Fina was sound asleep in my arms, Ivo sitting at my feet on the floor scratching symbols that only he could see with his fingers. Kiva was the first to hear the door.

"Someone's here." She lurched to her feet.

I stood and rocked Fina, a little girl of nearly two who was not quite able to walk. "Everything is fine," I cooed, my eyes traveling over each of the children. I squeezed my eyes closed and prayed that none of them would be hurt. No matter what happened to me, none of these little ones deserved a moment's pain.

Tabitha and Remy tried to play backgammon, but their attention wandered to the thundering footsteps. Gini walked into the kitchen, her hair wild and her eyes focused on me.

"Gini," I said gently, handing baby Fina to Tabby. I approached the woman and extended my arms. "I've returned. I'm so sorry to have worried you. I—"

The words died on my lips as Gini slapped me hard across the face. The children gasped, and I lifted my chin, rage on my face and fight nearly bursting in my heart.

"Don't you dare touch me," I seethed. I quickly realized that it was possible Gini didn't know I'd seen her at the manor. "You have no right. Am I your prisoner? Am I not free to come and go if I wish?"

"You're a godforsaken thief," she said, the finger pointed at me shaking with rage. "You stole coins from my purse and then left... To do what? To report this place?" She looked at the children, all of whom hovered together, watching with fear-filled eyes. "Did you know your beloved Brexia was a spy for the queen?"

She walked a wide, slow circle around me.

"That is not true." I glared at her. "I am not a spy. I did steal your coins. But after years in your service without so much as a quarter-penny's pay, I thought it my due."

"You are owed nothing." As she circled behind me, something seemed to strike behind my knees, and I dropped to the floor with a grunt.

"Don't hurt her!" Tabby cried, holding on to the baby as though she was a toy.

"I'm all right," I said, roughly struggling to stand. The illusion of being struck was over, so I stood tall and pointed to the baby. "Tabby, why don't you take Fina for a nap. Kiva, take the children outside so Gini and I can talk."

Valkiva's eyes widened, but I just smiled at her. It would be safer for her to leave me. Gini wouldn't waste energy controlling the girl if she was out of reach.

"It's all right," I urged. "We'll be right here if you need us."

Kiva nodded and hurried the children out of the kitchen while Gini again knocked me to my knees with a blow that only existed in my mind. My knees struck hard against the floor, the breath rushing from my lips. I would not give her the satisfaction of seeing my pain. I gritted my teeth and struggled to stand.

"You betrayed me," Gini said. "I know you did. You've consorted with spies of the queen. You mean to destroy everything I've worked for." She never took her eyes from me as she made her accusations, walking another long, slow circle around me.

I didn't move. Held my chin high. "I did no such thing. Do you think I would bring harm to the only home I've known? To the innocent children here?"

Suddenly, a blow struck me in the stomach, knocking the wind from my lungs. I staggered back, trying not fall. I leaned forward, my hands on my knees for support, as I tried to force air into my chest.

"I notice you didn't include *me* in that heartfelt list." Gini's voice was calm but bitter. With every accusation, every name she called me, she delivered another illusion that struck like a hammer against my body. "You're a thief. A liar. You've betrayed me, *and* you're common."

I coughed and sputtered but stayed on my feet. I knew if I fell, she might see the knives. It didn't matter what she did to me as long as I could stay on my feet.

"I...am...common." I coughed, gasping for air as I tried to

speak. "You know I would be put to death if I admitted I hid magic users. If I admitted I'd lived among the species these children are. Why would I do that? Betray you and sentence myself to death?"

"You wanted all of us out of the way." A sick smile on her face, she knocked me back against the wall, once, twice... Again and again and as she listed one by one the names of the foundlings now under her care: Valkiva. Tabitha. Remy. Ivo. Faustina.

I was breathless and in pain when vines of ice crept up my neck and tightened around my throat.

"I don't know what you mean," I sputtered.

"You ran away and took a vampire lover. How perfectly dishonest of you."

No matter what she said or did, I would never admit that I'd seen her at the manor. If she was going to kill me, she'd have to do so without ever hearing from my lips that I'd seen her. "I bought a horse," I wheezed, trying not to panic, trying to stop my hands from clutching at the choking vines that were not really there. "Didn't you see it outside?"

She seemed unmoved, silent as she glared into me. Through me. I braced for what was to come but was shocked by bone-chilling cold bathing my body. As though I'd been plunged into an icy pond, I shivered uncontrollably, unable to fight the illusion.

"I came home." I struggled to utter the words. Between the breathlessness of being struck and the ice that closed around my limbs, I could hardly move my lips. "I came back!"

She walked slowly up to me, each silent footstep reminding me that she was not human. She wielded magic against which I was common. Weak. Powerless.

My mouth was open, my tongue fixed in a soundless scream. I didn't know how to fight my way through the illusion.

My hands and feet felt as though they were dying, the limbs so cold I couldn't move them. Except of course the agonizing shivering, over which I had even less control.

"The damage you've done cannot be repaired. There is no forgiveness for you here." She closed her eyes, and suddenly my entire body went rigid, icy cold and unable to move. I was freezing.

"Please," I panted, forcing my lips and tongue to cooperate for just one, tiny syllable.

Icy fingers throttled my throat, and I closed my eyes. I felt pain through the frozen stiffness, my body reacting to what it believed was happening. I tried to look inside my memories. Although my eyes were open, I pictured the beautiful things I'd loved in this world. The warmth of Neo's body. The heat of the fire in the sitting room. The sweaty heat of running with the foundlings in play.

My mind was strong, but the power she wielded was stronger. I felt my lips go cold, and I started feeling drowsy, like I could fall asleep pressed where I was against the kitchen wall.

"You're...killing...me," I wheezed.

"This is not even a taste of what you deserve," she said, her rageful whisper soft as she focused every bit of vitality she had into the illusion. "Consider yourself lucky I don't have any interest in cleaning up blood, or this would be a very different kind of suffering."

I struggled to lick my lips, to ease the stiffness that made speaking so difficult. My head lolled back against the wall, and I let my eyes flutter shut.

"Brexia?" I heard Kiva's voice call to me from a far, far distance.

I fought to lift my face, to open my eyes, but the ice controlled my every move. I released a tiny whimper but could say no more.

"Brex!" A small, skinny body slammed against my waist. "Stop! You're killing her!" Kiva stood between Gini and me, her face buried in my dress. And yet the illusion in my mind was unbroken.

Kiva fumbled a shaking hand beneath my dress and a moment's relief broke through the numbing pain.

Run, I thought, hoping that if I died at Gini's hand, Kiva would at least stop the other children from coming to harm.

I chirped another sound, weak and poorly formed, when I heard crashing and shouts in my ears. The room began to spin, and I saw the ceiling as though I was inches from it. I knew I was starting to lose consciousness, but there was nothing I could do. This was the punishment Gini sought to inflict. I could only hope that my denying Neo would be enough to keep her from tracking him down. From going back to Omrora to punish the one she thought was my vampire lover after I'd perished.

Everything was so, so cold. I couldn't keep my eyes open any longer. I knew if I closed them, my spirit would separate from my body and my journey to Forráheim would begin.

Mum, I thought.

I imagined I was smiling. I imagined I was warming, my limbs coming back to life as I prayed my solemn goodbyes.

I heard a screech and the sounds of running, but I was already moving, leaving this Realm. I slipped a hand beneath my skirt, marveling that I could move it, and fumbled for the embroidered fabric I'd stolen from Neo's pillow. Gripping it in my hand, I was ready. Ready to make the slow walk alone into the misty unknown. I flared my nostrils, took a deep breath, and closed my eyes.

Collapsing on the floor of the kitchen startled me awake. I squinted one eye open, and then, in a panic, realized I was not frozen. I could move. I was still alive.

I blinked to clear away the fog and saw a puddle of blood seeping along the floor toward my face. Gini had one of my throwing knives in her belly, and Kiva had another gripped in a fist. She was crying, her shoulders shaking and her face wet with tears. Her arms were wrapped tightly around Neo's broad shoulders.

I was too weak to lift my head from the floor, but with a grunt, I lifted the hand clutching the embroidered flowers to my chest so the keepsake wouldn't be stained with blood. Then, I smiled and closed my eyes.

FOURTEEN

"I don't think you have a problem with stealing." The voice came through the mists of my sleep, rich and inviting. "I think you have a problem with pillows."

I opened my eyes to the smirking, scarred lips of my husband. He was lying on his side next to me on the tiny bed in my room.

We were still in the foundling home. I was still alive. And I was still clutching a shredded length of embroidered flowers in my hand.

"You have a problem with timing," I said, groaning as I tried to roll over to face him. "I needed you about a half hour before you actually arrived. Oh, by the gods..." I squeezed my eyes against the pain. "Those illusions leave very real bruises," I admitted. I couldn't wait to get the filthy day dress that had been like a uniform for so many years off my body. I tapped my thigh to ensure that the breeches and leg holster were still in place underneath the dress.

We faced each other, me lying on the less painful of the two sides, while he propped himself on an elbow and watched me.

"I need to know..." I started, not sure how to even phrase the question on my heart. After everything that had happened in the house, I was certain we were all safe, but there was far more to caring for people than simply keeping them out of harm's reach. "Neo, are the children...?"

"They are all right," he assured me, reaching between us to stroke the hair away from my face.

"And what of Gini?" I whispered, lifting my head to fit more closely against the curve of his palm.

He nodded, his lips a thin, hard line. "Her injuries were severe. She did not make it."

Hot tears burned my eyes, but not for the woman who'd tried to control me, then kill me. The "house mother" whose selfish demands had stolen years of my life away. I was worried for the poor young girl who'd taken my knife in her hand to protect me. And what she'd had to do to save my life.

"Where is Valkiva?" I asked, my lips trembling. "She is only twelve, Neo. She's seen so much already."

"Right now, she is calm. But she will need support to get through this." He nodded. "Last I checked, Flynn was putting on some sort of performance for the children. Even Kiva seemed amused."

He swallowed hard, the knob in his throat moving as he sighed. "Would that I'd been just a few moments earlier. I would have gladly done what that poor child never should have had to."

"I should have used my knives the moment Gini walked through that door." I was so furious at myself. My fists tightened against my frustration, but there was nothing I could do. I was too weak to move, too sore to pace the room and scream. All I could do was live with my choices, as well as their consequences. "I was wrong," I spat. "I'd hoped that maybe if she had me back, Gini would leave you and your family alone. All she wanted was me, so I thought... I thought if I abandoned my plan to kill her and just gave in, sacrificed myself to her…"

"And what of your freedom? Your happiness?" Neo's lips parted. He looked like a man staring into an endless pond, unable to fathom what mysteries lie in the murky depths. "You came back here to trade your life for my household's safety?"

I nodded. "It was a fool's offering. I should have known better. I hesitated to take a life, and my reluctance forced someone far more vulnerable to do the job."

"No one forced Valkiva to take that knife." Neo snaked a hand beneath my hair and cupped my neck. "She reacted out of love for you. Out of fear and anger at what Gini was doing. Probably what she'd done for many, many years. Caused pain to someone the girl loves. You cannot blame yourself for the child's choice."

I sniffed hard, unwilling to cry for Gini. But for Kiva? She deserved better than my cowardice, my hesitation. I would make sure she had love and care and support to put this behind her. I would give it all to her myself. There was no one else to do it now, and she would need me all the more.

I struggled to shift my weight again but simply couldn't. I groaned and rested a hand lightly on my ribs. "By the gods," I muttered. "I'm no use to anyone like this. Is Odile here? Did she stay back with Elgit?"

He nodded. "She's back at the manor, but I'm sure she will be anxious to attend to you when we get home."

Home. Just the thought that he would bring me back there, that he still considered his manor my home, brought a fresh wave of tears to my eyes. But I would not shed them. I knew I could never return with him. If it were ridiculous before… Now? Simply impossible.

"Neo," I said, shaking my head as much as my pain would allow. "I cannot return with you. These foundlings have no one else. I left them once thinking Gini would treat them as she always had—well enough, at least. But now? There is no one but me, and I will not leave them to uncertain fates."

Neo looked amused, perhaps even happy. "Gia and Rain are packing up Flynn's cart as we speak."

"Packing? I do not understand."

"Gia looked through Gini's records while you slept. Did you know she was selling these children?" he asked.

I sucked in a horrified breath. "Adopting," I corrected. "She found each child a willing, loving home, Neo."

He shook his head. "She kept extensive records. She placed the foundlings, but none would call those transactions adoptions."

"Where is she?" I demanded, struggling to sit up in the bed. "I'm going to tear the hair from her lifeless body!"

Neo kissed my forehead and urged me to lie still. "Let's not be in such a rush to desecrate a corpse. She is likely receiving the justice she deserves in Ástleysi, now."

I squeezed my eyes closed at the mention of the dark Realm. While all good must be balanced by evil, imaging that place, where demons and devils ruled, terrified me. Even for someone who had done the things that Gini had. Those things I knew of, as well as those of which I'd been painfully unaware.

Selling foundlings? I could not believe it.

My heart shattered as I thought about how my mother would feel if she knew where she'd left me. What kind of place this truly was. "My entire life here has been a lie," I said, my voice broken. "My memories. My emotions. Even the people I cared about—all the children I thought were loved and wanted, who went on to live happy lives. One of the only things that kept me going every day was waking up knowing that for most of the children, their time with us was temporary. I wanted them to feel loved and happy so they could meet new families and leave for exciting new lives." I swallowed back the sour taste of bile. "It's all been a lie. And I was part of it. My work here made her evil schemes possible."

I groaned as he tucked himself closer to me, leaning forward on one elbow so he could study my face. "None of what you lived was a lie," he insisted, his voice thick with emotion. "Have you considered that the gods chose you, Brexia? A common person among the most vulnerable foundlings in the Realm. Perhaps your destiny has always been thus. Only one who was trusted by Gini could get close enough to stop her."

While his words made sense, they did nothing to ease the chafing around my heart.

"There's still a chance for the foundlings downstairs. For a happy future and truly free lives." His optimism surprised me. Each of the children would be doomed to flee this Realm or live hidden. What hope of freedom could there truly be for any of us?

Questions and uncertainties pounded like an unrelenting rain through my soul. "They deserve that chance. I don't know how I'll afford their care, but I will manage it. I'll make sure they don't go a day without everything they need. Everything," I insisted.

Neo looked dubious. "There is a dead mage in the kitchen and, from what Kiva told me, a dead merchant buried some-place on this property. Staying here is not a good idea, Brex. There will be an inquiry into Gini's death. Perhaps not right away, but the shire-reeve will eventually come calling for taxes. That merchant may have family..."

"That merchant may have been a spy of the queen," I sighed. "Gini seemed convinced of it."

"All the more reason to depart this place and never return." Even though his voice was resolute, I did not see a way through this.

"What choice do we have?" I asked. "Where will I take the children?"

He raised a thick brow at me. "I have a manor and a sister-in-law who can help heal these foundlings, both in body and mind. I have a family and some means." He traced a finger along my lower lip. "And I have you. At least for as long as the contract remains valid."

"You would do that?" I asked. "Bring the lot of us to Omrora?"

He caressed my cheek and the ridge along my jaw, as if studying my features for the very first time. "I have a goblin, a teenage boy, and a thieving wife. I think what the manor lacks is a handful of foundlings."

The sun was beginning to set, casting a warm glow on Neo's face. Careful of my tender injuries, I reached a hand to touch him. He closed his eyes as I stroked the stubble on his chin, his cheeks, and the tiny fractures long healed on his parted lips. "Brex," he whispered. "Come home. All of you. Come home with me."

I tried to lean in to kiss him but fell back in pain. "I might need a bit of help with that," I said, trying to laugh through the aches of my very real injuries.

He looked like he was in pain watching me. "I can do more than help a bit," he said.

I knew instinctively what he meant.

His venom. He was offering to bite me.

"What is it like?" I asked. But then I shook my head. "I don't care. I don't need to know. I just want you to do it. Drink from me. Please."

He stood up from the bed and helped me carefully adjust into a sitting position. He wore only his tunic and breeches, his leather armor piled on a small table by the window. He climbed behind me, leaning his broad back against the wall and spreading his legs apart. Then he helped me scoot backward so my rear end rested between his splayed legs. He wrapped his arms around my waist and bent his head to brush his lips against my ear. He moved my hair away from the back of my neck, teasing my skin with soft kisses.

"You can hold your pillow flowers," he growled, a smirk in his voice.

I leaned back against his chest, letting his strong form support my weight. "What should I do?" I asked.

"I can drink from your arm or leg," he said. "But with how bruised your ribs and throat are, drinking from here will deliver the venom faster."

He trailed his fingers along the sensitive column of my neck, and I groaned, pleasure flooding through my body despite the pain.

"Yes," I whispered. "Please. Do it."

He lowered his lips to the side of my neck, his thighs anchoring mine in place. "You may feel..." He chuckled. "Good. Very good. But just relax. If you see colors or visions, do not think I am controlling your mind. It's not an illusion. I don't have magic. Everyone reacts differently to the venom. But you and I have a connection. So it's likely going to feel very stimulating."

I nodded, my long hair hanging over my shoulder, one side of my neck completely exposed to him. "I'll be fine," I promised.

I felt nothing but gentle pressure as Neo's fangs pierced my skin. For a moment, I wasn't sure anything was happening at all, but then... I felt like I was falling, and I understood why Neo had positioned himself behind me. His arms were tight around me, so even though the room moved as though I might tip out of bed, I was not afraid.

I happily gave in to the sensations. My eyelids drooped closed as I watched a cascade of colors behind the darkness.

Vibrant red, oceanic blue, and the unforgettable golden honey of Neo's eyes encircled me in a blanket of living colors. The sharp pricks of pain from my injuries loosened as my muscles relaxed, my vitality returning my body to not just a normal state of being, but to something far, far better. I sighed, a warm bath of sensation flooding my legs, arms, fingers, and toes. The intensity increased as it traveled through my core, a distinctly sensual heat hardening my nipples to peaks.

I lost control of my words, sound slipping from my lips as I uttered moans of delight. I felt free, strong, as if I could not just leap from bed, but could fly. I stretched into the sensation, aware of Neo's strong arms securing me, his thighs hot alongside mine. Just as I began to grow comfortable with the feeling —greedy, even, for more—it was over. My eyes ripped open, and I pouted. "Why? Why did you stop?"

I looked over my shoulder at Neo's lips, parted by his fangs, his eyes glowing a fiendish red. He stroked the spots on my neck and closed his eyes as his elongated fangs retracted into unmistakably normal-looking teeth. He swallowed then opened his eyes. The crimson color had faded back to the yellow-gold, but the intensity remained as he searched my face.

"Too much will kill you." He sighed and rested his chin on the top of my head. "If I drank any more, I'd be in danger of draining you dry. My Brexia. By the gods, woman..."

Enlivened by the lack of pain, the absolute bliss of his venom still coursing through my body, I wiggled out of his hold and turned to face him. Climbing between his legs, I straddled his thighs with mine. Reaching for his face, I parted my lips and probed his mouth with my tongue. He gripped my hips and tugged me against him, his arousal straining against his breeches. He fisted my hair while I tugged at his, our kisses a clash of powerful beings chasing an even more powerful high. Teeth clinking against teeth, we kissed with ferocious intensity.

Our hands grappled to explore each other's skin, our lips' breathless kisses matching the pace that our hips worked against each other.

This was not just the venom, not just lust. This was something deeper than blood and desire.

I leaned away from him and gazed into his eyes. "If we don't stop now..."

"We've only just been married, and yet already have five children," Neo agreed with a harsh laugh. "We may wish to slow things down."

"Six," I reminded him, "if you consider Elgit. Not so much a child, I suppose, but a dependent."

"Then I count seven," he growled, planting a gentle kiss against my lips. "I consider Flynn a dependent."

I laughed, and kissed him lightly, sweetly. A reluctant transition from passion to practicality. "Let's make dinner. We have a lot of packing to do."

"The sooner we leave, the better," Neo said, his voice growing concerned. "We'll wake the children at first light and make for Omrora as soon as the trolls and the vengersax have gone to sleep."

I held my hand out to him, and he climbed off the bed. I tucked the strip of pillowcase into my leg harness. Two of the knives were missing, but I was sure I'd find them downstairs. One might still be inside Gini's belly. "Do you think we're in danger?" I asked. "Did Gia see anything else in the records?"

He smoothed his mussed hair and sighed. "Whether it was true or not, Gini seemed terrified that she was being watched by spies of the queen. Gia found long, rambling passages—the thoughts of a woman nearly gone mad with the obsessions of her mind."

"Madness?" I asked. It made sense that something was afoot. Gini and I had lived together for years. It wasn't until the merchant arrived—and was killed—that I began to suspect something was very, very wrong. "Do you think Gini's magic was being used against her in some way? An illusion reflected back to create a belief in something she was afraid of?"

"I've considered it," he said. He smoothed his tunic over the bulge in his breeches that would have scandalized the foundlings if they'd seen it. To be honest, I was a little scandalized myself, but in the best possible way. "If Haeloc was dabbling in magic, he might have attracted the attention of the queen. If Gini sold a foundling to the wrong people..." He sighed. "One fire extinguished, but many others still burn."

He was right. We might have been safe from Gini, but there was still the massacre of the goblins and Neo's torturer, Rekker Haeloc, to deal with.

A high-pitched shriek and the pounding of several sets of feet distracted us from further conversation.

"I'm a sea troll! And I loooove eating kiddie meat! Raaaaawr!!" Flynn's voice boomed through my closed door, Remy's and Tabitha's distinctive squeals bouncing through the home.

"Flynn's about to become a very different kind of apprentice," I laughed.

Ivo, the stone-faced little boy who seemed unaware that smiling and laughter were expressions used by children, seemed to discover that his lips could curl upward when he was around Gia. The boy chattered to her nonstop and even reached his hand out to offer her a glimpse at something he held very, very dear: a lock of his hair.

"Oooh," Gia said, nodding, looking partly uncomfortable and partly touched. "Thank you for sharing that."

I ran my hand over Ivo's smooth head and bent down to explain what was happening. While all the children would need to understand that we were leaving, Ivo would need a little more time to process.

"Ivo, do you understand that Gini did some very wrong things?" I kneeled, eye-level with the child.

"Hmmm." His expression was flat but for the tiniest wrinkle between his brows. "She left us foundlings alone overnight. That was irresponsible."

I stifled a laugh, absolutely certain that the four-year-old had learned the big word just last night. Valkiva no doubt had used that very word to explain what was happening to the children.

"That's right," I said. I touched the hand that gripped the lock of his hair. "You remember when you made the decision to cut your hair off?"

He ducked his chin once, a barely perceptible nod. "It felt right."

I nodded. "And yet..." I lifted the hand that clutched his hair and kissed the back of it. "You're not really ready to let go, are you?"

He blinked twice very quickly but did not answer.

I stood up and waved a hand around the sitting room. The other foundlings were gathered about the fire where Flynn was standing on a chair impersonating some type of very large bird. I hoped he wasn't putting ideas of the vengersax into the children's heads so soon before bedtime. But both Rain and Neo had their arms crossed over their chests, amused smiles on their faces. Gia sat on a chair reading through notes inked in a leather-bound book she'd taken from Gini's room.

"This place has been your home for a very long time," I reminded him. "Do you remember living someplace else before here?"

He blinked twice.

"Hmm-mmm," I said, nodding. "You know that things change, Ivo. When something leaves your life, you may feel very, very sad about it. Or maybe angry. But you know that other things come into your life to replace those things that left. Wouldn't you agree?"

He didn't blink, just stared with his thin lips pressed firmly together.

"For example," I went on, "when you decided to cut your hair. Remember how beautiful it was? You had the prettiest long, dark curls. But you decided to cut them. That was a choice you made. And now, even though you may miss them sometimes, how do you feel about your hair?"

I gave a playful rub to the short bristles on his head.

"It was time," he said simply.

"Exactly," I said. "It was time to change from one thing to another. From curly hair to very short hair. Both are good, though. You lost your curls but gained a different kind of hair. The same thing happens with homes. Like the home you had before you lived here."

He blinked twice.

"And now that Gini has left this Realm…"

"She is dead," he said matter of factly. "Valkiva stabbed her, and she died."

I sucked in a breath and let it out slowly, thinking several steps ahead of what I wanted to say. "Yes, Ivo. That is what happened. But you know now that Gini is gone, we need to decide if we want to stay here."

He stared down into the fist that gripped his hair. "We cannot stay here. I don't want to stay."

I cocked my chin at him and put a hand on his shoulder. "Why? Why don't you want to stay here?"

"Scary," he said, sounding every bit the four-year-old he was.

I could understand how frightening this all must have been, and I was torn between pushing the child to talk about his fears or to focus on the news I needed him to adjust to.

"I think it's scary too," I said simply, filing away the word to ask him about later. When we had more time. "When I left the foundling home, I made some wonderful new friends. They have a beautiful home with horses and a very sweet dog. And some other surprises." I twisted my lips, excited to introduce the children to Elgit. I could not imagine how they'd respond, but I was certain it would be unforgettably cute. "Would you like to go live there? In the new house with my new friends?"

"You too?" he asked.

"Oh, of course, sweetheart. Absolutely, I will be there. My new friends and I will work together to take care of you. All of you, in fact. I'd like all the children to come."

Ivo squinted his eyes and flicked a quick glance at Flynn, who was now riding the chair backwards like it was a horse, with Tabby on his shoulders spurring him on.

"Him?" Ivo asked, wrinkling his nose like he'd just smelled something rotten.

I clapped a hand over my mouth to hold back laughter. "Well, Flynn doesn't live there now. He has a family, so he lives with them. But I'm sure he will be around a lot."

I looked up and noticed Neo was no longer watching Flynn and Tabby act like fools but was staring at me. I heated under the raw desire in his eyes. The way he licked his lips and watched me as I spoke to Ivo made my limbs loose with liquid fire.

I sucked my lower lip into my mouth and turned my attention back on the child. Ivo appeared to stare into the distance, his eyes unblinking, his lips unmoving. I let him stand there, quiet amidst the chaos of the performance. I just stood beside the child and waited. He watched everything taking place but didn't speak. Didn't even blink.

"Ivo?" I looked into his sweet little face. "It's all right to feel afraid. You can cry if you feel sad."

"You're wearing knives," he said. "Is that because it's scary here? Or scary where we're going?"

I took a breath before answering, measuring how much honesty the child could manage. "There are many scary places in this Realm, Ivo. But there are many safe places too. When you have people around you who love you, even the scariest of places can be safe. But that means sometimes being prepared. Like what happened today with Valkiva. I had the knives when something dangerous happened."

I didn't want to contemplate what might have happened if I hadn't been wearing them. If I'd never gone to the cutler's and armed myself.

"I don't want anyone else to die when we go to the new place." A single tear dripped from Ivo's dark lashes. He blinked twice. "Can I play with Fina now?"

I smiled. "Of course." He walked somberly away, his little arms and legs locked tight.

"Is the child all right?" Neo stood behind me, and I easily leaned back against his chest.

Gia and Rain sat together, Gini's books set aside, to watch the kids play with Flynn. Ivo had taken little Fina aside and was helping the baby try to balance on her chubby legs without falling over.

"He will be," I said. "Ivo is a very sensitive soul."

Neo laced his arms around my waist and rested his chin lightly against my head. "You'd almost think this entire room wasn't filled with creatures the queen believes should not exist."

"Most people like me refuse to believe you do," I murmured. "But I am so glad I know better."

He squeezed my hands, and together, the four adults put the five foundlings to bed. Flynn was so exhausted from playing, he passed out on the settee in the sitting room, snoring loudly with his mouth wide open.

"Leave him," Neo said, blowing out the candles and tossing logs on the fire so the room would stay warm.

Gia brought a blanket from Gini's room and covered Flynn with it.

"You take Gini's room," I said. "Neo and I can sleep in mine. We've slept in tinier spaces already."

While his brother and sister-in-law went to bed, Neo peered through the windows. He went outside and checked the horses, secured Flynn's cart, and walked the entire length of the property. Checking for what, I did not ask. Finally he returned, his torch illuminating the worried expression on his face.

"What is it?" I asked, his tension making my stomach turn knots. That and Ivo's solemn question about safety, about death, was making me generally feel uneasy. "Is something out there?"

He shook his head. "I don't think so. I would feel better if we slept in shifts. I don't like being here."

I nodded. I didn't either. Nothing about this place felt like home anymore. The familiar surroundings felt like ghosts, demanding wraiths determined to drag me back to another time. A time that knew it was doomed, but simply did not want to die peacefully.

"There are so many of us," I said. "Someone will hear something if anything goes wrong. Maybe it's just that Gini's dead body is..." I shuddered. It was too macabre to speak of.

I could tell he agreed. We traded nervous looks, but there was nothing to do. We were exhausted, it was late, and tomorrow, at first light, we would leave this place for good. He held his hand out to me. "I am certain we'll be all right. Let's sleep."

Neo followed me to my tiny bedroom, where we stripped off our clothes and climbed under the covers of my far too tiny bed. He wrapped his arms around me, and I wound my legs with his. My cheek against his chest, the sound of his breaths heavy against my hair, I had to ask the question on my mind.

"What will do about the bodies when we leave? Do you think there is any chance harm will come to Valkiva? Or to us for the crimes?"

"There was no crime as far as Gini is concerned. She was trying to kill you, Brex. Would there ever be an investigation, we have both adults and children who would bear witness to what happened here. But... I think I have a plan." He yawned, and I didn't think I'd ever seen him look less tortured. Unless I knew nothing about this man, he looked almost relaxed. "Sleep now, my love," he murmured against my hair.

My love.

I closed my eyes and burrowed my face against his chest. Our hair tangled together like that first night on the settee, but somehow now, falling asleep with Neo satisfied something in me I'd never known I wanted. Never had the imagination to dream of.

"Tomorrow night," I murmured, my body relaxing against his. "I'd like to sleep in a bed that was actually built to hold two."

He chuckled. "When we're in a bigger bed, Brex, I don't think either of us will get much sleep."

I lifted my face to his, and he kissed me goodnight, his lips gentle, probing. Then we touched noses, a tender goodnight that promised more. More nights like this. More tenderness. Then, the last night I would ever spend as a foundling, I drifted off into a peaceful, dreamless sleep.

THE NEXT MORNING, after the children were fed and Flynn's cart loaded with everything we could salvage from the house, we sent Flynn and Gia ahead with the children piled into the cart. Rain and Neo dug up the body of the traveling merchant and threw his rotting corpse on the dirt floor of the kitchen. Then they dragged Gini back to the kitchen as well and left her remains there.

Rain went to the front yard to clean himself up with a bucket and refill it with fresh well water for Neo to use later. We couldn't take to the road with the two of them looking like they'd buried something or been buried. Once Rain went into the yard, Neo and I stood together in the kitchen, staring at the wreckage of the last thirteen years of my life.

"Do you wish to be alone?" Neo asked, dirt and sweat streaking his cheeks.

I wasn't sure what I wanted. Wasn't sure that what we were about to do was right.

I thought of my mother. Of the day she'd left me in Gini's care. I lowered my head and closed my eyes. I had no words to say. Nothing but anger and pain for what Gini had done. Had taken from me.

"Stay with me?" I asked.

My husband stood close by while I dropped into a kitchen chair and rested my face in my hands. I thought back to the day I'd arrived. The rats Gini had tried to feed me, believing I needed blood to drink like my mother. The face of my sweet mum in my nightmares. And all the years of not being able to leave here. Of being needed and manipulated and controlled and insulted.

It had taken me years to find a way to leave this place, to strike out on my own and seek my own horizon. But I knew no matter how long I lived, I would carry Gini, her thoughts, her beliefs, with me always. If I'd thought that her death would rid my soul of the stains of her actions, I was wrong. I would carry that woman along with my mother and part of each of the children who had come through this place with me always.

I only hoped the stronger I became, the lighter the weight would be to carry. The softer the sting of memory.

I stood from the chair and took the scrap of embroidered fabric from my leg harness. I tugged the hag stone from around my neck and set both items on Gini's chest. Then I reached for a candle.

Neo cocked his chin at me, puzzled. "I thought you had an uncommon fondness for that pillow," he said, sounding genuinely concerned.

"I took those flowers to remind me of you. Of what you are. Of how happy I was with you. I don't need a reminder anymore, a shred of something small when you've offered me you. Your home. Everything. For maybe longer than the time we're bound to by contract."

I dared to hope that maybe in time my husband would grow to truly love me and I, him.

I bent to Gini's hair and touched the candle to the blood-matted strands. Then I dropped the candle on the filthy folds of her dress.

"What are you doing?" Neo asked, his arm protectively around me.

"Things never burn the way people think they will," I said. "I need to watch. I need to see her burn."

We stood together watching the flames consume the clothes and hair of Gini and the merchant. The morbid crackling of fabric and skin, the charred stench had Neo dragging me from the house far sooner than I would have left on my own. He quickly washed up in the yard, and we mounted our horses.

Rain had already taken off after his wife and Flynn's cart loaded with foundlings.

Neo prodded Sedda to canter and took off, his hood covering his head, his short sword sheathed at his side. I covered my hair with my hood and stroked Sara's neck. But before I could leave, I turned the horse around. I looked at the wildflowers, the vegetable garden, the trees, and all the plants I'd known and tended to for so much of my life.

As the fire spread from the wood and straw structure, the dry fall grasses and plants began to ignite. I watched as they too burned. The last landmarks of where I'd lived. Everything about who I'd been, what this place was would soon be gone, ashes scattered by the wind.

With a prayer on my lips for what was ahead and with gratitude in my heart, I turned Sara and rode my horse home.

FIFTEEN

Our return home was uneventful, which was a welcome reprieve from the recent turmoil. Neo and I rode side by side behind Gia and Rain, trying to ignore the sounds of Flynn's stories. He spoke with so much passion and gusto, I absolutely believed he'd missed his calling. He might have been an apprentice thief, but the boy could have made a good living in any corner of the Realm as a bard.

The late fall sun warmed my back, the light breeze carrying fresh, cold air down from the mountains in the east. If I breathed deeply, I could still scent hints of smoke clinging to the loose hair that escaped my hood and danced before my face. Soon, all traces of the foundling home would be washed from my skin. That would be a start toward healing the pains in my heart.

As we rode, Neo and I traded looks and smiles but spoke little. There would be much to do when we returned to the manor, and I was grateful for the time to be quiet. Without the charm around my neck, there was nothing tying me to my past but my memories, and the long ride through the sunshine seemed the perfect time for my thoughts to run free.

Despite the comforting rhythm of Sara's walk and light-hearted conversations around me, I could not stop the flood of memories. I saw the faces of so many children over the years as I wondered where they were now. If they'd found loving, happy lives. Or if, like me, they looked back on their own histories and saw dark and chilling tales. Guilt over the ways in which I'd perfected my skills as a thief heated my cheeks and brought my chin low, as if I could duck beneath my hood and hide from myself.

Gini hadn't just taught me well; she'd relied on me. Any family seeking to adopt a foundling would undergo an interview in their home. While Gini played the part of the concerned guardian, I would be sent with the child to explore the place they might—if the adoption was approved—call their new home. As I explored, I had one mission: searching hearths, pouches, under beds, in drawers.

Gini was certain that if the family did ever notice a valuable item had gone missing, they would never think to blame the innocent girl who'd held the hand of their future adopted child. The house sister tasked with making the process of leaving the foundling home for a new life easier. Gini could have used her illusions to ensure we were never caught, but that became messy and complicated to maintain. She preferred to use her magic only as a last resort, so the burden of becoming a capable thief fell entirely to me.

I was instructed to take as much as I could find. Nothing that held sentimental value, of course, as those items would be missed almost immediately. Jewelry and easily identifiable items were less attractive to Gini, who would have had a hard time explaining how she'd come by the merchandise when she tried to sell them in the village. That meant quickly observing and deciding what to steal, as well as what to leave.

In the early years, I'd felt sick with guilt over things I'd taken. Eating blades, cutlery, loose hair pins... Anything small enough to be carried away in my sleeve or a pouch beneath my cloak.

For a short time in my late teens, I became more daring. Willing to risk being caught if only to spite Gini. I'd pick up an item and ask a question about it. Admire its beauty or condition. That way, later, when that item was discovered to be missing, the family would remember my interest and maybe, just maybe, come to the foundling home to investigate or accuse. But the beatings I'd received once Gini and I returned home quickly cured me of the thrill of rebellion.

I eventually soothed my aching conscience by taking only those items that I was certain would never be missed. I took more from those who could spare it—the wealthier parents who would likely blame a single missing spoon on the carelessness of a butler rather than the sticky fingers of a houseguest.

There were times a family had simply nothing of value but food. In those cases, I risked the most severe penalties from Gini. If she'd decided I could have taken an entire loaf of bread but I'd left it behind for a family who clearly had stretched their means to provide some hospitality to us, I would be denied food for a day. Never so long as to be noticed by the other children, but long enough that I would suffer for my lack of compliance.

Misery bent my shoulders and lowered my chin as I thought about all the crimes I had committed over the years. And now, I was married to a thief, although I had very little idea whether Neo actually stole anything. As far as I was concerned, brokering deals with goblins and raiding for treasure sunk deep in the sandy shores of Tutovl was far from criminal activity.

I felt Neo's gaze on me, heavy and curious, but I put a smile on my face and refused to reveal the depths of my shame. I wondered if there was a way to heal me of the evils I'd committed, or if guilt would bend my back for the rest of my life. The thoughts echoed in time with the hoofbeats of the horses until finally, we reached the road that would lead us home.

By the time we arrived at the manor, the children were too excited to stay seated. Tabby and Kiva stood as Flynn directed the cart toward the front gate, which was being ably repaired by Syndrian.

Neo leapt down from his horse and clapped the man on the shoulder. "This is most unexpected," he said. "You're a versatile craftsman, Syndrian."

The big man grunted and hooked a thumb over his shoulder. His light hair was tied back to expose the shaved sides of his head, several lengths of leather binding the long hair in segments behind his back like a horse's tail. "I hadn't planned to fix this," he admitted, "but my mother sent me looking for Flynn when he didn't return home last night."

Neo shook his head, an apologetic frown on his face. "I'm sorry to have worried your mother. Flynn is an indispensable help to us."

"Right glad to hear that." Syndrian took note of the five foundlings, two of whom were climbing on Flynn's lap, and twisted his lips into a smirk. "I noticed you had some damage here, and with the visitor inside and none but the butler at home, I figured I'd stay." He cocked his chin at Neo. "To be fair, the man says he's a friend, but I don't have a good feeling about him."

At the news that there was a visitor, the entire party seemed to tense.

"Syn, none but the butler is at home? Do you happen know where my sister is?" Gia asked.

He nodded. "Ms. Antonia said Molle Noll called her to assist a troublesome birth."

"The midwife," Gia said, nodding. She threw a nervous look at Rain and handed him the reins to her horse. "I'll summon

Dale to help with the horses and find out what's going on inside."

Neo was steps ahead of her, already striding through the front door of the manor.

"Thank you for your trouble, Syndrian." Rain clapped the man on the shoulder. "Please, stay and let us pay you for the work."

Syndrian waved a hand dismissing the offer. He gave his brother a look, while I fought a rising panic. I called to Kiva and handed her the reins to both Sara and Sedda. "Hold these until I'm back, okay?" I asked. "I'll be just a moment."

"My brother and I will take care of all this." Syndrian's eyes were wide as baby Fina started cooing and reaching to be picked up from the cart.

"Thank you," I said, wishing I could tell him what fine instruments his throwing knives were. But that conversation, if we ever had it, would have to wait.

I rushed up the stone stairs, passing Dale on his way out.

"Welcome back, milady!"

I had so many questions, but Dale's chipper demeanor settled the tension in my shoulders to a tolerable tightness. "Is everything all right inside?" I asked.

He gave me a lopsided grin. "Couldn't be better. See for yourself! Your patient is at rest, and Neo's got a visit from an old friend." He narrowed his eyes at the children climbing over Flynn's lap and the toddler Syndrian was holding like the girl was a mess of quivering shapeless goo that he didn't know quite how to keep still. "I see we have a lot of catching up to do. I'll attend to the horses."

I went inside, a slightly slower pace driving my feet forward. *It can't be Haeloc*, I assured myself. Would the deranged vampire show his face here and expect to survive Neo's wrath?

As I walked into the main hall, Neo was talking excitedly

with a man I recognized. The un-pretty friend he'd shared dinner with back in Fish Head End.

"Oy!" The man stomped his foot. "You promised me more than just a job. I'll take a bit of healing from that sister-in-law of yours, don't forget."

The fear that there was another danger in the house gave way to a more complicated feeling: jealousy.

"The job is no longer available. Isn't that right?" I interrupted, narrowing my eyes at Neo.

My husband seemed inexplicably delighted to see his friend. His eyes sparkled, and his plush, scarred lips stretched in an amiable grin. "Brexia," he called. "You remember Trond."

A shadow crossed the man's face as he cocked his head at me. "Can't say I remember this one," he said, looking me from head to toe. "And I think I'd remember a pretty face like that."

My mouth tasted sour at the implication in his voice and his unblinking stare.

"I'd prefer you not look at me like I'm food on your table." I walked up to the man and flared my nostrils. "While that tone in your voice might persuade barmaids to go home with you, most decent women would be insulted. Since you're a guest here, I'll take no offense and simply remind you to sort your manners for as long as you intend to stay here."

The scraggly mess of moustache on his face drooped as his mouth dropped open. I tried not to flinch at the stench of his breath while I looked at my husband with annoyance.

"Would you care to introduce me to your guest?" I asked.

Neo looked completely lost, torn between not fully understanding why I wanted to verbally eviscerate this man and why his friend seemed to immediately despise me. He for once was speechless but recovered quickly.

"Trond, this is Brexia Eloise, Lady Oderisi. My wife." His words were wooden and felt stiff, lacking any of the warmth they'd had before. I never wanted to hear him say wife that way again, as if he were almost embarrassed to say it.

Trond's eyebrows quivered, and he burst out laughing. "Wait... Is this a prank, Neo?" He looked from my husband to me and then back. "I know this girl from someplace..." He scratched his head, his florid, hairy cheeks puffing out as he breathed. "Aren't you that... That rogue! The little thief from the pub the other night!"

Neo clamped a hand on Trond's shoulder, no doubt seeing the color in my face rise murderously. I raised my chin, but before I could open my mouth, Neo seemed to find his voice.

"This is no joke," he said seriously. "Please give my wife the courtesy she deserves. She is lady of this manor now." He looked at me with a slightly tortured apology in his honey-gold eyes.

Trond slapped his knee and then held a hand out to me. "Well, Lady Oderisi it is, then. Pleasure to meet you."

I would have preferred to avoid the disgusting man's hand, but I shook it firmly, squeezing harder than necessary to let him know I was no weakling. He squeezed very hard in kind.

Antonia came from the kitchen with a cart of snacks and tea. "Oh! You're back!" She clasped my hands in greeting. "I'd love to hear all about your time away, but I wonder if you could help me upstairs. You recall Odile's patient. The one who was so sick that we gave him shelter here?"

I nodded, squeezing her hands. "Has the patient been moved?" I asked, concerned how they'd managed to hide the goblin from Neo's visitor. I refused to call that man friend.

"Aye, we moved him, thanks in no small part to Syndrian. When Odile was called away to assist the midwife, he moved the patient upstairs to the bedroom. Figured it would be easier for Dale and me to manage his care closer to Odile's tonics anyway. Would you care to check him?"

I lifted my chin and, without a word to Trond, headed upstairs. Antonia followed behind and slipped a key from the front of her apron.

"We had to move him," she said, her eyes wide. "That Trond character came calling for Neo this morning. Thank the gods Flynn's brother came calling even earlier. I sent Trond to the stable with Dale to sort out his horse while Syndrian moved our dear friend." She smoothed her fine white hair away from her forehead. "That Trond has been asking a lot of questions. What happened to the front gate, where Neo is, where Rain and Gia went off to." She unlocked Odile's door with a trembling hand. "I don't care for that man," she said.

"Neither do I," I said, suddenly incredibly disappointed in my husband's choices. "How are he and Neo acquainted?"

Odile's room was dimly lit. Some kind of fabric covered the window glass to the keep the place bathed in shadows. Whether that was Odile's design or Antonia's, I was relieved for it. From the doorway, Elgit looked like little more than a bundle of blankets on a settee. I approached the lump while Antonia explained. "He's a raider friend. He and Neo have known each other for years. Went on a few adventures together before Neo's turn of fortune with Rekker Haeloc."

Once I saw the goblin, all my disgust at Neo's friend Trond disappeared like smoke in the wind. The tiny man's eyes half-fluttered open as I took hold of his hand. "Hello, my friend," I whispered, my heart nearly bursting with that promising sign of life. "You're still with us."

He didn't respond to my words, but I was certain his fingers tightened weakly in mine.

"I'll be fine up here with him," I said. "We have more guests than just Trond, I'm afraid."

I told Antonia about moving the children from the foundling home, and just as I was apologizing for the additional work and cost, the butler dropped down onto a chair and took a rag from her apron. She mopped her brow as tears fell from her eyes.

"The gods have blessed us," she said, her voice shaking. "Dale and I were never able... We have no family of our own. So many times I've prayed and wondered why. Why not us? Would we not have made fine parents?" She stared off into the distance, lost to her private pain. "I've been dedicated to Neo and Rain since they were young, and I love those boys as if they were my own. But they had a mother and a father, and later a stepmother who loved them dearly. But these foundlings... Will they stay?" she asked, the raw hope in her voice bringing a tear to my eye. "Will you raise the little ones here, under our roof?"

I nodded. "I believe so, but Neo and I haven't discussed the specifics yet. Antonia, I know this will mean so much more work for all of us. Disruption of your routine, more cleaning, more food..."

She leapt from her chair and grabbed my hands, holding them to her lips. "You brought this, this...blessing," she said quietly. "There is no need to apologize to me. Don't you think again about it. A house full of little ones? You've been sent by the gods to heal us. I've never been more certain of anything." She cried quietly a moment, while, speechless, I let her. Then she released my hand and wiped her face. "Now that that's finished, I have five hungry mouths to feed. And I could not be happier to take on the task."

I bit my lower lip before breaking the news to her. "Flynn and Syndrian are still here," I said. "That means even more mouths."

She clasped her hands in front of her chest and bustled toward the door. "I'd best get every morsel I can find ready for lunch." She stopped and turned back to me. "Lady Oderisi, I'm so very happy you're home," she said. Then she dashed off for the kitchen.

Alone in Odile's room with Elgit, I breathed deeply the air scented lightly with the tonics and ointments, dried herbs and fresh plants that Odile kept in a workspace at the far side of her bedroom. The scents were comforting, and I wondered about the love tonic she'd anointed me with on my wedding night. Maybe she had a tonic that could help me forgive myself. Love myself a bit more. I poured a cup of fresh water and was looking for the special sipping spoon Odile had left for Elgit when there was a soft knock on the door.

Gia peeked inside. "May I?" she asked.

I waved her in. She looked over the small patient and nodded. "He looks as though he's improved."

"Your sister is indeed a gifted healer," I agreed. "Am I a fool to still hold out hope he will survive?"

"You're far from a fool," she said, "unlike that Trond." She rolled her eyes. "Harmless, but tiresome." She motioned toward the door with her head. "Are you all right with this?" she asked. "With everything that's happened? I know we're hardly sisters yet, but I feel as though we already have been through so very much together. You can talk to me, if you need a friend."

I smiled. "I would still like those sewing lessons," I reminded her. "With five more in the house, I expect I'll be making a lot of clothes."

She laughed but covered her mouth to soften the sound. "What a difference a few days makes."

I sighed. "I can only imagine. You must feel as though I've come in and completely upended your life."

"Yes, but I mean that in the best possible sense," she assured me. "I admit I'm concerned about having a house full of foundlings with the work Rain and I do, but...the change in the rest of us..." She looked down at Elgit and smoothed a hand over the end of the blanket, tucking his feet in a bit more snugly. "My sister and I have known so much loss, so much pain. We dealt with it in different ways. Odile hid away in our cottage, afraid to leave. She cared for patients but lived only to serve, to work. It helps that she loves what she does, but she's far past the age when she should have started her own family."

"Does she have a heart for foundlings?" I asked, a half smile on my lips. "Because we have family in abundance at the moment."

Gia shook her head, muffling another laugh. "You're not like my sister and me," she said. "I admire you for that."

"Admire me?" I asked. "I cannot see how you'd feel that way, though I'm sincerely flattered by your opinion."

"You're a fighter. And despite everything you've been through, you have a capacity for compassion that rivals any I've seen. I'm not the only one who feels that way," she said with a grin. "Neo is completely smitten with you. It doesn't hurt that you're beautiful, but you're also just simply good for him. I dared not hope for as much when I witnessed your marriage contract, but I do believe he's falling in love with you."

After just a few days, that seemed impossible. Or would have seemed impossible if I wasn't curious about the same type of stirrings deep within my own heart. And what those feelings might mean for my relationship with my husband.

"I like him," I admitted. "*Like*. But he can be a real pain in the—"

"Excuse me." A soft knock at the door had Gia and me laughing behind our hands. "Am I interrupting?"

"Not at all, brother." Gia winked at me and gave Elgit's foot a loving pat before she got up. "I'll leave you now."

"You might want to help Flynn," Neo said, a concerned look on his face. "He has children climbing all over him. He's now more tree than boy."

Gia nodded and closed the door behind her, leaving Neo and me alone. He walked up to the settee and peered down at Elgit.

"How is he?" he asked, his deep whisper sending sensual heat sliding down my spine.

"He seems better," I said. "He squeezed my hand just a bit when I held his fingers."

"Good. Very good." Neo avoided my eyes as he spoke. "Brexia, about Trond..."

I huffed a sigh. "Will he be staying long?" I asked, trying to manage a bit of polite interest in my husband's unsavory "friend."

"No," he said, "he won't be staying. I'm taking him to Haeloc's manor."

My head snapped up so quickly my teeth banged together. "What do you mean, Haeloc's manor?"

Neo lifted his chin but still refused to look at me. "He'll be staying there. He's come for the job, Brex. He's accepted the offer I made in Fish Head End."

I flew to my feet and grabbed Neo's sleeve, tugging him away from Elgit. "You can't be serious," I said. "We've five new mouths to feed under this roof, and you're going to hire an outsider for a job you know perfectly well I wish to do?"

Neo's jaw set and his yellow-gold eyes narrowed. "We've discussed this."

"We have not discussed anything!" I spat, keeping my voice a harsh whisper so as not to disturb Elgit's rest. "You've told me you wouldn't hire me, but you've never once given me the chance to discuss it with you. And now, you'd give the work to someone else? To that...snake?"

Neo's face hardened. "Please," he said sarcastically. "Snake? The man is an old friend, Brex. Rough around the edges, but he's the sort who will do exactly what needs to be done." He leaned down and stared into my face, his eyes softening. "Tell me you'd kill Haeloc if it came to that. By the gods, Brex, why would you wish to put yourself in that kind of danger? After everything you've been through, why seek out more death? More injury to your troubled soul?"

I stepped away from him, every bit of affection Neo had earned burying itself deep. "Do not use my vulnerabilities and honesty against me. Because I failed to do what needed to be done with Gini, you question that I would protect you? Would protect anyone I loved against any threat?"

Neo tried to reach for me, but I stepped farther away. His touch would melt my resistance. The spark of something true I felt for him burned inside me, wanting his comfort. Seeking his love. And yet, my mind and heart were hard. "Is this because I am common? Because my only weapons are pretty tools and not magic or terrifying red eyes and fangs?"

"You wield far more power than you give yourself credit for," he said cryptically. "I wish you would consider things from my view."

"What I wish is that my husband would talk to me before squandering our already stretched resources on a man who is not part of this household." I tried to soften my approach. "I don't like him, Neo. He...he..."

Neo turned his back to me, his hands clenched in fists this sides. "I've known Trond for quite a bit a longer than the mere days you've been my wife. I offered him the job back in Fish Head End, and he has accepted. I will not go back on my word."

"And yet you'd disappoint your wife? Endanger the good of the family you've invited into your life?"

Neo's back stiffened, his black hair loose over his shoulders. "I'm sorry to hurt you," he said. "The decision is made."

I crossed my arms over my chest. "Go, then. I will not stop

you. And may Trond be the true friend you seem to believe he is."

Neo slammed the door a little more roughly than was necessary. I could not shake the disappointment from my heart. I couldn't believe that he would offer the job of guarding Haeloc's manor to a man like Trond. Perhaps before we were married, but now?

I paced the room, trying to make sense of my wild emotions. I hadn't had the stomach to kill Gini, even though I had every reason under the sun to do so. If Haeloc returned, I was absolutely certain I would protect myself from him. Kill him to protect my husband without a moment's hesitation. But if it were true that Haeloc dabbled in magic, Neo's concern about me facing him, especially alone, would be well-placed. As much as it hurt to admit, I was only a common woman with a harness full of throwing knives and a heart full of angry vitality.

But my instincts were what I had relied on through nearly every decision I'd made—and they had never let me down. I trusted the wild idea that Neo should marry me to protect his secrets, as well as mine. I believed that Gia and Odile were good women, capable of adding me to their blood-made sisterhood. I trusted Flynn and Syndrian and all of the people under this roof, even when I had no reason to believe that their goodness would last. That their kindness was real.

I believed that a tortured vampire, his history marred across his face and back, could be the man I would grow to love. To let into my mind, heart, and body, not out of desperation. Not manipulated by illusion. Because I'd chosen him. Just like he'd chosen me.

I may have hesitated with Gini, but my instincts here were clear. Trond was not to be trusted. I was certain of it. And I would prove it to my husband.

SIXTEEN

I ran to the stable in search of Rain, but he was nowhere to be found. The foundlings were running through the open grass behind the stable, with Flynn somehow playing on two different teams, one made up of Kiva and Ivo, with Tabby and Remy on the other. Baby Fina crawled through the grass with Odile's dog, Joi, keeping watch as only an elderly dog could.

Rain's and Gia's horses were gone, and without either one of them, I'd have no way to find Haeloc's manor. I groaned and punched my fists against the stable wall as Syndrian came in to ready his horse.

He lifted a dark brow at me. "Everything all right?"

I shook my head. "No. I do not know. Yes, in fact I'm certain everything is not all right."

Syndrian tilted his head toward the road, his long ponytail swatting his enormous shoulders as he moved. "This have anything to do with Neo and that trencherman?"

"Trencherman?" I echoed, unfamiliar with the term.

Syndrian wiped the sweat from his brow with the back of one hand, a look of contempt on his face. "A man who goes where the food is and eats his fill." He shook his head. "Seems like the type. Values nothing so much as he does a free meal."

A free meal...

"Syndrian," I said worriedly, my heart throbbing in my chest. "Do you know the way to Rekker Haeloc's manor?"

"Haeloc?" The cutler's dark brows drew together in a defensive scowl. "Let's just say I've run across the man from time to time."

"Can you take me there?" I begged. "Now? I am certain Neo's friend Trond is..." I suddenly was not certain. But I knew that the life of my husband might depend on me trusting my instincts and acting on them. "I fear Trond is to blame for everything. The massacre at the sanctum... He made the introduction to Haeloc that started this trouble for Neo in the first place. I don't understand how, but I have a strong feeling."

Suddenly, Syndrian's countenance changed. His dark brows lowered, and he stabbed the air with a powerful finger. "Arm yourself," he suggested. "With everything you've got. That one dabbles in magic, Brex."

"Haeloc?" I asked.

"Aye." Syndrian slung a long, thick leg over the back of his horse and adjusted a menacing-looking mace in the scabbard at his waist. "Ready?"

"Give me a moment," I said. "There's something I need to bring."

I ran back inside and raced upstairs, praying that Neo had left the goblin dagger someplace I could find it. I did not have to look far. He'd left it on top of a small table beside the bed. I checked the fittings on my throwing knives and held the goblin dagger in my hands. I needed a way to carry it. I searched the room for the scabbard that Neo had used for it and, finding it, spent a moment fumbling with the pommel and tilting the blade back and forth in my hand. The long yellowing fangs slipped from the hidden compartment into my hand. The tips were pointy but surprisingly dull, perhaps from so much handling. But the opposite end, the side that retracted from the jaw itself was irregularly shaped and chipped, as if someone had tried very hard to make sure Haeloc suffered every second those things were being torn from his mouth.

With the scabbard and dagger secure under my cloak and my throwing knives tight around my leg, I tucked the teeth into my tunic. I wasn't sure why I felt so strongly about this, but I believed that if the fangs inside that dagger were important, separating the fangs from the dagger was doubly so. Once they were secure between my underclothes and my skin, tucked close to my heart, I ran back to the grassy field, shouting for Flynn.

He dragged himself toward me, panting and drenched in sweat. "Did you want to play, Lady O?" he asked. "The kids are..."

"Not now, Flynn, and please—" I wrinkled my nose "—don't call me Lady O. I need to leave the manor with Syndrian, and I'm not sure where Rain and Gia are. Can you take the children inside and keep them safe? Let Antonia and Dale know we left and our patient is upstairs alone."

"Will do," Flynn said, giving his brother a saucy wave.

"And Flynn," I said, gripping the boy by the shoulder. "Secure the house. Let no one in or out who isn't family. If we're not back by nightfall, send word to the shire-reeve."

"Lady Brex..." The boy swallowed hard, the knob in his throat bobbing up and down. "Is everything all right?"

"It will be," I said. "Keep the children safe. Promise me."

He nodded, and Syndrian and I took off.

~

I EXPLAINED to Syndrian what I knew as we approached the property that must have at one time been a fine manor. But there was nothing fine about the scene before us now. The low, rolling hills that surrounded Haeloc's manor looked dead. As if years had passed without a bit of rain, the tall grasses were stiff and brown, hollowed-out tinder just waiting for a stray ember to burn. I shivered as I thought about the property around the foundling house. It must have looked like this now. All the healthy, green plants met their deaths because of the evil contained in that home, but here... It looked as if evil had marked every tree, every shrub, every blade of grass unlucky enough to grow within the Haeloc estate.

Syndrian slung a leg over his horse and sniffed the air. "This place has been touched by dark magic," he said, stepping heavily on the dusty earth. "I can smell it."

He tied his horse to a leafless tree, its brittle branches like dead vines sagging toward the barren soil below. He motioned for me to do the same.

"Let's go on foot from here," he said, his voice low. "Don't wanna give 'em any cause to expect us."

We crept along the scorched path that led to a crumbling wall. Syndrian peered over the scattered boulders and stones, dry straw and mud clinging to the fallen rocks. He climbed over the lowest point in the wall and jumped behind it, his shoulders and bright-white hair visible above the highest pile of intact stones.

He extended a hand over the wall. "Climb on the loose rocks," he urged. "They're steady."

I stepped onto a boulder as big as my head and grabbed Syndrian's hand. With his help, I too jumped over the wall and landed roughly on the ground on the other side. He crouched low, scanning the property for movement. He pointed to me with a finger and then nodded at the door.

The door of the manor wasn't ajar, as if carelessly left open by the last one to pass through it. The center of the ornately carved wood had splintered all the way through the middle, sharp shards breaking through the exterior as if something had burst through the door from inside. As we crept closer, familiar voices echoed from the hallway.

"I did this for you, Neo. *Because* we're friends." The sound of Trond's greasy voice made my skin pebble like plucked gooseflesh.

Syndrian and I listened a moment, unable to hear anything but the faint, deep rumbling of Neo's response. I couldn't make out his words and tiptoed closer, desperate for a glimpse of what was happening.

"Oy! We have company, love." A third voice had me squinting with the tug of memory. I'd heard her voice before but couldn't remember where or who she was. "Ya might as well come on in, girlie. We ain't gonna bite." A hideous laugh grated my ears. "Although Haeloc would, if he had the teeth fer it."

Haeloc.

As soon as I heard that name, my feet took control of my body. I sprinted past the broken door, roughly shoving my shoulder into the fractured wood. Syndrian followed, his heavy footfalls thundering through the quiet.

The manor itself looked far less wrecked than the land outside but still reeked of death and decay. The stale air was rank like fetid breath and spoiled lard. Dust motes big as horseflies fluttered through weak shafts of light coming through the broken panels. No lamps or candles burned, and the chill in the air made the place feel still and empty as a tomb.

"Is this everyone, Lady Oderisi?" Trond said my name like it was distasteful in his mouth. He punctuated the greeting by spitting a wet mass from his sloppy lips onto the floor. "Come in, then. We're just doin' a little business here."

"Brex... Stay back. Do not come closer." Neo's voice was painfully tight, like threads pulled taut just before they snapped.

Syndrian stood beside me, his steady presence silently agreeing with Neo's warning. Next to Trond was the woman whose voice I hadn't been able to place.

"So we meet again, you little thief! What a treat." It was the woman from the pub. The server I'd conned. She leaned over to Trond and planted a noisy kiss on his cheek. "This one meets a lord, and two days later he makes an honest lady of 'er. How come you ain't married me yet?"

Trond grunted and turned his mouth to kiss hers. "If we make enough money on this deal, Corabel, I'll do whatever you'd like me to."

I looked away from the hideous display, my stomach roiling in my belly. Neo stood close to a small, wretched-looking man, his back bent and his grizzled face filthy and wrinkled with age. *Haeloc.* I tilted my head, trying to puzzle through why Neo was beside Haeloc, almost as if he was allied with him, but Trond started barking orders.

"Hey!" He pointed at Syndrian. "Ya giant! Why don't ya put that mace on the ground. We're all friends here. Just a bit o'pleasant negotiation."

Haeloc snorted, long panels of oily hair hanging in his face as he trembled.

"Don't mind Haeloc," Trond said. "He's what's bein' negotiated. Now, you. Put that mace on the floor."

Syndrian held the weapon in one hand, casually resting it over one shoulder. "I'm not going to do that, stranger." His voice was cold as ice, but the words stalled on his lips as a powerful blast of air flew from the pub woman's hands and knocked the mace to the floor. Just inches away, I recognized Neo's sword. She'd no doubt blown it from his hands to disarm him long before we arrived. While Syndrian staggered back, gripping his shoulder, a stream of curses passing through a grimace of pain, I looked at my husband's empty hands. Both he and Syndrian were completely without weapons.

Corabel cackled and looped an arm over Trond's shoulder. My stomach twisted again. She was a mage. I started quickly thinking through all my defenses. Now that Syndrian was unarmed, all I had were the knives under my cloak and the goblin dagger. I tried to assess what her abilities were as quickly as my mind could process, but I needed more information. Could she manipulate objects and people? I hated to assume, but based on her appearance and manner, she had to be a low-level mage, likely a sorcerer. Born with one limited ability, and in the absence of dedicated study, she'd have nothing more than one trick up her sleeve. Not all that different from Gini.

"Leave them out of this," Neo gritted, his eyes flaring red. "This is between you and me, Trond."

"You and me and Haeloc," he corrected. "All I want is the goblin, Neo. And this mess is all yours."

I glared at Haeloc, curious why he wasn't fighting for himself.

Neo shook his head, long and slow, and it hit me that he was still processing that his old friend was not the man he'd believed him to be. "Allow me to explain to my wife what she's missed." He flicked me a quick look, but I had no idea what he meant by it. Was he apologetic? Angry? "It appears my friend Trond saw an opportunity a bit bigger than the job I offered him."

Trond wagged a finger in the air and walked a little closer to me. Neo lurched forward, but Corabel moved fast and darted forward to get between Neo and her man. "Do that again, ya filthy vamp, and I'll blast your pretty head off."

That told me all I needed to know. Corabel had one trick.

Trond's cracked boots creaked as he paced the dusty floors. "You see, girlie, I'm the one who introduced these two, way back in the day. Neo was running short on coin, and Haeloc needed a patsy. Some pretty noble who'd never worked a day in his life but had a thirst for adventure. For the sea." Trond belly-laughed, thick droplets of spittle flying from his yellowish tongue. He held up one finger from his right hand and looked at it. "One desperate vampire..." He held up the other index finger. "A second, equally desperate vamp." He looked altogether too proud of himself as he linked his fingers together. "Even I didn't have to work too hard to figure out a deal was mine for the taking."

"Trond was behind the sunken cog," Neo said.

"Just insurance." Trond waved a hand. "What Haeloc needed was money, and not just a purse of it. He needed an income. Keeping you in his debt should have provided a steady flow of riches. But this one didn't have patience." He paced up to Haeloc, stood behind him, and grabbed hold of the back of Haeloc's filthy hair. "Godforsaken fool." He spat the insult right into the vampire's ear.

He roughly shoved Haeloc, sending the raider stumbling toward Neo. "So he ran through the Realm trying to find the cheapest mage he could find."

"I thought that was me!" Corabel cackled, her cleavage heaving as she screamed with laughter at her own joke.

"Haeloc tried to use magic to outrun his debt," Neo explained. "But that brought him a whole different kind of attention."

"Who's he indebted to?" Syndrian asked, his face suddenly devoid of color.

Trond pointed a dramatic finger at Syndrian and jabbed it in the air. "You sound like you know a thing or two about the business. Criminal enterprises are as common in this Realm as..." He looked at Neo. "Useless landowners."

My mind whirled as I fit the pieces together. Haeloc was in debt to a crime family, and Trond was what, then... A low-level thug? An enforcer?

"Haeloc's problem isn't the attention. It's that he has no vision." Trond glared at the wrecked man, whose wasted limbs flinched at the scrutiny. "He screwed up with you, Neo. He should have done what I said. Beat you senseless to send a message and then let you go back to raiding until all the debt was paid off."

"You wanted Neo in debt to you?" I trembled with hatred as I looked at the filthy mongrel. "I thought you'd hired Neo to help him."

Haeloc's murderous gaze turned on me, but he said nothing.

"Haeloc had no intention of helping me," Neo said stiffly. "By sinking the cog, Haeloc planned to force my brother and me into servitude. Make us take on the risk to bring in the treasure he needed to pay off his debts."

"And if the godforsaken vamp had followed the plan, this all would have been easy. You'd still think we were friends. I'd still be collecting my percent of Haeloc's debt payments. But instead of a steady income made on your very capable back, Neo, Haeloc got greedy. He wanted to suck every last penny out of the Oderisi assets to pay off my bosses as quickly as possible. By consulting with goblins on enchanted items that he could use or sell or gods only know what to try and hide if his plan didn't work. But we all know how that turned out."

"You?" Neo's fangs broke from between his lips and his eyes

glowed a vile, sickly red. "You killed them? You're responsible for the massacre in Vlareq's sanctum?"

That explained so much. The force of Corabel's blast would have been enough to break a half dozen goblin bodies, while Trond followed behind and cut them up.

"This fool," Trond spat, "brought the spies of the queen upon my employer!" He shook his head, his overgrown orange-gray eyebrows lifted. "We can't have that. When Haeloc didn't show to drop off his scheduled payment, we followed him right down that cute hidden shaft in the ground. Not so hidden when an idiot like this leads you right to it. All I did was make sure those greedy magic workers couldn't take the money that belonged to my employer!" Trond was screaming now, his voice hoarse and his cheeks flushed an angry red.

"So, Haeloc missed a debt repayment and you killed an entire group of goblins just to prevent him from using money that he should have given you to buy some goblin craft."

"Pretty an' smart, that one." Corabel looked at Neo with a seductive snarl that made me want to tear the lips from her face.

Trond tapped his temple and nodded. "Not too smart, though. That's why I always liked you, Neo. Too bad this one had to come between what could have continued to be a very profitable friendship." He jerked a thumb at Haeloc, who coughed, a rattling, sickly sound.

"But there's a chance for both of us to recover a bit o'profit here, eh? Thanks to you, I found the last remaining goblin. A survivor who I trust will have no memory of what happened in the sanctum. But just in case he does... I'd like to make a trade."

I could tell what was coming. If Trond released Haeloc to Neo, he knew—had to be certain—that Neo would kill Haeloc. That was, after all, exactly what Trond had been hired by Neo to do. But if Neo gave the goblin up to Trond... Neo would have his nemesis and he'd have his revenge. But another innocent goblin would die just to cover up what Trond and Corabel had done.

"Do you really think Tarqeq will believe Haeloc murdered his cousin and nearly two dozen of his kind? By himself?" Neo pointed to the withered vamp beside him. "And even if Haeloc is dead, do you think the goblins won't come seeking revenge?"

"Revenge against who?" Trond demanded, a menacing sneer on his face as he twisted the ends of his moustache between sooty fingers. "The only ones who know what really happened are in this room. If we all go back to being friends, I'll trust that you, your pretty new wife, and all the rest of your family—including all those little ones I saw back at your manor —want to avoid the same kind of fate that poor Vlareq suffered." He raised his brows and drew a finger across his thick, pimpled neck.

I closed my eyes and pictured the faces of the children, of Gia and Odile, Antonia and Dale. Gini's abuse would look like a mild summer rainstorm compared to what Trond and Corabel could to do our household. I prayed that Neo wouldn't—no, he couldn't—sacrifice Haeloc for Elgit. If these two killed Elgit, forevermore Neo would look over his shoulder. Forevermore, none under the Oderisi household would be safe.

If Neo wasn't able to see what he had to do, I'd not let the moment pass. If Haeloc and Trond both didn't die today, and Corabel too, we'd never be able to sleep behind an unlocked door again. I would not let someone else take action in my stead again. I'd come here with a vague idea of what that goblin dagger might do. I only had to choose the right moment to act.

"Eh, Neo? What'll it be? You give me the little one, and you can have Haeloc. And you can do whatever it is you want with him. As long as you kill him. In front of me. I'll need to report back to my employer that they aren't the only ones Haeloc's cheated." Trond paced the dusty hall, never wandering too far from Corabel's side. I imaged her power only lasted a certain distance, and if he walked too far away from her, he was as good as exposed.

"And if I refuse to sacrifice the goblin?" Neo barked. "What then, *friend*?"

Trond shook his head. "See, poppet?" He tenderly stroked Corabel's chin. "This is why I can't go anywhere without you. If you'd been with me at Neo's manor, we could have taken care of the goblin and had Haeloc. Had our cake and eaten our fill."

She shrugged, pouting her fat, wet lips. "Someone had to stay here with this one. He's weak, but he's not dead yet."

Now I was certain that the only magic Corabel had was controlling air, wind blasts, nothing more than that. If she'd stayed here to guard Haeloc while Trond came to the Oderisi manor to lure Neo here... I wondered why she hadn't just tied Haeloc up and left him here alone, but then I realized Trond had never told Neo that he and Corabel were together. And the mage probably wasn't entirely sure what, if anything, Haeloc had obtained from the goblins. She wasn't so powerful that she wouldn't have a healthy fear of stronger magic. Who knew what Haeloc had threatened her with? And I guessed that killing Haeloc before his debt was paid would bring Corabel and Trond some trouble with their employer. Which meant the only one who could kill Haeloc was someone who didn't know or didn't fear the greater consequences.

Suddenly, the impossibility of the situation became much, much simpler.

We had to kill Corabel and Trond first. I just had to be smart about it. And that meant not doing it myself.

"If you refuse the deal, I'll kill Haeloc myself right now," Trond said, sounding murderously excited to do just that. "And I'll make sure my employer sends word to Tarqeq that a certain vampire lord murdered his cousin, and as you said, all his kin.

Kept the sole survivor as a hostage. Who would you rather have angry at you, Neo? The goblin lord of Tutovl, or the people who pay me to do what I am so very good at doing?"

Neo's shoulders were tight, and his nostrils flared. I knew he was about to make a decision and do something that would change the future of everyone we knew. Everyone I cared about. I couldn't let him make the same mistake I'd made before. I was certain I knew how the dagger worked, was certain I understood the enchantment Haeloc had sought from the goblins. The mistake Trond and his mage had made was not finding whatever it was Haeloc was there to buy. I slipped my hand beneath my cloak and released the dagger from the scabbard.

"This is your fault!" I screamed and ran for Haeloc, throwing myself on top of him. I knocked him onto his back and plunged the dagger with all my strength into his shoulder. He screamed and kicked his legs in pain, but as I hovered my face over his, I nodded slightly at the intricate hilt of the goblin dagger. His vile, bloodshot eyes flicked to the dagger, and he seemed to understand it was his. His head lolled to one side, his mouth open, his legs and arms splayed motionless. Not dead—he couldn't be from the well-placed stab wound—but he played the part well. The hilt of the dagger stuck ominously from the flesh between his shoulder and his chest.

In a split second, a blast of air threw me from Haeloc's body. "You fool!" Corabel shrieked, knocking me halfway across the hall.

I rolled as best I could, my shoulder and elbow taking the force of my fall. I groaned and scrambled to my feet, watching as Corabel rushed to stand over Haeloc's motionless body.

"You killed him, you…" But Corabel's shrieks bubbled in her throat as Haeloc's claw-like hand flew up from the ground, hooked behind her neck, and pulled her close. His other hand yanked the dagger from his own shoulder, and he plunged it straight into her heart. Corabel dropped to the floor, crimson blood staining the bodice of her dress.

Trond flew into a rage, reaching for a dagger at his hip, but Neo and Syndrian were upon him, fists and boots flying in a tussle on the ground until finally, a sickening slash across the front of Trond's throat ended the scuffle. Neo covered his mouth with his hand and wiped away the blood of his former friend that had sprayed his face and neck.

Syndrian leapt to his feet and offered Neo his hand. Neo gripped it, surged to his feet, and ran to my side.

"Are you hurt?" he demanded. "Brex, talk to me!"

I was bruised, but far less than I'd been at Gini's hands. I shook my head. "I am all right," I assured him. "I'm all right."

Trond and Corabel were dead, but the fight here was far from over.

"You filthy mongrel," Haeloc snarled, looking down at the blood pouring from his shoulder. "You've brought the wrath of all the devils of Ástleysi upon us! Do you know who those two worked for? Do you have any idea!" He started pacing the floors, swearing and muttering incoherently about how they would find us and kill us all. "You owe me! You owe me. You've got to help me escape."

"I don't owe you a godforsaken thing," Neo thundered. He released my hand and crossed the floor, while Syndrian came to kneel beside me. Neo raised his hand as if to strike the pathetic vampire, but Haeloc stabbed the dagger toward Neo's heart.

Neo leapt back, narrowly stepping out of Haeloc's reach, while I reached for Syndrian's hand. I pulled it close to my thigh, looked into his eyes, and nodded. He slipped a throwing knife from its fitting, jumped to his feet, and, with an expert flick of his wrist, tossed the knife. His blade sailed through the air and cut a neat slice in Haeloc's forearm. Screaming, Haeloc dropped the goblin dagger. Neo it picked up, and without hesitation, my husband plunged it into his enemy's belly.

And that fast, it was over.

Syndrian helped me stand, and Neo rushed to me, picking me up off the ground and holding me against his chest. "Are you hurt?" he demanded, holding the back of my head in his palm.

I shook my head. "Are you?"

We held each other, our raging heartbeats pounding, our sweat and tears mingling with the last traces of Trond's blood.

"Somebody's gonna be looking for these three," Syndrian said, immediately walking the scene. "We leave the dagger in Haeloc's hand. Touch nothing. Try not to step in blood." He crossed his arms over his chest and tore the sleeves off his tunic with one fierce tug. "Go," he said, motioning toward the door.

Syndrian covered the soles of his boots with the fabric of his sleeves and dragged his feet through the footprints and other impressions we'd left in the dust on the floor. "This is a story that tells itself. A scuffle. Fighting. Corabel blasting things around. There'll be no trace of our footsteps. Just a debt collection gone wrong." He walked carefully past Haeloc's body, picked up the throwing blade, and wiped the blood on the front of his breeches. "Not bad," he said appreciatively, admiring his handiwork.

Neo released me and picked up his sword. "We need to get home. We must get Elgit back to his people and tell them what happened. If he's improved, perhaps a bit of venom will fortify him enough to make the journey."

"Whoever these two worked for, I wouldn't want Tarqeq hunting me. A goblin fueled by revenge..." Syndrian whistled, shaking his head. "If you need a guide to Skickligera, that's a road I've traveled."

We looked over the bodies, and I contemplated saying a

prayer for each of these horrible creatures. But I remembered I had Haeloc's teeth in my tunic. I reached my hand in and pulled them out. "What should I do with these?"

Neo's eyes widened. "Why do you have those? What did you do?"

I pointed to the dagger. "We didn't know how the dagger worked, but I figured it was enchanted in some way. It wouldn't make sense to create a compartment to hold the fangs otherwise. I assumed any power it had to help Haeloc was connected to the fangs. I thought separating them from the dagger would weaken its power. But I guess it didn't matter after all."

"Maybe it did," Neo said. "That injury to the shoulder should have taken him out. He should have passed out, lost more blood. Perhaps the dagger was enchanted so that as long as he held it, he couldn't be killed. Injured, sure, but a vampire only needs blood to heal. That was a wise conclusion. I can't say I would have reached the same."

Syndrian nodded. "Don't leave the fangs here," he said. "Be cautious if you keep them. Consider throwing 'em in the sea where no one will ever find them. There may still be some magic attached to them."

I looked down at the fangs in my hand, two more objects that connected to me a dark power. To the darker side of magic. But this time, I was the one in control. I tucked the fangs back into place beneath my clothing. "Where is Sedda?" I asked.

"I hope she's in the stable," Neo said. "Until I came inside and discovered Haeloc here with Corabel, everything seemed... Trond and I were..." He lowered his eyes. "It doesn't matter now. That was never a true friendship. I'd best leave it to die here with the man's body. Let's go home."

Together we walked to the stable, the eerie silence of the barren land making the entire estate feel haunted. Sedda was tied up and seemed completely untouched by the darkness of the afternoon. Neo led her back to Sara and Syndrian's horse.

"What should we do with Trond's horse?" I asked. There was only one horse, so I assumed he and Corabel had ridden one. "Maybe they released Haeloc's so he couldn't get away?"

"Leave it to me. I'll make sure it finds a safe home in a day or so," Syndrian assured us. "I'll send word to some of my associates. Someone's going to discover the bodies in this manor. May as well be someone who'll report it to the shire-reeve and do right by the animal."

We climbed astride our horses, Syndrian armed with his mace and Neo with his short sword. I tapped the fangs beneath my tunic to make sure they were still there. This was one touch-stone I dared not lose.

And then, all together, we rode for home.

SEVENTEEN

Back at the manor, we cleaned up and wished Syndrian well. I hugged the man hard and thanked him for leading me to Haeloc's manor. I couldn't bear to think what might have happened if I'd not trusted my instincts and followed Neo. I couldn't dwell on what might have happened if he had not believed me.

"Haeloc? Don't know the name Haeloc, I'm afraid," Syndrian said, a slight smile on his lips. "But I am glad to find that my brother is staying out of trouble and that I was able to do some repair work while I was here. *All* afternoon," he said, giving me a knowing look.

Neo clapped the man hard on the back and whispered something in his ear.

Syndrian nodded and mounted his horse. "Send my brother home before dark so our mum doesn't come hunting him down herself," he said. "Although I dare say the boy likes being a older brother. He's quite a bit better in the role than I was."

With a wave, he took off, his ponytail bouncing against his back as he rode.

Gia and Rain returned and immediately started asking questions, but Neo gathered them together in the sitting room.

"What happened? Where is Trond?" Rain demanded, but Neo held up his hand.

"We are safe from Haeloc. He is dead, and I believe any other threats that may have lingered have also passed. We must not speak of the events of today again. Are we agreed?"

Gia and Rain traded nervous glances and looked at me, as if expecting me to explain or tell them more. I was exhausted and sore from Corabel's blow. Drained from nearly losing everything just moments, it seemed, after I'd finally, *finally* had anything to call my own. A husband. A family. A home. I would have sacrificed myself and killed Haeloc today. Could have been killed myself. I agreed with Neo, though. There was nothing more to say, so I gave a weak nod of agreement.

Rain studied my face and then gripped his wife's hand. "As you wish, brother," he agreed. "We'll speak of it no more."

Gia pressed her lips flat and nodded. "What will become of the children?" she asked. "Antonia has been creating quite the fuss about room assignments and bedding, and..."

Neo waved a hand at his sister-in-law. "Anything she wants," he said. "Set the children up in rooms. This is their home now." He looked at me. "Assuming that's all right with their mother?"

I pressed my lips into a smile and nodded. "Perhaps let's call me their aunt? I don't think anyone in the village will believe I'm mother to a twelve-year-old."

"Aunt it is," Neo said. "And while you're at it, why don't we have Antonia make up a space for Flynn. We may need the boy on hand more often. The gods know he is a better caretaker than he is apprentice."

Gia and Rain left to gather the children, leaving Neo and me alone. I'd not said a word to him since we'd left the wrecked manor. I would have to start training myself to not even think the vampire Haeloc's name. With a crime family missing a mage and a debt collector, not to mention a debtor, the safest course would be to remove any trace of Trond, Corabel, and Haeloc from my memory. Those were memories I'd gladly lose.

Neo held a hand out to me, and together we retired to our bedroom. Dale was pouring water into Neo's tub, while Antonia set fresh linens and clothing out for us to wear once we'd cleaned up. She said nothing as she left the room, just paused and cupped my cheek with a hand, her eyes glassy with tears.

Neo unfastened the ties that held my cloak and tossed the filthy item aside. Then he stripped off my tunic and breeches, while I held on to him for balance. I was sore and tired, yes. But after what we'd been through, all I wanted was to lean on him. To feel him, alive and vibrant, beneath my fingers. I slipped off my shoes and held his hand while I reached into my under-clothing for Haeloc's fangs. I set them on the table beside the bed where I'd found the goblin dagger then pulled off the rest of my underthings.

I stood naked before Neo, his honey-gold eyes intense as he took in my curves. My skin pebbled, and I watched as he too shed his clothing. His body was perfect—sculpted and hard, his hair falling loose to his chest. His scars, his size, the heart that beat beneath the cage of his ribs. In this moment, I wanted nothing in the Realm more than him. He held out his hand, and I took it. We climbed into the bath together, and I tucked myself between his legs.

Inside the steaming water, fragrant with scented oil, I leaned back against Neo's chest. The ends of my hair were submerged beneath the water, and I teased the hairy tops of my husband's knees with my fingertips, stroking his skin and kneading the dense muscles of his thighs with soothing strokes.

"I'm sorry you were betrayed by a friend," I whispered. "I'm sorry you had to take a life."

"I am as well," he said, his voice tight, his arms circling my waist.

The fire cracked and the candles flickered in their lamps, casting shadows over the darkening bedroom.

Neo's whisper was warm against my hair. For just these few moments, I wanted to believe we were safe. Completely safe. Just the two of us submerged in truth and honesty, bound anew by shared secrets. "More than being sorry for what I've lost, I'm sorry that I let you down. I'll endeavor to never lapse in judgment again." Neo lifted a wet hand to my chin, turning my face slightly toward him. "I will put you, and our family, first in all things. From now on."

"At least for the next year," I reminded him, turning my face away.

"I'm going to burn that contract," he said, a bit of humor softening his words. The lips I yearned to taste, scarred and beautiful, curled into a smile.

"Things never burn the way people think they will," I teased. In the depths of my heart, I was certain he meant it. This marriage began in necessity but would continue by choice. I did choose Neo and *would* choose him, over and over again. For the rest of the days of my life.

I turned to face him, and all the fear and shock and sadness of the day melted away. What was left was hope. The possibility of what might grow between us. I lifted my mouth to his. The first kiss was light, gentle, reminding me of why this man felt so right. His taste, the texture of his skin beneath my hands. His pretty hair and his battered heart. He was mine. For as long as he'd have me.

He swept his tongue into my mouth, his hands on my breasts, my nipples between his fingertips. I felt things change between us again. The grief of the day gave way to passion. Our wet hands explored each other, my hands fisting his hair. He took my mouth, whispering promises between every luscious sweep of his tongue against mine.

"Wife," he breathed, cupping my face, my bottom, my sex.

"Husband," I panted, welcoming every touch and giving back every bit of pleasure he gave me.

Ecstasy flooded my body as Neo's arousal found my core. We licked and tasted, laughed and loved each other until the bath had cooled and half the water had splashed to the floor. When we finally stood, my legs trembling, Neo's body forever joined with mine, we clung to each other, wet and shivering. Washed free of the dust and blood and stains and shame of the past. Reborn to a life uniquely ours, made by us.

I climbed naked and dripping into bed, but before he joined me, Neo stopped at the sight of Haeloc's fangs at the bedside. He touched them lightly, almost reverently.

"May I have these?" he asked.

I nodded. "What will you do with them?" I asked. "Make a touchstone to wear around your neck?"

Neo shook his head, a wry grin curling his perfect, sensual mouth. "I mean to make a trade." He walked around the room, bathed in firelight, his skin glistening and bare. He dug in a drawer for a small box then lifted the lid and dropped the fangs inside. He pulled something out, then walked back to join me beneath the covers in bed.

He climbed in, and I immediately settled my head against his chest, tucking my body beneath his arm. I could hear the steady beat of his heart, a sound I wished to sleep to, wake to, and work beside every day forevermore. He held me close and breathed deeply until I thought he'd fallen asleep. But just as I lifted my face to check on him, he opened his hand and showed me the token he'd taken from the box.

"This ring was given to my mother by my father when they were married," he said. "When my father died and my mother found love again, she kept the ring that my father had given her but added these stones."

I held the ring in my hands and peered closely at the design stamped into the round gold face.

"Is that...sedum?" I asked.

Neo nodded. "My mother came from nothing," he said. "No land, no dowry. She loved this place, the Oderisi land, so deeply that my father had the Dragon's Blood Sedum stamped into this ring as a symbol of everything their union meant. This place was not just a home, not just a farm. It was the symbol of the power love had to transform their lives. I believe it's why even when my mother had the chance to leave, to find sanctuary in other parts of the Realm, she simply couldn't abandon this place. Of course, we didn't have blood moss growing here at that time, but these rubies?" He pointed to tiny red stones that looked like tiny pinpricks of blood set into the sedum. "My mother added them when she met Jaenelle. This became the ring my mother gave her wife on their wedding day."

He slipped the ring over my finger. "I'd like you to wear it, if it pleases you."

I closed my eyes against burning tears of joy. This was the first gift anyone had ever given me. Selflessly. For my own pleasure. Not the hag stone, with its manipulation and control over me. Not the borrowed breeches from Dale or Odile's shoes. This ring had been passed down from one loving union to another. And now Neo was giving it to me. A symbol of what our union was and what it might be.

"It would be my honor," I whispered, kissing his eyes, his nose, the slope of his cheek, and his beautiful lips. "Thank you, Neo."

I settled back beside him in bed, my drying hair mingling with his. "You know," I said, tracing my fingertips along his bare chest. I watched the rubies in my ring sparkle in the firelight as my fingers danced. "You've never told me what Gia and Rain do. What is their part in the Oderisi family criminal enterprise?"

Neo grinned and closed his eyes, groaning in pleasure as my hands explored his body. "You realize Antonia will summon us for dinner any time now. The bedroom door isn't locked," he reminded me, "and we have a house full of little mongrels running about."

"I'm well aware of the foundlings and the hour and the locks," I crooned. Soon we would have to get out of bed, dress, and break the sweet seclusion of each other's company. But I wouldn't mourn it, as I knew this was only the first night of many, many nights and days to come when Neo and I would share passion and pleasure and pain. Everything required of a true family.

Neo scrubbed a hand over his face. "I'll need to find a way to get Elgit safely back to his kind," he said. "As soon as he's well enough to move. I'll try drinking from him tonight. We'll test the effects. If it speeds his healing along... Who knows? We might save this goblin yet."

I nodded. "Perhaps we can bring Ivo. His talents are especially suited, I think, to communicating with goblins."

Neo widened his eyes. "Hmmm, I look forward to learning about these foundlings. May the gods bless Flynnie. That boy is going to have his hands full."

"Flynnie?" I gasped. "Is that a note of affection I hear in your voice?"

"Don't be a fool," he barked, tugging the blankets up higher and wrapping his arms ever tighter around me.

"I won't be distracted, you know," I reminded him, sneaking

another peek at my ring. "Gia and Rain? Their work? What's one more secret between husband and wife?"

He sighed and closed his eyes. "Brexia, please. If you would prefer to live as the mistress of this manor, steward of foundlings..." He opened his eyes and held my gaze with his. "You may leave the thieving life behind you. I will support you through my own sweat and labor. Protect you from the harsher realities."

I lifted a brow at him, ignoring his noble but entirely ridiculous sentiment. "I have no intention of being protected from life by you, Neo. If there are harsh realities ahead, I intend to share them with you. And perhaps even protect you from them."

Neo's body seemed to shudder as he looked at me with raw affection. Purity of emotion that one day, I was certain, would be profound and lasting love.

"So are they pickpockets?" I asked. "Thieves of...ideas? Do they steal the songs from the mouths of bards?"

Neo shook his head, sighing through a resigned chuckle. "They are grave robbers," he admitted. "They have a network of...I'll call them friends, who spread the word through the shires when a wealthy person dies. They specifically seek out the worst of humanity. Wife-beaters, cheats, murderers. You'd be surprised the means some will go to for riches. They locate the grave of the recently departed villains, take any jewels or gold the person was buried with, and return the body to its final rest. Just a little less fancifully attired."

"What of the vengersax?" I asked. "That sounds like dangerous work, digging graves out under cover of darkness?"

"Don't forget the trolls," he agreed. "It is dangerous work. Very dirty, very complicated, very dangerous work."

"I'm going to need clothes that suit the job. Some breeches that actually fit," I said. "And shoes. Gia can teach me to outfit myself appropriately for the work. Thankfully, I'm already well-schooled in stealing. I have only one condition," I added.

"Hmmm, what's that?" Neo stroked the hair back from my face and kissed my forehead. "My perfect little thief?"

I wove my legs between his and breathed a dozen light kisses against his lips. "No graveyards in Fish Head End," I said.

ACKNOWLEDGMENTS

This book would not have been possible without the thoughtful comments from my amazing team of betas. Bob, Rachel, Shanyn, Kelsey, and Julie, you are amazing. Your attention to detail, your honesty, and your cheerleading mean the world to me. Every emoji that let me know I'd nailed it (or not...), every text, every email...every minute of your time is the most amazing gift. Thank you, thank you, thank you!

Thank you to my copyeditor, Jenny Rarden, for your work on this one. I will someday master the correct spelling of grey/grAy, but until then, you've been a lifesaver.

I cannot heap enough praise onto the artist who I've been blessed to work with for several projects now. Matt, your talent inspires me to write a strong enough story to do your artwork justice! You captured Neo the exact way I saw him and made Brex even more kick-butt than I imagined she could be. Thank you so much for sharing your unbelievable talent with me!

Michael Lee designed the typography as well as the book, set up my newsletter, and did only about 1,000 other things to make this book possible. Michael, how dare you, sir! No, really, a trillion thank yous for taking my career and my dreams to heart.

To my friend Dr. Laura Scott., DVM, cVMA, cVPM, for your

support and friendship over the years, but especially for answering horse-related questions. Any inaccuracies/errors/creative stretches taken with respect to the treatment and behavior of the horses in this book are mine!

I want to acknowledge the many podcasters and YouTubers whose passion for the Medieval period and all things fantasy/gaming helped me stay inspired and in the headspace I needed to be in while I was writing.

And to all the readers willing to give a new-to-you author a try. Thank you, thank you, thank you!!

About the Author

Callie Chase lives in Los Angeles and has way too many books on her desk and in her brain at any one time. She passionately believes in happy endings, magic, and outsmarting monsters of all kinds.

Lover of mythology, mermaids, zombies, and dogs, she credits strong coffee and all things chocolate for helping her bring her ideas to life.

Find out more at www.calliechase.com

Chat with Callie about all things books and fantasy in her Discord community!
www.calliechase.com/discord

If you'd like to leave a review of this book, I'd sincerely appreciate you sharing your thoughts with other readers!
www.calliechase.com/review

facebook.com/calliechaseauthor

twitter.com/c_chaseauthor

instagram.com/authorcalliechase

amazon.com/author/calliechase

tiktok.com/@calliechaseauthor

www.ingramcontent.com/pod-product-compliance
Lightning Source LLC
Chambersburg PA
CBHW051132190726
48290CB00006B/1810